OUT OF SIGHT

Isabelle Grey grew up in Manchester and graduated from Cambridge. She began her writing career as an arts journalist for national newspapers and magazines before going on to write television drama, including screenplays for several popular crime series. Under her maiden name, Isabelle Anscombe, she is the author of five non-fiction books. She lives in London.

OUT OF SIGHT

Isabelle Grey

Quercus

First published in Great Britain in 2011 by

Quercus
21 Bloomsbury Square
London
WC1A 2NS

A CIP catalogue record for this book is available
from the British Library

ISBN 978 0 85738 316 7

10 9 8 7 6 5 4 3 2 1

Typeset by Ellipsis Digital Limited, Glasgow
Printed and bound in Great Britain by Clays Ltd, St Ives plc

PART ONE
Sussex 2005

Patrick leant forward a little towards the woman in the chair opposite. 'I've explained that an increase of symptoms is a sign that the remedy is taking effect,' he said. Still worried, she looked back into his eyes, wanting – needing – to trust his words. He regarded her steadily, sure from long experience that this was the crisis, the moment when the internal fever, so to speak, would break and the temperature – an emotional temperature, in this case – would subside. As she held onto his gaze, he felt that she was willing from him an essence of the reassuring wisdom she sought.

'How can I start to feel better when I still don't really understand what's wrong with me? I know you've explained, but–' She grimaced apologetically.

Patrick smiled. His desire for the satisfaction of healing was every bit as deep as hers: the healer also reaped powerful rewards. And he sensed how this woman would feel more profoundly healed if the cure he offered were given up at some psychic cost to himself. He knew, without understanding or even questioning the process, that it was because he could and did pay this price that his patients recommended him so highly. Exactly what the cost was he chose never to analyse, though he sensed that it was his reticence to which his patients responded most power-fully.

He spoke kindly. 'It's about past emotional trauma, do you remember?'

She nodded doubtfully. Although twenty years older than he, she nonetheless craved both his authority and his authenticity.

'An inherited predisposition,' he continued. 'It may be in your life, or your family, or even your distant ancestors, something that leaves a residue which has a negative impact on the vital force.' He held her anxious gaze. 'Eat healthily, attune yourself to nature's cycles and seasons, and the remedy I've given you will stimulate your body's healing powers to restore absolute well-being.' He leant forward to cradle her right hand in both his own, his eyes crinkling at the corners as he smiled. 'Trust life. Allow yourself to be healed.' Her shoulders dropped. She sighed deeply, briefly closing her eyes as if in silent prayer. When she opened them again, he could see that the immediate crisis had come and gone. She had accepted his permission to feel better.

Ten minutes later, he saw her out, his last patient of the day. He always welcomed that moment of silence alone in the office. Now that the practice had achieved some success, it was inefficient not to employ a receptionist, but he resisted the loss of this solitariness. Patrick never liked to feel observed; he refused to conform to the logic of someone else's work patterns, and felt this private moment as his reward for having faced the needy, coaxing, prying eyes of his patients all day.

He tidied away his repertories and other books, the dilutions, tinctures and additional preparations of his *Materia Medica*, closed down his computer, stowed the day's cheques in a desk drawer. As he locked the door of the former shop to which he'd re-located after Daniel's arrival – there were plenty of such premises available around Brighton, village stores forced out of business by out-of-town supermarkets – he took his usual pleasure in the brass plate screwed onto the wall: Patrick Hinde DipHom, RSHom. It was an idyllic summer's evening. The shadows of the elm trees across the road were beginning to lengthen, and he straightened his spine and breathed in the quiet air as he walked up past the side of his building to the yard at the back where he parked his car. He still felt guilty that he drove here every day from Brighton – he who counselled his patients to live natural, organic and carbon-neutral lives – but needs must. He looked at his watch, feeling the first stab of anxiety.

But Daniel seemed fine when he picked him up. He was a stalwart little boy of eighteen months but, every so often when left with his childminder in the mornings, he would grow distressed and cling to his father. Then Patrick found

5

his son's hot, tearful face unbearable, and felt himself enacting a terrible betrayal every time he clawed himself free of the child and handed him over to Christine. She was a no-nonsense, comfortable woman, the same age as he – thirty-five – yet already, unbelievably, a grandmother. On these occasions, shutting himself into his car outside Christine's unruly terraced house, Patrick would briefly wonder what negative emotion he had passed on to his son, what shameful residue that he was helpless to relieve. Next, he usually found himself with his key in the door beside the brass plate, the drive on to Ditchling accomplished without conscious awareness. But returning this evening he found Daniel chatty and bouncing, wriggling like a trout as Patrick buckled him into his child seat, and gave in to his son's demands for his favourite CD of nursery songs for the drive back through the velvety Downs.

At home, Daniel's buoyant mood continued and Patrick assured Belinda that he would bath the boy and get him ready for bed while she made supper. In echo of the homeopathic premise that water retains an energetic memory, he relished the amphibious pleasure of a baby in water. Since Daniel was a few months old, he had regularly taken him swimming, though he dreaded to think what compounds the Lido at Saltdean might contain. So bathtime was pure fun, especially with summer sunlight still streaming into the narrow room onto Daniel's sturdy wet limbs as he thrashed at the water, releasing delicious throaty chuckles as his father willingly let himself be soaked.

Patrick read Daniel a bedtime story then, retaining the warm imprint of the boy's sleepy body against his, re-entered the kitchen where Belinda was tossing a salad. Ever since first meeting her, he had enjoyed watching Belinda prepare food. More even than when she played the piano or her violin, her actions seemed to sum up who she was: precise, yet tolerant of mess, exercising instinctive judgement about how much or how little was required, tasting as she went along, unreflectingly optimistic about the results. He sat down at the table, smiling.

'Good day?' he asked.

'Very. Emma heard she got an interview with the Royal College of Music.'

'Well done.'

'Even the principal was pleased.'

'That's a first.'

Belinda grinned as she placed the salad bowl on the table. 'Do you want bread?'

'I'll get it.' As he reached around her, he nestled his hand into the curve of her waist; she was as willowy now as when they first met, less than a year before she fell pregnant.

She turned, placing her hands on his chest, pressing herself against him. 'Hello.'

In answer, he kissed her, losing his other hand in the warmth beneath the mass of hair that covered the back of her neck, anticipating the pleasure of later love-making. Then both went about the business of putting food on the table and sitting down to eat. He valued the ease of their silence, their shared assumption that all would undoubtedly be said in due course in a tangle of naked limbs and urgent mouths. Whatever it stemmed from – maybe her brain was hard-wired for music rather than for speech – he found his wife's constitutional incuriousness about words immeasurably restful.

When she did break their comfortable silence, it was, as usual, to deal with practicalities. 'I'm afraid I ran up a huge bill shopping for your parents. I'll make fish pie for tomorrow night. Will your father survive without meat for three days?'

'There's nothing he likes more than having something to be unhappy about.' He threw up his hands theatrically. 'Why the hell can't they stay in Europe and retire to the Italian Lakes rather than move to bloody Esher.'

'Or France, near your grandmother.'

'Ha!'

'What?'

'Dad can do business in three and a half languages, but outside of work he refuses to converse in any of them. Except for emergencies.'

'Remind me which one's the half?'

'Dutch.'

'Oh yes. Impressive.'

Soothed by the security of Belinda's disinterest, Patrick went on eating, but the familiar nest of vipers had been disturbed and, after a few more mouthfuls, he found himself thinking aloud. 'It'll be Josette's ninetieth in October. I guess Maman will think she has to throw a party.'

'Well, it'd be nice to meet Josette at last. For Daniel, too.' Spearing another tomato, she missed Patrick's unconscious glance towards the door, the nearest escape route. 'He's her great-grandson, after all,' she continued. 'Be fun to get a photo of them together.'

Patrick's mouth tightened. He pushed away his plate.

'Anyone else you want to invite over while they're here?' she asked. He shook his head. 'Pudding? There's a bit of lemon pie left.'

'You have it.'

'Maybe later. I want to practise that sonata again, if you don't mind?'

'I'd love it,' he said, letting out a breath of relief.

He cleared the dishes then followed the sounds of the piano into the sitting room. Belinda, intent on the score, didn't register his presence. He lay back in his favourite armchair, admiring her total absorption, her graceful movements. Gradually the tiny surge of flight-or-fight adrenaline that had hit him in the kitchen subsided. Focusing now on the differences of speed and emphasis in each repeated passage of music, he was glad to be able to relax his guard. He settled down, suspending all thought until, forty minutes later when she had played the entire piece through to her own satisfaction, she turned, ready to be rewarded with his slow smile of approbation and desire.

*

Patrick heard his parents' Audi draw up on the gravel outside the house. There was room for only one car in front of the semi-detached Edwardian villa, so he had already moved his to the street. He picked up Daniel, who protested mildly at having his play disturbed, and, shielded by his son, went out to greet them. He saw Agnès in the passenger seat, waiting for Geoffrey to open her door. It would never occur to his mother to sit like this except when it was her husband driving, and Patrick resented how the familiar mixture of love, exasperation and pity arose in him almost the moment he set eyes on her. His father clocked him, nodded curtly, and continued on around to open the passenger door for his wife. When Agnès emerged, she went immediately to plant warm *bisous* on the cheeks of her son and grandson, while Geoffrey retrieved their small suitcase from the boot. Only then did he shake hands with Patrick and pat Daniel approvingly on the head.

'Come in, come in.' Patrick went to the bottom of the stairs and called 'Belinda!' just as she appeared at the top. Watching her descent, he couldn't prevent himself glancing at his father, hoping that he too took in her beauty, her sensuality. Belinda, who had previously met her expatriate in-laws only three or four times, greeted them with due consideration.

'Tea? Coffee?' she offered. 'Or would you like to go up to your room first? Patrick will take your case. Here, give Daniel to me.' She disappeared with the boy into the kitchen, leaving Patrick to show his parents the way. Suddenly the staircase seemed narrow and steep, the house small and insignificant, and he a child again. Not that Geoffrey and Agnès had lived in luxury; the procession of rented apartments and houses in Brussels, Geneva, Frankfurt and elsewhere that had been the lot of a middle-ranking multinational company executive had been comfortable, good for entertaining, but somehow never suitable for full-time occupation by a boy or teenager.

Now his parents were house-hunting in Surrey, where a few former colleagues had washed up contentedly enough; and this was the topic of conversation over a cup of coffee and slices of Belinda's banana loaf. Something modern, hassle-free, where they could grow old without having to worry about repairs or too big a garden. The lease on their apartment in Geneva was up in two months, by which time they hoped to have chosen a new home and could decide how much of their furniture and possessions to ship over.

Patrick noted that Agnès nodded blandly to virtually every suggestion, even when contradictory, all the time watching Daniel in his highchair fussily picking minute pieces of walnut out of his loaf. Her hands fluttered nervously as if she might catch the morsels before they were scattered on the floor. Regarding this as a brilliant new game, Daniel instantly sought to outmanoeuvre her, happily pulverising his cake to create new supplies of ammunition. Patrick laughed as his son responded to her ineffectual attempts to calm his giggles by flinging crumbs even further afield. But, at the point at which Agnès glanced surreptitiously at Geoffrey, Patrick's heart sank. A louder squeal of delight caught Belinda's attention, and, laughing, she whisked Daniel up out of his chair.

'Little monkey!'

Belinda's obliviousness to Agnès' muted cry of relief caused a sugar-rush of love in Patrick towards his wife, enabling him to ignore Geoffrey's infinitesimal frown. He got to his feet, placing an arm around her shoulders, conscious of the image they presented of the happily united family. 'Let's go out somewhere!' he cried.

The sea was sparkling, almost painful on the eyes, and the weekend beach crowded. Belinda walked beside Geoffrey, who had taken control of Daniel's buggy. Agnès had linked her arm through her son's. 'Patrice,' she murmured lovingly. 'Patrice.'

Out of earshot of his father, Patrick questioned her. 'Will you be happy in a modern house, Maman?'

'Oh, I've never minded that much about the roof over my head. You know that.'

'But it's different this time. This will be your own house at last. A proper home.'

'It's wonderful that Belinda goes on teaching, with the infant.'

'She works four days a week. And of course gets the school holidays.'

'And I suppose you can fit your hours around him, too. That's wonderful.'

'Would you have liked to work, if you'd stayed in one place long enough?'

'Me? What would I have been any good at? Besides, I had you to look after. There was always so much to do at home.'

Out of habit, Patrick let it pass unchallenged. 'So what's your plan for retirement? Are you sure you wouldn't enjoy a garden?'

'I don't think so. And Geoffrey doesn't want the bother of hedges and grass to cut.'

'What about a cat? Or a dog?'

'Didn't I tell you? For our anniversary, he gave me a pair of yellow canaries. The infant must come and see them. They're in a sweet little cage, like an antique.'

Patrick looked at his father and hated him anew. Now Geoffrey was stopping at an ice-cream van, the kind that sold a sugary emulsion extruded from a machine into a cone, and telling Daniel that, because he had been such a good boy and not made a fuss, he could have one as a treat. Belinda caught Patrick's eye. He merely shrugged: let it happen, they were helpless.

Daniel buried his little face in the creamy confection, and Geoffrey tried to instruct him how to lick, not suck. Belinda laughed, while Agnès hunted in her bag for a clean tissue. Patrick left them, walked over to the railing that edged the promenade and looked out to sea. In both directions, hundreds of people – families, couples – covered the beach: did all of them, he wondered, find life so hard, so overwhelming? The gears of life always grinding and clashing, never meshing perfectly so one could effortlessly accelerate ahead and get clear? He fought the temptation to thread his way through the crowds and simply walk into the sea, let the waters meet over his head, enclosing him in silence. He felt a hand on his back, heard Belinda laughing: 'I wish I'd brought the camera! Just look at him!' He turned, smiled at their son's incredulity at the joyous mess he was making, and chided himself. He was being ridiculous!

Re-joining the others, he ignored Daniel's futile protests and wiped his face clean. They strolled on along the seafront. Patrick returned the pleasant half-smiles from strangers who wished shyly to acknowledge the harmonious group they presented, three generations enjoying a day out together, and resolved to view his family as others clearly did.

At dinner, Geoffrey jovially introduced the inevitable topic that Patrick dreaded. 'So, found a cure for cancer yet?'

'Homeopathy doesn't really deal in cures. It has more to do with healing.'

'The placebo effect!' declared Geoffrey, delighted to win the first point so easily.

'I'm not going to fight with you, Dad.'

'Who's fighting? Don't tell me your ideas can't withstand some healthy debate, a little honest scepticism.'

'Nearly everyone in France uses homeopathic remedies,' murmured Agnès.

'Absolutely,' crowed Geoffrey. 'Billion-euro industry. There's big money in astrology, too, I daresay.'

'Patrick is having to turn away patients,' said Belinda proudly. 'People come from miles away to see him.'

'If he's that good, then all the more shame he threw away a medical career. He could've been a top surgeon by now.'

'I like what I do. The way I do it.'

'You never would be told.'

'No.'

'Your fish pie is delicious,' Agnès addressed Belinda. 'You must give me the recipe.'

'Thanks. It's very easy. I'll write it out for you.'

'You wouldn't treat Daniel your way, though, if he was ill?' demanded Geoffrey, adding, out of politeness, 'Or Belinda, either, of course. You'd take him to a proper doctor?'

'Of course he would!' declared Agnès.

'We're perfectly responsible parents,' said Belinda lightly, starting to clear the dishes. Patrick pushed his plate towards her, wishing for silence to engulf him.

'Children go down with things so rapidly at that age,' fretted Agnès. 'You used to get so ill when you were little.'

'I didn't, Maman. No worse than any other kid.'

'But I used to worry so.'

'I left my glasses upstairs.' Geoffrey pushed back his

15

chair and walked out of the room. Agnès looked at Patrick wide-eyed.

'It's all right, Maman. Everything's okay.'

They heard a door close upstairs then, a few moments later, the chirruping sob of Daniel woken from sleep.

'He's disturbed the baby!'

'No,' soothed Belinda. 'He'll turn over and go back to sleep.'

'He won't be used to hearing strange people in the house! He may be afraid.'

'No one's afraid, Maman.'

'But—'

'Everything's fine. Nothing's happened. Dad's only gone to get his glasses. He'll be down in a minute for his pudding.'

'It's fruit salad,' offered Belinda. 'Or there's some cheese,' she added hopefully.

'Why is she like that?' Belinda asked as Patrick got into bed beside her. 'Does he beat her, or something?' He sighed, not saying anything. 'What's she so scared of?'

'Nothing. He's never hit anyone. He hardly ever even shouts. He means well, he just can't imagine anyone not desperately wanting precisely what he wants. And he's so incredibly tense all the time. They both are. They think it's normal.'

'How on earth did you cope as a kid? All by yourself, not even a brother or sister?'

He made a joke of it. 'Who says I coped?' Before she

16

could say more, he pulled her to him, covering her mouth with his, his hand already stroking her hip. Both relaxed into the kiss, in no hurry to take it further. He twisted round to switch off the light, then let his conscious mind contract into the single easy focus of his desire for her. But, as they touched each other, he picked up the murmur of his father's deep voice through the wall, a couple of feet away from his head, heard the bedhead knock lightly against it as one of his parents moved. He groaned, rolling away onto his back.

'Never mind.' Belinda kissed his cheek and turned over, snuggling her behind close against him. 'Sleep well.'

But he couldn't sleep. He lay there, almost expecting to hear, as he had done in his childhood when his father was abroad on business, the sound of his mother getting up and tiptoeing around the house, checking the locks, making sure the kitchen taps weren't dripping, that the gas was off. Repeatedly. Sometimes eight, nine times, up and down the stairs, in and out of the kitchen, before she finally remained in bed long enough to fall asleep. The more Geoffrey stayed away, the worse it got. Or, as it had finally occurred to Patrick to wonder after he'd left home, was it the other way around? That the worse it got, the more his father chose to stay away?

The next morning, the family set off to climb the Downs. Patrick led the way, Daniel in a carrier on his back, smothered in sunscreen and wearing a cute cotton hat.

The footpath was steep, but he preferred this route because it was less frequented than the more popular trails, especially on a Sunday in July. The sky was cloudless. The hot weather had held for several days now, and was forecast to continue for the rest of the week. Patrick enjoyed the exertion, feeling the muscles in his calves and thighs begin to stretch and relax. Agnès came up beside him, catching at Daniel's waving hand.

'You like being up high, with your papa!' she said to him brightly. Patrick smiled at her. Perhaps today they'd all relax and begin to enjoy one another's company. 'You're a lucky little boy,' she continued. 'I never even met my papa.'

'We're hoping maybe this year we'll start a brother or sister for him,' Patrick told her happily.

'Oh!' As usual, he could see that her genuine delight was almost immediately clouded by a rush of anxiety as all the catastrophes that might attend a pregnancy and birth engulfed her.

'Wouldn't that be great?' he instructed her firmly.

'Yes. Oh, yes, Patrice, of course.' Bravely, she banished the dread, yet he watched her hand flutter to the buttons on her shirt, then pat her pocket to ensure the handkerchief was not lost, before checking both earrings were still in place.

'Maybe I could give you a remedy that would boost your confidence, Maman. You deserve to enjoy yourself once you're all settled here.'

'A remedy . . . yes. Not that I need anything, I'm really quite all right. But if you'd like me to have one, I'd like that. I'm sure it would help, if it came from you.'

When they reached the top, there was the slightest of breezes and, with the detail lost in the heat haze, a view of Sussex that seemed timeless. Belinda gratefully removed her own backpack, which contained the picnic, then lifted Daniel out of the carrier. While she handed out cups of water, followed by a splash of white wine, Patrick kept watch over his son's explorations. He was amused at how swiftly Daniel became engrossed in an investigation of the striped snail shells and dried-out rabbit droppings he discovered in the cropped grass.

Tired by the hot climb, the adults were content to pick at the food – French bread, Brie, green olives and tomatoes – and enjoy the view in companionable silence. Conversation resumed as Daniel napped on his special blanket in the shade of an umbrella propped up on the grass beside him, and Patrick was pleased that their quiet talk of music and concerts and changes in the countryside flowed in an easy way, skirting any potential rocks that might have sunk their pleasant Sunday afternoon torpor. At that moment he felt proud of them all for being a normal family; then, with a cynical laugh to himself, reconsidered the thought: surely no real 'normal family' would ever give themselves a pat on the back for being one.

Once Daniel woke up, he wouldn't sit still. Stumbling on

the uneven turf, the toddler discovered that he could roll a little way down the slope. Shrieking with theatrical fear, he began to throw himself down deliberately, rolling over two or three times before Patrick, stationing himself below, caught him and placed him back on his feet, ready to do it all again. Geoffrey watched approvingly: a proper boy, he'd be a good sportsman one day, but each time Daniel began to roll a little further, Agnès became alarmed. She tried to hide it, to join in the laughter, but eventually was overwhelmed. 'He might tear his clothes!' she protested anxiously.

'Won't matter,' answered Belinda, not appreciating the scale of her mother-in-law's distress. 'He's nearly grown out of them anyway.'

'Surely that's enough, now?' Agnès pleaded. 'He'll be sick.'

'He's never sick,' Belinda responded stoutly, still unaware.

Agnès kept quiet, but her hand flew to her mouth when it looked at one moment like the child might wriggle out of Patrick's grasp. Finally her fear escaped her: 'What if he hits his head on a stone?' she cried.

Patrick took the cue, caught Daniel and held him firmly. 'That'll do, young man. Let's find a quieter game now.'

But as Daniel struggled to escape his grip, Patrick's foot slipped slightly on the short grass and he trod backwards a single step. He easily regained his balance, but too late to stop Agnès scrambling to her feet in terror, crying, 'They're going to fall! They'll fall!'

Before Patrick could get to her to reassure her, let her

touch her grandson and feel for herself that he was perfectly safe, Geoffrey was beside him. 'For God's sake, get that child out of here!' he hissed. 'Can't you see he's upsetting her? Take him away.'

Stretched out on either side of them were the smooth, massive humps of the South Downs, above them a vault of clear blue sky. There was nowhere to go.

Supper that evening was a subdued affair. Agnès commented apologetically that maybe they'd all had a little too much sun, while Geoffrey failed to grumble even about the lasagne being vegetarian. In an effort to distract them, transport them to another time and place, Belinda cheerfully asked what plans they had for Josette's ninetieth birthday. Maybe they could all go to France together? For a moment no one spoke, then Geoffrey observed that Agnès usually went on her own to visit her mother. 'Now Josette is so old,' he added, 'she may find it confusing to have strangers descend on her en masse.'

'Strangers?' queried Belinda. Patrick parried her look of incredulity.

'She's as sharp as she's ever been,' answered Agnès. 'I'm sure she'd like a celebration. And she loves children. Doesn't she, Patrice?'

'Yes, Maman.'

'You were very happy there with her, just the two of you, weren't you?'

'Yes, Maman. Always.'

21

'She would love Daniel, just as she loved you. And me.' Agnès turned to Belinda. 'My papa died at the very end of the war, before I was born. *Ma mère* never remarried. Once I left France to marry Geoffrey, she was alone.'

'It seemed a kindness for us to let Patrick spend the school holidays with her,' expanded Geoffrey, and Patrick recognised the familiar dialogue. 'Much better for a boy to have space to run around instead of being cooped up in an apartment.'

Patrick saw Belinda's head shoot round in surprise. 'You never said you spent holidays with your grandmother.'

It was Agnès who answered, in well-worn phrases. 'It gave him continuity. It would have been unnerving for him to keep coming home from school to different houses, different countries. Josette offered him familiarity, a home from home . . . didn't she, *mon chéri*?'

'Yes, Maman.'

'You were seven when you started boarding, weren't you?' asked Belinda. Patrick nodded dumbly, concentrating on swirling his wine around the glass.

'British executives who worked abroad had their children's public-school fees paid by the company,' Geoffrey informed her, with subtle pride.

'So when did you three get to see each other?'

'I didn't spend the whole of every vacation in France.'

'And remember, I was travelling on business all the time,' added Geoffrey, seeking to clarify matters. 'I wouldn't have been around much anyway.'

'So it was Josette who more or less brought you up?' Belinda made no attempt to disguise her amazement at only now discovering this about her husband.

'I told you I used to stay with her,' protested Patrick. 'And Maman used to come, too, sometimes.'

'Yes, but I thought it was just an occasional visit. I've not heard you talk about her as if she was such an impor- tant part of your life. I never realised—'

Patrick could see that Belinda was stumped. He wouldn't have blamed her if she had risen from the table, picked up her violin and begun to play, immersing herself in a language that made perfect sense and evading the chaos contained in this ostensibly sensible conversation. But instead, she was staring at him, her forehead uncharac- teristically furrowed.

'You didn't even invite her to our wedding!'

'She doesn't speak English,' explained Geoffrey patiently. 'Never leaves France.'

Patrick gave Belinda the open, candid look he gave his patients when they were confused or distressed. 'I guess a child's memory of time is different. I was pretty young.'

She nodded, but continued to observe him as if for the very first time. He shrank from her sharp gaze, imagining himself as some chemically stained organism taped under a microscope.

'Well,' said Geoffrey, leaning back in his chair, 'that was quite a meal, Belinda. Thank you.'

The expression on Belinda's face as she looked at them

all around the table, thought Patrick, was the same as when she accidentally struck a dissonant note on an instrument. But, with a slight shake to clear her head, she set about removing the plates. As she went to the fridge to fetch the apple snow she had made for pudding, he became aware that he was breathing through his mouth, that his heart was beating rapidly. Fearing to give himself away, he fought the urge to make a run for it.

After Agnès and Geoffrey had gone up early to bed, he told Belinda he would clear up. That done, he sat at the kitchen table, tracing the grooves in the scrubbed pine surface with a finger, waiting for silence above. Only when he hoped his wife was fast asleep did he go upstairs.

It was with relief that Patrick shut himself in the car the next morning for his drive to Ditchling. Belinda didn't teach on a Monday, so Daniel didn't go to the childminder. It had been arranged that Geoffrey and Agnès would stay until Tuesday, but although Patrick had re-scheduled some of his patients, he apologised that he nonetheless had to go to work on Monday, though he would come home early. Meanwhile, Belinda would take them out somewhere, maybe to Charleston Farmhouse or Firle Place.

At Ditchling he parked in the yard and walked down the side of the building, opened the door to his office, and breathed in the still air of rooms unoccupied over the weekend. The solitude acted like a balm, and by the time his first patient arrived, promptly at half-past ten, he felt less bruised, more able to deride his susceptibility to his parents' dysfunctions. Really! So his poor mother's anxiety had developed into Obsessive Compulsive Disorder, and his father, given half a chance, tended to be avoidant. But hadn't he escaped from all that, made his own life? He had stopped considering his parents as 'home' when he left school. Though he admitted that marriage had been largely Belinda's idea, he'd been content to go along with it. He loved being a father and everything seemed to be working out pretty well. Now, sitting opposite him was a forty-year-old man in loose faded jeans and work boots, a local builder, who had originally come to him with a bad back and open scepticism and was now arriving at the point where he could admit to having sexual problems. What could be better, on a Monday morning, than to win the trust of a decent, unassuming man like this, and perhaps even be able to help him?

And yet, as the day wore on, that ability to help, to heal, seemed to elude him. All practitioners got stuck from time to time, hit an invisible wall when none of their insights proved useful, when none of the selected remedies, so carefully thought out, appeared to make the slightest difference. And he knew that at such a disjunction his colleagues would advise confidence, clarity and vigour, the courage to see homeopathy as not just a science but an art – an art that took depth and originality to accomplish well. He was experienced enough not to blame his patients for their lack of beneficial response: it was he who was stuck, not they. And it wasn't as though he had far to look for the reason! His negative state of mind had left him susceptible to an accumulation of unresolved past actions which had imprinted on his vital force. When he had time, he would consult a colleague for a remedy to dispel such influences but, meanwhile, the awkward frustrations of the morning forced him to acknowledge how much his ability to heal others sustained him, too. Yet he resented the insight. He needed such self-awareness to remain unthought, to stay just out of reach, so that the alchemy of the healing encounter remained unself-conscious. The moment that healing became a conscious act of will, an act, then something precious, the something of value he offered his patients, was irretrievably lost.

And so, when he reached home, even though his family had enjoyed their day out, he was unable to shake off his impatience. Agnès was touched that he had remembered to bring her the promised Rescue Remedy and was certain it would do her good, even though she was equally certain she didn't need rescuing. Over dinner, the others chatted about their visit to Daniel's favourite zoo park, fondly recounting his delight in the otters' aquatic acrobatics, and Patrick admired the scarf Geoffrey had bought Agnès in the Charleston shop. Yet, despite the positive mood of the evening, Patrick could barely wait for Tuesday morning when his parents would leave.

*

It started in the spare bedroom with a tussle over who should carry the suitcase down. As Patrick had anticipated, with Agnès' anxiety provoked by their imminent parting, breakfast had been tense. Now Geoffrey took his son's appearance in the doorway as a challenge to his dominant position in the pride of lions and, glad of a release for his tension, began roaring that he wasn't so past it yet that he couldn't carry his own luggage! So Patrick followed his father submissively down the stairs to the hallway, where Belinda was getting Daniel ready to go with Patrick once Agnès and Geoffrey had departed.

'What's the best route onto the M23?' Recognising Geoffrey's man-talk as a peace offering, Patrick gave the appropriate responses. Agnès came out of the kitchen, where she had insisted on washing up the breakfast things, and stood watching uncomprehendingly as Belinda put on Daniel's shoes. She turned to Patrick. 'Doesn't the infant stay home with you?'

'Patrick's working,' explained Belinda.

'Oh,' exclaimed Agnès, relieved. 'He goes with you to work. I didn't realise.'

'He comes with me, yes.' Patrick looked at Belinda, willing her to interpret correctly his appeal to say no more.

But her head was bent over the shoes. 'Patrick drops him off at the childminder,' she said carelessly.

'The childminder?' queried Agnès. 'I don't understand.'

'We should get on the road,' chivvied Geoffrey. 'Everything's packed up.'

27

'You leave him with a stranger?'

'Hardly a stranger!' said Belinda. 'Her name's Christine. Daniel has a good time there with the other kids.'

'Go and powder your nose, or whatever you need to do,' Geoffrey ordered his wife.

'He's little more than a baby!'

Belinda straightened up to put an arm around Agnès, giving her a hug. 'Honestly, Agnès, he's absolutely fine with Christine. We'd never leave him if he wasn't. Would we?'

She appealed to Patrick, but he found it impossible to look at any of them. He longed to bend down and pick up his son, hug the child to him, but he was frozen.

'You never told me he went to a childminder,' cried Agnès, 'to a woman you barely know.'

'Time to go!' Geoffrey put in desperately.

But Agnès could not be distracted. 'How can you be sure if he's happy or not?' Her voice rose. 'You can never tell how your child is, if you are not there!'

Geoffrey dived at Daniel, scooped him up from where he sat contentedly at his mother's feet, and thrust him at Patrick. 'Take him away! Get rid of him!'

Startled, Daniel began to cry. Patrick cradled him, cradling himself, too, against the little body.

'What's wrong with you?' Belinda demanded of Geoffrey, but he was hauling Agnès towards the door.

'Get in the car! We're going now. We have to go.'

'No, wait!' Belinda's words made Geoffrey pause in the doorway. 'Please wait.'

Patrick could hardly bear to look at Agnès standing distraught beside her husband. He knew what he would see: his mother was alternating between wringing her hands in a compulsive gesture that seemed almost comic and checking the buttons on her blouse. He sensed rather than saw Belinda's mute appeal for him to say something, do something.

'Stay and have another cup of tea. Don't leave like this,' Belinda begged, while he continued to stare fixedly down into Daniel's soft, downy hair.

Geoffrey now spoke more gently. 'You can see it's hopeless. Best we get off. Give you a ring tonight.' He picked up the suitcase and shepherded his wife outside, leaving Belinda to follow them out to their car and see them off.

Patrick stood in the hallway, rooted to the spot, holding Daniel, slowing his breathing as he counted each golden hair, until he heard the crunch of gravel as the car drew away and Belinda returned. 'What was all that about?' she asked, stroking Daniel's head. Patrick said nothing. 'Poor baby,' she crooned. 'Silly old them. Just silly-billies, aren't they?' Calmed, the child nestled his head in under Patrick's chin, his thumb in his mouth. 'He'll probably sleep in the car,' Belinda said to Patrick. 'Maybe you should just go, then he can drop off. He'll have forgotten all about it by the time you get to Christine's.'

Patrick's next conscious action was turning his key in the lock beside the brass name-plate and entering his Ditchling office. The rooms already felt close and airless and he opened the windows before crossing to his desk to check his diary for the day. Seeing an extra name scribbled in, he remembered that a regular patient had rung the day before requesting an urgent consultation, and he'd agreed to fit her in over his lunch break. Two other appointments were with new people, which he always enjoyed. He looked at his watch, surprised to see he still had ten minutes to himself.

He was mildly aware of a dragging undertow of distress but, determined not to let it rise to a point where it would disturb his interaction with his patients, he turned on the computer. He would chase a few late payers before the first arrival, when it would be vital to block out all personal distractions, all conscious self-reflection. It wasn't that he didn't listen to people's actual words, but he needed simultaneously to attend to tone, hesitation, body language, in which he could perceive at an innate, intuitive level what they were striving to communicate. He always looked forward to entering the set phase of solid concentration which an appointment with a new patient demanded. He found the experience intensely calming. He once heard a heroin addict describe on television the sense of well-being that flushed through his system on taking the drug, and recognised the same cravings in himself: he thought how lucky he was to have discovered a way to self-medicate without opiates.

The bell rang, and Patrick went to greet his first patient.

Over the course of the morning, during which he saw three people, each with a very different ailment, he was aware that, as usual, there were several phone calls while he was occupied. Sure enough, at lunchtime the message light was blinking, but he only had time to grab an apple and a cup of tea before his extra lunchtime appointment, so he left the calls to deal with later.

Meghan, who soon arrived, had been coming to him for a couple of years. She both amused and exasperated him. She often requested a last-minute consultation like this, presenting with some acute physical symptom, but the core issue to be resolved generally turned out to be something that she had said or done and now regretted. Meghan made him feel like a priest in the confessional, granting absolution; before she began coming to him, she had no doubt sought similar relief from her GP or her hairdresser. But he was willing to offer it because, while she might not be prepared to admit her faults directly to herself, she was nonetheless attempting in this roundabout manner to account for her sins. For that measure of self-awareness he liked her and was prepared to indulge the moral subterfuge. Today she'd come because she'd had a falling-out with a neighbour on some village committee – a sure sign, she told him, that she was out of balance and needed a new remedy.

Patrick's next patient was already waiting as he showed Meghan out. This stranger was his second new patient of the day, and he was carefully writing up his notes

31

afterwards when, at three o'clock, he became aware of the sound of a siren. A moment or two later he glanced up to see blue flashing lights through the trim Venetian blinds, followed by the noisy bulk of a fire engine pulling up against the big shop window of his office. For a few minutes he went on with his notes, but now found it impossible to concentrate. He went to the door to investigate just as one of the fire crew came looking for him. The man was bare-headed; his face was white and his sweat looked clammy and cold in spite of the heat of the afternoon.

'Is that your Renault parked round the back?' he asked. 'If so, we need the keys.'

PART TWO

France 2010

I

The pharmacist, whose crisp make-up and white tunic were pristine thanks to the fierce air-conditioning, indicated over Leonie's right shoulder, '*Mais, c'est lui-même!*'

Leonie turned to see a long-legged, tallish man with very blue eyes. The pharmacist, introducing him, took evident care to pronounce his name correctly. 'Monsieur Hinde.'

'You're English?'

'English father, French mother,' he replied. 'Patrice. Or Patrick. Take your pick.' He smiled – an attractive smile – and held out his hand. She shook it happily.

'Leonie Treadwell. I work for Gaby Duval, and one of our clients needs an English-speaking homeopath. How perfect is this!'

He frowned slightly, looking to the pharmacist for clarification, but she was already attending to another customer.

Leonie explained. 'We do holiday lets – bastides and farmhouses – and we're on call for any snags. There's a six-year-old with an allergy to something in the house and the parents hope a homeopathic remedy might do the trick.'

'More than likely.' He fished in his wallet and handed her a printed card. 'Here's my number. I'll do my best to fit her in quickly.'

'Him, actually, but thanks. I'm sure they'll call you straight away. They're threatening to pack up and go home if the poor kid doesn't stop wheezing.'

He smiled down at her again, and Leonie found herself wishing there was more to say, something to detain her beside this man whose presence she instinctively liked. But, thanking the pharmacist, she said her goodbyes, left the shop and returned to the July sunshine.

The phone rang as she was closing the office shutters at the end of the day: it was the parents of the allergic child, singing their praises for the homeopath's prompt and effective help. They were sure the remedy he supplied would work, and they could now stay on for the full three weeks they had booked. Leonie added Patrice Hinde's details to the database and all but forgot him until, a busy week later, she was crossing the square at lunchtime when the persistent ringing of a bicycle bell made her turn. Without thinking, she greeted him familiarly with a *bisou*. It was his infinitesimal recoil, like some wild creature too wary to approach, that instantly endeared him to her. Yet, despite that momentary flare of alarm in his eyes, it was he who suggested they take their baguettes and sit together on a bench in the shade of the medieval church.

When they parted, he said nothing about meeting again, and during the course of the long, hot afternoon she recalled with shame how they had each talked about their work: he spoke engagingly of imbalances, stored griefs, chronic conditions and relieving distillations; she told of mice, blocked lavatories, extra pillows and where to buy baby food late at night. Why had she imagined such an apparently thoughtful man would be interested in the mundane concerns of her job?

As she came outside at the end of the day, she found Gaby watering the pots in the courtyard. Gaby maintained a robust liking for people and revelled in, rather than despaired of, the peculiarities of some of their weirder holiday clients; her four children joked that the only reason she'd married the local *notaire* thirty-odd years ago was so that nothing could ever happen in this small town without her hearing of it first. Deciding to tell Gaby about her lunchtime encounter, Leonie lingered to hear whatever Gaby might have gleaned about Monsieur Hinde.

'He's popular, built up a fairly large practice,' Gaby informed her readily. 'Lives in his grandmother's house. One of those ghastly ornate Belle Epoque villas near the river.'

As a frequent guest in Gaby's immaculately restored house, Leonie had observed how her employer's taste veered towards minimalism.

'He spent a lot of his childhood there, apparently,' Gaby continued. 'Came back when she died, about four years ago.'

'Did you know him as a kid?' asked Leonie. 'If he grew up here?'

Gaby shook her head. 'Madame Broyard, his grand-mother, kept to herself. Very correct, old-style *bourgeoise*. War widow, I think. Must've been coming up for ninety when she died. I heard he's restoring the house, doing the work himself.'

Seeing that Leonie appeared mildly intrigued by her thumbnail sketch, Gaby went on. 'I'm not aware that there's ever been a wife on the scene, sweetie. And if he has had women friends, he's been very discreet about them.'

For the past year Gaby had been encouraging her to find a new man, but Leonie refused to rise to the bait. 'See you tomorrow,' she laughed, waving, and making for her car.

Her tiny rented apartment on the edge of town wasn't far. The old Citroen had come with the job, and in the summer heat she was glad not to have to walk home. Nevertheless, she liked having something fresh to mull over on the familiar drive. She still regarded her stay in the Dordogne as temporary, even though it was well over a year now since she and Greg had broken up. Her French was pretty good, but discovering an unattached Englishman here was – what? *Was* she interested? The very notion of having her feelings entangled again was a possibility she couldn't have imagined earlier in the year, and might even be a cheering sign that she was getting over 'things': Greg telling her that he didn't want to get married or have kids with her; watching her pack and letting her leave after eleven years together, these memories were still too brutal to recall in any detail. He'd suggested once that he visit her in France but she put him off, and though Stella said he wasn't seeing anyone else (too lazy, Stella said), he hadn't asked again. So – Patrice Hinde. Should their paths cross again, who knew what might not happen?

It was three weeks before Patrice rang her one morning at the office, offering no explanation for the arbitrary timing of his call. But she accepted his invitation to dinner readily, resolving on this occasion to appear less banal.

They met, as Patrice had suggested, at the bench beside the church – an arrangement Leonie teased herself for already finding a touch romantic, as if this was to become 'their' bench. Not knowing where they were going for dinner, she had been indecisive about what to wear. Settling for a patterned summer dress that showed off her slender waist, but fearing it might not be dressy enough, she had added strappy heeled sandals, and wound her hair up into a coil, clipped with a bright artificial flower that Stella had given her. When she spotted him waiting with his bicycle and a rucksack, her heart sank. She must have misjudged the situation, and now she felt wrong-footed and awkward. Making no move to greet her with *bisous*, he nonetheless appeared friendly and relaxed.

'I like your flower. Thought we'd have a picnic.' He patted the rucksack, in which metal chinked against glass, and she noted a folded rug in the bicycle basket. 'I know a

perfect spot – if that's all right with you?' he added courteously.

'Sounds perfect. Be a shame to sit inside on such a lovely
evening.'

He led the way downhill, and, as they turned onto a
gravelled track, quickly noticed the unsuitability of her
sandals. Leonie was mortified, though his laugh was
kind. 'Here, hop on. I'll push.' He hung his rucksack
from the handlebars and held on as she clambered onto
the bike; it was years since she had ridden one. With
one hand on the back of the saddle and the other guiding
the machine so she didn't have to pedal, he strode on.
As his shirt-sleeve brushed her bare arm, he smiled
comfortably. His face was close to hers, and after a little
while she found her attention dwelling on the narrow
margin between the denim collar and his light brown
hair. Leaning back slightly, she caught herself thinking
inappropriately how nice it would be to stroke the sun-
browned skin, to explore with her fingertip just a little
way below the faded collar, and almost laughed out loud.
He caught her look of private amusement, and smiled
once more. She found his evident ease with their silence
somehow touching.

They crossed the bridge and headed along a path beside
the river. Although only a metre or so deep, at its lowest
mark now in late August, the brown water ran with quiet
power between the wooded banks before opening out unexpectedly into a small sunny meadow.

'Oh, how lovely,' she told him. 'I thought I'd explored the area thoroughly, but I've never been here before.'

'What brought you to Riberac?'

'I spent a few months here as a student. My degree's in French. I had such a good time that, when I wanted to get out of England for a bit, I wrote to ask Gaby if there was any work going. Nothing moves around here without her knowing about it.'

'I'll remember that!'

'Anyway, she offered me a job herself, so here I am. Didn't exactly recapture my carefree student days, but I'm kept busy and Gaby's incredibly kind.'

He nodded; while rather frustrated that he wasn't more curious, she liked the consideration he showed in not yet asking why she might have wanted an escape from England.

There was further evidence of Patrice's solicitude when he laid out the rug for them to sit on and unpacked the rucksack. He had not only brought cold white wine and local bread onto which he sliced for her tomatoes, artichoke hearts and Brie, but two huge linen serviettes, soft with age, to serve as plates and even a small citronella candle which he lit to discourage gnats and mosquitoes from the river. Leonie, enchanted, was plunged into tender and forgotten longings: she couldn't remember when Greg had last shown such thoughtfulness, such delicacy of feeling. Pretending ignorance of the little that Gaby had told her, she asked Patrice in turn what had brought him here.

'My grandmother died and left her house to me. I came over intending to clear it up and sell it, but . . . I found I liked it better here.'

'Were you close to your grandmother?'

He shrugged. 'In a way, I suppose. I used to stay with her during school holidays, but I wouldn't say we were close. She was strict and old-fashioned. Doing what was right and carrying out her duty were what mattered most.'

'Sounds a bit bleak.'

'Not really. Besides, one doesn't know any different as a child.'

'I suppose not.' It became clear he wasn't about to volunteer more, so she prodded gently. 'Do you have brothers and sisters?'

'No, just me.'

'Lonely, then, with your grandmother?'

He shrugged once more. 'A bit isolated, yes.'

'You still have connections in England, though?'

'Some.' He paused, looking towards the water. 'I was married briefly. Only lasted three years.'

'Do you stay in touch?'

He shook his head. 'We're divorced. I doubt she'd want to hear from me.'

'What happened? Do you mind me asking?'

He shrugged again. 'I let her down. There was no future for us together.'

Leonie wondered if he meant he'd had an affair, but she didn't dare ask; not yet, anyway. Instead, she encouraged him to expand by offering information about herself: 'My ex and I weren't married, but we'd lived together for almost twelve years.'

'You don't look old enough!'

'I'm thirty-four.'

'A youngster!' He topped up her wine, shooting her what she hoped was a flirtatious glance.

Leonie waited for Patrice to ask her about herself; when he seemed content with silence, she ploughed on, wanting him to have a sense of her, to push through to some kind of intimacy, impatient to get something underway between them.

'When I started talking about our future, Greg said he didn't want the same things. So I left.'

'And came here?'

'Yes.'

'So we're both refugees.' He raised his wine to her in a mock toast. She touched his cup with her own, looking into his eyes, noting the fine white lines around them disappear when he smiled. He met her gaze. 'You've told me what you do here for Madame Duval, but that can't be what you did in England?' His tone was matter-of-fact, intimacy apparently not yet on his agenda.

Disappointed, Leonie answered, 'No. It wasn't. I used to work on various specialist journals for a big publisher, buying in articles from foreign publications and arranging translation. Very absorbing, but rubbish money. When Greg and I split up, I realised I couldn't afford to buy a place on my own in London. And I was—' she took a deep breath and decided to go ahead and say it '— pretty heart-broken.' She looked covertly at him to see if this struck a chord. Unable to read his expression, she pressed on. 'Life just didn't seem fair, so I ran away. Hoped a bit of summer heat would do the trick.'

Patrice winced. He tried to disguise it, but it was unmissable: she had touched a nerve. He, too, had been wounded. Fearing she'd gone too far too fast, she gave a false laugh, trying to cover her tracks. 'But I'm over all that now. No idea why I stuck it out as long as I did. I love it here. Don't you?'

'I've made a life here, yes.'

She heard the pain beneath his words and, aware of some kind of tension underlying his reticence, longed to discover what untold story lay buried there. But he was clearly a private man, and if he were unwilling to offer the information then it was far too soon to go digging into his romantic past. She studied him as he sat watching the flow of the river, and berated herself for her clumsiness. She found his modesty deeply appealing; it was more than shyness: once again the image came to mind of some wild creature that dreads becoming lethally trapped by coming too close. Leonie felt an excited, confused curiosity, and, observing his expression react minutely to the swirls and eddies of the water, her heart went out to him. In that moment she decided that, while she was now certain of her desire to know him better, she must be careful not to

barge in on his sense of discretion, and to let him dictate
his own terms.

Answering Gaby's questions in the office next morning,
Leonie found it hard to account for the intensity of her
emotions. Though Patrice had chivalrously insisted on
wheeling her on his bike back to where she had left her
car in the now dusky square, he had bid her goodnight
without any form of kiss and, without even waiting until
she'd driven away, cycled off without a word about seeing
her again. It was ridiculous to feel so let down, and so she
refused to admit to Gaby that it had been anything but a
pleasant evening spent in the company of a compatriot.

Meanwhile, though Gaby had been indefatigable in her
researches, she had so far failed to come up with any further
information about Patrice Hinde. Highly prizing her own
intelligence-gathering skills, Gaby had little option but to
regard this unusual lack of background gossip as signifi-
cant.

'No one remembers him as a child,' she informed Leonie.
'He didn't go to school here, only spent the holidays with
his grandmother. But my sister-in-law Sylviane, you met
her at Thierry's birthday celebrations—' She broke off to
answer the phone, and while she dealt with a change to
a client's booking Leonie thought back to the party Gaby
had thrown for her husband, where she had indeed chatted
to his older sister. Sylviane was a pleasant woman in her
early sixties who, despite never having left the small town

45

in which she was born, bore that air of remarkable sophistication for which Leonie most envied French women.

Her call ended, Gaby returned to her story. 'Sylviane remembers Patrice's mother, Agnès, when she was a girl. They were at school together.'

'What was his mother like?'

'Sweet-natured but timid. Even when Sylviane reminded Thierry, he didn't remember her at all, and he was always one for the girls. Apparently Madame Broyard was heavily pregnant when her husband, Patrice's grandfather, was killed, right at the end of the Occupation. He'd been active in the Resistance, I gather, and got a bullet in the neck for his efforts. Anyway, Sylviane says Agnès was always in her mother's shadow.'

'Gosh! Madame Broyard never remarried?'

'There were few enough men to go round after the Liberation as it was.'

'I guess so. And presumably when Agnès married, it was to an Englishman?'

Gaby nodded. 'Sylviane and Agnès didn't stay friends much after school, but Sylviane remembers the upset her marriage caused. Madame Broyard had barely let the girl out of her sight as she grew up, and now she was leaving France altogether. Deserting her. People said Agnès sent Patrice to Madame Broyard every holiday to propitiate her mother for staying away herself.'

'Well, I know how I felt when my mother chose to go off to Canada with my stepfather,' Leonie affirmed. 'And his two daughters,' she added, recalling her old sense of being second best. 'But tough on Patrice. Especially as a kid, with only a strict old lady for company.'

'He's still a loner, by all accounts.'

'More shy, I suspect.'

Gaby looked at her shrewdly. 'I hope you're not going to fall for the idea that being a loner is romantic.' Leonie blushed, and Gaby shook her head reprovingly. 'Loners are people who have no friends. And if you look hard enough there's usually some good reason why,' she said firmly, before adding in a softer tone, 'You know I'm all for you finding a good man, sweetie, but we need to find out more about this one.'

Leonie nodded submissively. But she pictured Gaby's well-ordered life, every corner taken up with husband, business, married children, infant grandchildren. What had she experienced of heart-break and recovery, of second chances and the pain of regeneration? Leonie understood all too well what it was to be wounded, could empathise with the impulse to withdraw into oneself, to appear to others to be a loner. Although she considered Patrice to be carrying the deeper hurt, she too was a refugee. Yet he had awakened sensations in her which had renewed her belief that wounds could heal – and be healed.

Her musings stopped when she caught Gaby observing her. 'Be sure your heart is properly mended first,' counselled the older woman.

'Don't worry about me,' Leonie reassured her, while a

rebellious inner voice crowed that the heart knows best, that sometimes it's necessary to undergo a little pain in order to win something precious.

And so, when an entire week had gone by without hearing from Patrice, she found herself inventing an excuse to call the number she had entered on the database, ostensibly about another villa client who might require a homeopath. He sounded pleased to hear her voice, so she ventured, as she had planned, to mention an outdoor concert to be held in the grounds of an abbey about fifteen miles away. Might he be interested?

'That's a lovely idea, thank you, but I don't drive.'

'Oh, no problem. We can go in my car, I don't mind.' She cursed herself for gushing.

'No. I don't use cars. At all.'

'Oh.' This time she managed to keep the disappointment from her voice. 'That's very ecological of you. You must have firm principles.'

'Well, it's a decision I took when I moved to France,' he explained.

'No, really. I admire you for it.'

'I even walked here. Followed parts of the Way of St James.'

'Wow, that's amazing! If only we were all so strong-minded.'

There was a lengthening pause. Leonie felt she could hardly suggest a second reason to meet, but he broke it. 'It'd be nice to see you again, though.'

She hid her triumph. 'I'd like that.'

'I'll call and we'll arrange something,' he told her, his tone purposeful. 'Bye for now.'

The phone went dead. Not until this moment, when her hopes plummeted, did she acknowledge how much emotional responsibility she had unreasonably placed on Patrice's shoulders. She was behaving as if she were in the grip of a schoolgirl crush, and vowed to stop this nonsense!

As always by the start of September, work was busy. Most of the properties had been continuously occupied since May, and the wear and tear was taking its toll. It never ceased to amaze Leonie how disrespectfully some clients treated the houses in which they stayed, failing to report breakages, leaks or stains, dragging furniture outside, leaving bathroom towels in sodden heaps by the pool. And worse.

After her frustrating call to Patrice, she headed up into the hills to sort out an infuriated summons from a family from Reading who had arrived that weekend. It was not yet eleven o'clock when she parked beside a top spec Range Rover. She found the husband, who was about her age, down beside the pool, a can of lager in his hand, his hairy and reddening belly straining against outsize swimming shorts. His three young sons, their shoulders and noses also already painfully sunburned, stood in a row wearing full snorkelling regalia.

They stared at her through their masks as their father

ranted about how much he had paid to rent the villa and the disgusting condition of the pool. In fact, as she knew, he'd opted to keep his kids out of school for the first week of term in order to get a slightly cheaper rate, but, as Leonie looked at the pool, she had to agree. Potato crisps floated atop scuzzy water that was already turning cloudy. Through the murk she could make out a Coke can resting on the bottom. It had not been there on Saturday when she'd done the pre-arrival checks, but she didn't think it was a good idea to point this out. Instead, she commiserated and, in the client's hearing, made the call on her mobile to the pool guy to come that afternoon. As she returned to her car, she didn't blame the unfortunate wife for keeping out of sight: men like that gave her a lot of sympathy for Victorian women who embraced invalidism. It was definitely better to be alone than to be with the wrong man.

Resolving to make the most of pleasures that did not require a romantic partner, Leonie decided to take her lunch break early so she could stroll through the Friday market in the square before returning to the stuffy office. She was sure Gaby, who insisted on the finest and freshest ingredients, would not object; indeed, they'd probably bump into one another at the busiest of the charcuterie stalls. Leonie made a first circuit to see what fruit and vegetables were in season, making mental notes of which seller had the best greengages and corn on the cob.

She was on her way back around, beginning to enjoy

the clamour and the easeful warmth of the sun on her back, when she spotted Patrice buying chanterelles at the stall that she'd ear-marked to buy some for herself. What to do? If she continued as she had intended, he might imagine she had engineered a meeting. After the abortive phone call this morning, it would look like she was stalking him! On the other hand, why should his presence force her to alter her natural behaviour? As though reading her mind, he turned his head, spotted her and beckoned her over.

'Hello! These look really good. Let me get you some.'

The artlessness of his offer made her regard her thought processes as conniving and artificial, and she stood there like an idiot while he bought a second bag of mushrooms. Their hands brushed as he handed it to her, his blue eyes sparkling into hers.

'Here. A taste of autumn. Enjoy.'

Before she could even mumble her thanks, he turned and wove away through the crowd. She stayed put, and asked for a couple of corn-cobs while she willed the hot blush to fade from her cheeks.

When she dared to look again in his direction, he was gone. Dazed, she carried on with her shopping, but the allure of the ripe fruits had faded, and she bought mechanically, smiling only from politeness. Carrying her bags, she made for Gaby's office, where she could hide her shame and the ringing phones would banish her confusion.

But Gaby already had fresh intelligence from her

sister-in-law to impart. A friend of Sylviane's, Catherine, had been close to Agnès at school. When Agnès used to send Patrice to stay with his grandmother, Catherine would ask the boy over to play with her children, who were the same age and all seemed to get on well. But Madame Broyard nearly always made difficulties about it, and never invited Catherine's children in return. Though their kids had been given little chance to become friends, Catherine and Agnès had managed to remain in touch for over thirty years, and would always catch up whenever Agnès visited her mother, which she had done diligently once or twice a year.

'Patrice must've come too, at least once in a while, to see his grandmother?' suggested Leonie.

Gaby shook her head. 'Apparently not. And,' she added with emphasis, 'when Agnès and her husband came for the funeral, Agnès barely spoke to anyone, then left without even seeing Catherine. Catherine's not had a single word from Agnès since; she's actually extremely put out. Thierry wonders whether there might have been some disagreement over the will,' Gaby continued with relish. 'Madame Broyard apparently left almost nothing to her daughter. Although Catherine thinks that may be because Agnès was perfectly well provided for by her husband, and this way she would've been saved the bother of disposing of everything.'

'So Patrice didn't come for the funeral?' queried Leonie.

'Not that Catherine knew of. Which also makes it all the more odd that Madame Broyard chose to leave her house to him.'

It was clear to Leonie that the subject had been thoroughly discussed amongst Gaby's family and friends. While she didn't want to miss out on any possible scrap of gossip that might shed some light on her elusive new friend, she resolved to be extra careful in what she chose to tell Gaby from now on. Especially when Gaby declared, 'We'll all have to rely on you to find out for us, sweetie!'

When Leonie reached home that evening, she had no appetite and left the chanterelles to wither in their bag. Instead she rang her best friend Stella in London.

'Am I falling in love?' she demanded.

Stella laughed: 'You've only set eyes on him, what—?'

'Four times. Okay. But isn't that what being in love's all about?'

'I guess so.'

'Being certain straight away that somehow it's right?'

'Look, if you're that stuck on him, go ahead and see what happens. It's a chance to get laid, if nothing else!'

'It's more than that,' protested Leonie.

'Go easy, Lennie,' said Stella. 'What's all the rush? You hardly know this guy yet, let alone what he might be after.'

'Well, he's not exactly trying to jump my bones, is he?'

'Maybe not. But is this really what you want? To feel so . . . nervy about someone. At least get a better sense of who he is before you start investing yourself like this.'

'I'm not handing him my life savings!'

'You've only just got back on your feet after Greg.'

'I've got to take a risk again some time.'

'Listen, I'm sure your instincts are good. Take care, that's all. I don't want ever again to see you as upset as you were last year.'

Trying to ignore the obscure resentment evoked by Stella's sensible warning, Leonie switched the discussion to her friend's new job. After several stressful years working for an adoption agency, Stella had recently moved to a charity which reunited adopted adults with their original birth families. Hearing how her friend was already benefiting from a more optimistic working environment, her intrusive thoughts about Patrice took a back seat.

And yet, in quiet moments over the next few days – driving to work, waiting for a kettle to boil, removing her make-up, falling asleep – Leonie found herself stubbornly turning over like a pebble in her mind the conviction that her heart had begun to nurture some renegade life of its own. Stella was right to urge caution; she hardly knew this man, and reassured herself that she could still as easily turn away from the startling feelings she had for him as welcome them in. But nevertheless she was intrigued, excited, fearful – not of Patrice, but of the prospect of some fresh dimension of experience. It was time for her to change, to grow. And she was now absolutely certain that some entirely new way to feel would open before her if only she could draw near enough to Patrice to let it happen.

*

Leonie assumed, when Patrice rang to invite her laughingly to the 'grand opening' of the salon he had restored in his grandmother's house, that there would be quite a few other people there. She was more than curious to meet his friends and, flattered by the likelihood that she was about to be accepted among them, was almost disappointed to discover she was the sole guest. He had waited for her arrival to open a bottle of champagne, but she suspected from his slight clumsiness in pouring the wine that this was not his first drink of the evening. She took his evident jumpiness as a further sign of how favoured she was to have gained entrance to his home.

The marble fire surround, window shutters, plasterwork and parquet flooring of the salon had all been painstakingly renovated. The amount of work involved was clear from the dilapidated state of the entrance hall and other ground-floor rooms, all of which Patrice showed her. It appeared that he inhabited only a narrow study, the quaint black-and-white-tiled kitchen, designed as the domain of servants rather than of the original owners of the house, and, presumably, some sleeping quarters upstairs. Leonie was aware from the address on the card he had given her that he saw his homeopathic patients at a modern rented office in the centre of town.

After the tour, which included the beautifully kept garden at the back of the house, they perched decorously together on a Louis *seize*-style sofa, tightly upholstered in a faded satin of red and white stripes, and placed their glasses on an incongruous Sixties glass coffee table, which was the salon's one other piece of furniture.

'It must seem strange to you that I live like this,' Patrice observed lightly.

'No, I like it.'

'I'll be forty next birthday. I ought to be more settled at my age.'

'Why? People should live how they like.'

'The house was already starting to get shabby when I was a boy. Josette had spent forty years here by then.'

'Josette?'

'Yes. She didn't like to be called *grand-mère*. She didn't much like children, come to that.'

'What about when you were older? Did you get on better then?'

'I never saw much of her. Not as much as I should, I suppose. I drifted rather, after university and everything, and she never seemed particularly to care whether or not I came to see her.' He took a reckless gulp of champagne. 'I was named for my grandfather. A hero of the Resistance who was killed at the end of the Occupation. I'd catch Josette looking at me, and knew I was never good enough.'

'Yet you don't mind living here?'

He looked around, surprised, as if this question had never occurred to him before. 'No. No, I don't. But then I couldn't imagine existing anywhere else. It's a house that absorbs outcasts. A kind of safe house for three generations that failed to belong elsewhere.'

'Is that how you were made to feel, when you were sent here in the holidays?'

He was puzzled.

'An outcast,' she repeated.

'Oh, then. Yes. I suppose I was a bit. Certainly abandoned. Unwanted. You must remember how kids get about things. I always believed it was my fault that my parents sent me away, didn't want me with them; another reason why Josette was always so unforgiving about having me.' He gazed around the room, where lozenges of evening sun were lengthening across the newly polished parquet and shadows were beginning to pool in the furthest corners. 'I've enjoyed the work. It's very meditative. A psychologist I saw once thought I should take anti-depressants, but sanding and painting and varnishing are far more effective.'

She looked at him in surprise.

'I want you to learn the worst about me,' he said in a rush. 'I don't want you thinking I'm a good bet when I'm not.'

She was moved. 'Is anyone?'

'I'm sure you are.' Embarrassed, he topped up their glasses while Leonie glowed at the compliment. 'I'm in two minds which room to do next,' he went on, before she could speak. 'Maybe it should be the hall. What do you think?'

'It would look rather grand.'

'The hall it shall be, then.'

He contemplated the room once more, dwelling with obvious satisfaction on his craftsmanship. But after his avowal she felt relaxed enough to bear his silence. Then, to her surprise, and without looking directly at her, he reached out and took her hand, wrapping both of his around it as if it were the most natural gesture in the world.

'It's rubbish that I was abandoned, of course,' he said. 'My father worked for multinational companies that kept moving him around all over Europe at fairly short notice, and I boarded at school in England, so it made sense for me to come here. Though I suspect I was right about Josette being resentful. I think she felt my mother showed a lack of respect in expecting her to look after me. Like it meant that Josette lost face somehow in the eyes of the town. She was a very proud woman.'

'Are they still alive, your parents?'

He nodded, and at first she assumed he wasn't going to say more. 'Poor Maman,' he said at last. 'They say it's not Alzheimer's, but she's not sure who I am any more.'

Leonie filed that away to tell Gaby; it might explain why Agnès had failed to stay in touch with Catherine, her old friend from school.

'Dad and I keep a distance between us. After he put Maman in a home in Surrey, he found a grateful widow to take care of him and moved to Bournemouth. So that was that, really,' he ended drolly.

Leonie couldn't help laughing. 'My parents divorced, but

I get on fine with my stepfather and stepsisters. He's Canadian, and they all moved back there when I finished university, so I don't see them much. My real father drifted away years ago. Can't say he was missed.'

Patrice squeezed her hand, and she caught his eye, hoping he was about to kiss her, but he didn't. 'I hope you like risotto. Come and talk to me in the kitchen while I stir.' Managing to pick up the nearly empty champagne bottle without letting go of her hand, he led her through to the kitchen. Once there, he placed his hands on her shoulders, guiding her into a chair at the wide table while he lit the gas, took down an ancient iron pan and set about chopping shallots and fresh herbs.

Leonie looked about her. Nothing in the room appeared to be new. The image of Miss Havisham flitted into her mind, and she couldn't decide what to make of this bizarre set-up. Why return to the scene of his not-happy child-hood? If his marriage had ended because of another woman, maybe his heart had been doubly broken and, like Leonie herself, he had run away. Yet why, having returned here, had he failed to alter and renew things? He didn't come across as a man who was stuck in his ways, was neither fussy nor self-neglectful. So what was going on?

She studied his movements as he discarded vegetable peelings into a bin for the compost and reached up for a box of arborio rice from a cupboard, and her growing fasci-nation with his psychology melded with the first real stab of desire. She resisted the strong temptation to stand up, wrap her arms around him from behind and inhale the smell of him.

'Tell me more about homeopathy,' she requested.

'Sure? It's a huge subject.' His tone was light and amused.

'How did you get into it?'

'Drawn to it, I suppose. Poor Maman was anxious, obsessively so, and as a kid I had the usual omnipotent fantasies of finding a magical cure that would make her better, make her happy. Orthodox medicine failed to appeal to me, but I was always interested in ideas about treatment and healing.'

'I know next to nothing about it.'

'I'm still learning. It's an endless challenge.' He proffered a misshapen box grater. 'Fancy doing the Parmesan?'

It felt good to stand and work alongside him. One of the things she most missed about Greg was having someone to cook with. Though Gaby was endlessly hospitable, she was an unimaginative cook and had little patience for tasting, adjusting and thinking 'what the hell' with new combinations. But Patrice was dextrous, observant, well-attuned, and the thickening risotto smelt delicious. Glancing up at him as he judiciously added a last ladle of stock, she found her gaze wandering to his top shirt button, once again imagining tracing the brown skin beneath his collar. He caught her eye and briefly held her gaze. She stopped breathing, sure this time that he would kiss her. Turning off the gas, he announced, 'It's done. Let's eat.' And he busied himself setting the table with mismatched silverware and chipped, old-fashioned plates.

They ate opposite one another at the kitchen table, and now he did ask her where she had grown up, about her student years, her affinity with this part of France. She realised that he had an easy way of eliciting feelings rather than facts; yet, when their fingers touched as she handed him her empty plate, she saw once again a shyness, a physical reticence. She found it endearing, the lure of unavailability erotic. She, too, was essentially modest, but if there had been no women in his life since he returned to France – and four years was a long time for a man – then maybe he needed to be both enticed and reassured. She wasn't sure she could bring herself to make the first move, to seduce him, but, on the other hand, what did she have to lose? A little dignity? She was old enough to survive that. And why else, after all, would he have invited her alone tonight and then exchanged confidences as he had done so readily?

Patrice served a *tarte aux pommes* from the local patisserie and strong coffee in tiny cups, while answering more of her questions about homeopathy, explaining miasms and susceptibility and dyscrasia. Normally she would have dismissed such unlikely concepts as hocus-pocus, but tonight she was ready to suspend her critical faculties and respond instead to his genuine commitment and belief. His hopefulness and earnest wish to help the people who came to him in distress reminded her of Stella. Only a cynical beast could mock such well-meaning and oddly astute idealism. Their conversation petered out, and Leonie looked at her watch: eleven-fifteen.

'I should go,' she offered, not meaning it. They both rose awkwardly to their feet. In the embarrassed stumble towards the door, she turned into him, placing her hands against his cotton shirt and holding up her face for a kiss. Even then he hesitated. Impulsively she placed her lips on his. They were cool and soft, and she realised she had been right: although he had evaded the role of seducer, he now pulled her to him and kissed her as if he could draw from her mouth some elixir of life.

He soon led her upstairs, where the house was, if anything, even more neglected. He left her outside the bathroom, where a giant sink and claw-foot bath were both streaked with green below crooked brass taps, and the wood of the lavatory seat was worn smooth as silk. The window overlooked the silent garden, and as Leonie swiftly washed her face and rinsed her mouth she gazed out into unfamiliar darkness. Emerging, she tiptoed across the hall towards the light shining from Patrice's bedroom. He had switched on a rosy-shaded lamp and turned back the worn linen sheets on a narrow double bed that looked too short for his height.

He laughed at her surprise. 'I had this room as a boy. We'll manage, won't we?'

'Yes!'

'Back in a minute.'

To her dismay, he went out, brushing his fingertips across her collarbone as he went. She sat on the bed to take off her shoes, wondering whether to undress. Unsure of the etiquette – she hadn't done this with anyone other than Greg since she was at university – she decided, with a shiver of excitement, to wait for his return. Besides, she almost appreciated a moment alone to take in his room. There was a vaguely religious framed print over the bed, matching bedside cabinets edged with brass fretwork, one piled with paperbacks, the other bearing a modern clock-radio and the lamp. The curtains of faded *toile de Jouy* were an odd choice for a boy, and Leonie guessed intuitively that this had previously been Agnès' room before she married and went away. A small rag rug on the parquet floor by the bed, a chest of drawers, a cupboard built into the alcove beside the disused fire-grate and an incongruously ornate dining chair with a broken stretcher made up the rest of the furnishings. It was all strangely comfortless.

Patrice soon came back. He'd already taken off his shirt, which he laid on the chair as he kicked off his shoes beside hers. He stood a moment, uncertain and apprehensive, the lack of sunburn beneath his shirt making him appear especially naked. She went to him, stroking the warmth of his bare shoulders before putting her arms around his waist, her fingertips exploring the muscled contours of his back. He dropped his lips to her neck, then locked his mouth to hers, strained to help her to drag off both their clothes and groaned when their naked limbs met under the sheets.

Leonie awoke in the small hours from a deep sleep. He too stirred and folded himself around her. Breathing in the redolent scents of his bed, she felt a deep rush of joy.

II

By Sunday evening, Leonie was beside herself. She couldn't remember when she'd last felt like this, and could hardly bear to believe that she'd fallen so headlong into the cliché-ridden trap of waiting for a man to call and wondering if he ever would. Nearly forty-eight hours earlier, awake in Patrice's arms and smiling into the darkness of the unfamiliar room, she had allowed the fantasy of happy-ever-after to wash over her. She'd been unable to explain to him before they went to bed on Friday how Saturdays were her busiest days at work, and so she'd have to scramble off at dawn. He had woken with the light and, apart from saying good morning and asking how she'd slept, had set about making love to her again without further speech. Then she had decided that, for once, she could be late, even though afterwards she'd had to rush off without even a cup of coffee, apologetic, embarrassed and glowing from the unaccustomed sex.

All day, she'd been a grinning fool with a spring in her step. When she had come home on Saturday evening exhausted from work it had simply never occurred to her that he wouldn't want to speak to her. She had even hummed to herself as she took leftovers out of the fridge for her supper, sure he would call and interrupt her meal at any moment. But as bedtime had come, and the instrument of her torture remained infernally mute, terrible forebodings had begun to take shape. Was her rushed exit that morning the reason he'd not rung? Had he wrongly assumed that work was just an excuse, that she'd dashed away because she regretted being there? In which case, ought she to call him? But she knew that was impossible. She may not have had much experience of starting relationships, either before or after Greg, but she knew it was mandatory for her to wait for him to call.

And so she had lain in bed that night, watching the clock. This could not be! Before she'd left his house, she'd scribbled down her home number – maybe he couldn't read her handwriting? Or had lost the piece of paper? Eventually she slept, but all Sunday morning she had hovered near the phone. To keep busy, she had set about spring-cleaning her small apartment. By mid-afternoon, it was spotless, so she had driven to the nearest Carrefour to stock up on essentials she didn't need. And now, at eight o'clock on Sunday evening, she was exhausted and climbing the walls.

She would just have to accept that she was a one-night stand. She could live with that, she told herself; she was a grown-up after all. It had been heavenly to be reminded what it was like to be touched, aroused, desired, held. Extraordinary to remember, to realise how the body could forget pleasure as easily as it forgot pain. She had no regrets. She just had to pull herself together. Okay, she'd obviously been wrong about Patrice, but not for her the agony and humiliation of persisting in a belief that it had been anything more than it was. She might have been a bit naïve, assuming he felt the same way as she did, but being a bit naïve wasn't going to turn her into an object of ridicule. Or pity. She'd simply have a good cry before she went to sleep, and hold onto a glimmer of the sexual afterglow.

Leonie was very glad to reach the haven of the office on Monday morning, despite having to maintain constant guard against Gaby's acuity. The busy phones were a welcome distraction, so she was taken completely by surprise when, answering routinely, she heard his voice.

'Hello. It's Patrice. How are you this morning?'

'Fine.' She tried to keep the incredulity out of her voice. 'How are you?'

'Very well. I've got something for you. Spent most of the weekend on it.'

'Oh!'

'Would you like to come for supper tomorrow night?'

'Tomorrow?'

'Then I can show you.'

Leonie made a rapid emotional calculation: 'Yes. Thanks. What time?'

'Come when you like. I'll be home by seven.'

'Okay.'

'Bye!' And he hung up.

The weekend had given her enough of a scare to hide her relief and delight as much as she could from Gaby. But she felt elated, exonerated, reprieved, as if the story with the happy ending could now be resumed.

On Tuesday evening when Leonie saw what Patrice wanted to show her, she was enchanted. She forgave him utterly for all the misery he had unwittingly put her through over the weekend.

'It's been rusting in the shed,' he told her. They were in his garden, where he had wheeled out a woman's bicycle. 'I cleaned it up and oiled it, and I got new tyres and brake blocks. It'll be a hundred per cent safe, I guarantee. Nothing much I could do about the saddle, I'm afraid. It's a bit tatty. Otherwise all it needs is a basket.'

'And a bell! At least until I learn to ride in a straight line.'

'Do you like it?' he asked shyly.

'Yes!'

'Good. Then we'll be able to go places together.' Patrice looked at her with such transparency that her heart melted. It was clear to her now that she had completely misunderstood how new relationships were managed. She'd been a student when she met Greg, but thirty-somethings obviously had all sorts of priorities beyond some juvenile headlong rush into romance. During those long hours over the weekend while she had been mentally accusing him of just using her for a quick fuck, he had been innocently planning ahead, imagining picnics, outings, grown-up time spent together. A future. She resolved never to doubt him again.

'It's adorable! Thank you. Thank you so much.'

She went to kiss him and saw that same little flicker of alarm, of hesitation, that he had shown the day they ate their baguettes together on the bench by the church. As before, she was engulfed by tenderness. Then he kissed her back, and they did not make supper until after they had led each other upstairs to bed, hungry for warm, smooth skin, ravenous to reach inside one another and find release.

He held her hand as they went back down to the kitchen, hungry now for food and wine. 'We're pretty good together, aren't we?' he said, squeezing her hand, and giving her a sideways grin.

Patrice made salad and a hastily prepared omelette. Leonie sipped red wine and watched him handling the bowl, reaching for the eggs, adjusting the burner on the stove; she smiled to herself, imagining all over again with each of his deft, confident movements the pleasure contained in each touch of his fingertips. They ate in rested silence, mopping up their plates with bread, then she dried the dishes while he washed up, making a joke together of her attempts to work out where things were to be put, habit having superseded any rational storage system decades ago. They chatted in a desultory way, too satiated with physical knowledge to enquire into anything much beyond the present moment.

Before returning to bed, Patrice opened the garden door and they stood, his arm around her shoulders, listening to the night sounds – small rustlings, a passing car, the inevitable barking of a distant dog – and enjoying the cooling air on their faces. As he switched off the hall light and followed her up the stairs, Leonie had a vivid sense of eternity, of male and female together, forever approaching the same inevitable conclusion. They undressed again without self-consciousness, and he nestled in behind her in the narrow bed. He stroked her hip for a while, then they dropped effortlessly into sleep.

Over the next few weeks, during which they settled into a pattern of meeting every three or four days, Leonie found it hard to believe that she could look forward with such luxuriously matter-of-fact assurance to something as exqui-site and exalting as their love-making. It gave her almost as much pleasure to think about Patrice during the days she did not see him – and sometimes not hear from him, either – as to be with him. And when they were together, his ability to read from her body language what kind of day she'd had, and then wordlessly either soothe her or elicit and share some small elation, created a wonderful intimacy.

She had no memory of it being like that with Greg. She

possessed more energy than she'd had in years. Her life seemed whole, as if she were constantly on the point of effortlessly winning a race, throwing out her arms and flying past the tape. The very last of the grimy rim of misery that had clung to her since she left London was rinsed away. She felt cleansed of unhappiness – and vindicated: it was not she who was unloving, unlovable. There could be nothing wrong with her if she could feel like this with Patrice.

'I'd better book a ticket and come meet this man,' declared Stella, when Leonie attempted to explain her happiness over the phone. 'I want to relish the sight of a loved-up Lennie!'

After Leonie ended the call, she forced herself to analyse why her instant, though luckily unvoiced, reaction had been to tell Stella not to come. Stella was her closest friend. Not once had she ever been apprehensive at the idea of spending time with her. Why should she be reluctant now? It wasn't that she was afraid of Stella not liking Patrice. She was sure Stella would discover everything in him that she herself so adored. It was, she decided, merely that she and Patrice were still in that initial starry-eyed lovers' bubble into which, so far, no third party had been invited. They hadn't even yet gone out for a meal, preferring the intimacy and spontaneity of eating at home. Patrice had spent a couple of nights at her apartment, but mostly they had tacitly opted for his house – a place which, to her at least, had itself become magically set apart from day-to-day reality. She had been charmed, though, at how he took note of the type of breakfast tea and jam she had at home and produced them the next time she came to him.

Now, examining her reluctance to see Stella, she acknowledged how she'd repeatedly put off arrangements with a couple of the friends she'd made locally – Audra, who dealt in *bricolage* and garden and kitchen antiques, and Martine, who worked for the private catering company they recommended to some of their wealthier villa clients. She had declined their invitations because she couldn't always be certain in advance which night Patrice might suggest meeting, and she wanted to be sure of seeing him as often as she could. But that was not a good pattern to fall into. Not that she minded him not making fixed dates, she wasn't insecure about it; he always promised to call her and he always did. But equally, she instructed herself, she ought not to go on sacrificing her own arrangements, the infrastructure of friendships and appointments that had supported her life here – friendships that, when she first arrived, battered and fragile, she'd worked hard to establish. She picked up the phone, called Audra and fixed to meet in three days' time.

Sure enough, when Patrice called her the following evening, he said he'd like to meet up that same Thursday.

'Oh, I can't, Patrice. I'm going out with a friend.'

'Well, never mind.'

Leonie could hear that he was slightly taken aback, but squashed her craven impulse to say she'd cancel. She waited, breathless.

'Did you sort out the problem with the cots?' he asked.

'Yes. Gaby had to borrow a travel cot from one of her daughters. You'd expect people to shout well ahead that they had triplets. How many rented houses are going to have two cots, let alone three?'

'True. I had an interesting new case today. I'll tell you when I see you.' Patrice liked to discuss his work with her, although he never identified his patients.

'You could come along on Thursday if you want to,' she offered, cringing at herself. 'You'd like Audra. She's good fun.'

'I won't intrude. Another time. What are you up to this evening?'

Her hopes soared. 'Not much.'

'I'm ironing. Run out of shirts.'

Disappointed, she wondered whether she dared suggest going over there.

'And been watching the swallows gathering,' he went on. 'They'll be starting to leave soon. Nights are already drawing in, don't you think?'

'Oh, don't say that! Summer's not over yet.'

'I imagined you'd prefer it out of season. A lot less busy.'

'I don't mind. Anything rather than getting up and coming home in the cold and dark. I always hated the lack of daylight in London, so I'll take every last bit of sunshine and heat I can get.' When he didn't reply, she prompted him. 'Wouldn't you?'

'It gets a bit stressful. Some relief when autumn comes. Call you on Friday . . . Bye for now.'

73

Alone, she looked out of her kitchen window at the swallows endlessly swapping places on the telephone wires across the road, calming herself with the image of the birds' mysterious voyages as a direct link to Patrice on the other side of the town. She reminded herself of the powerful part his elusiveness played in his attraction for her. That such an essentially shy man should be lured by her willingness not to rush him, by her ability to coax him with stillness and waiting, emphasised her sensitivity and empathy. She couldn't help but like such a reflected image of herself. And Patrice was the complete opposite of Greg, whose failure to commit had stemmed from immaturity, a lack of depth. Patrice, she felt instinctively, suffered from an abundance of depth, profound places where he wrestled with difficult memories.

She hoped one day he would tell her what they were. She was sure they were bound up with why he was drawn to homeopathy: the wounded healer. He had all but explained himself to her when he outlined the theory of miasms, of past or inherited damage that causes an endless repetition of symptoms, of aches and pains caused by old and invisible injuries and diseases. She wasn't sure she believed in every last word of homeopathy, but she certainly believed in the healing power of love. She had only to be patient, and, she was sure, they would free one another from their pasts.

Unexpectedly, Leonie really enjoyed catching up with Audra. They compared one another's latest clothes and shoe purchases, chatted about random stuff, laughed over nothing much. She started to relax properly for the first time in weeks, and was on the point of ordering two more glasses of wine when her mobile chirped. She looked at the screen. Apologising to Audra, she moved away so she could speak in private.

'Patrice?'

'Hello. I realise you're with your friend.'

'Yes.'

'But I thought maybe you could come here afterwards.'

'Oh!' Leonie was confused. Maybe it was the wine on an empty stomach, but she resented his assumption that he could summon her like this. Yet a ripple of desire told her she would go anyway. It also reminded her that she did not have her contraceptive cap with her. 'I could be a while,' she hedged. 'I haven't seen Audra in ages, and we've not even ordered any food yet.'

'Doesn't matter. I'll be waiting.'

The insubordinate ripple made itself felt again. 'Okay.'

'See you soon, then. Bye.'

She returned to her companion, making out the call was work related, but her earlier lightness and ease had gone. They ordered, and, while they ate, Leonie asked diligent questions about Audra's business, what she'd managed to buy at a recent auction, whether the Dutch were still chasing after old enamel cookware. But all the while she couldn't help wondering how late it was, and when she could decently leave.

When, at last, Leonie parked outside Patrice's house, she sat in the car, trying to work out why she was feeling so ambivalent about going in. It was already eleven o'clock, and they both had to work the next day. He hadn't wanted to fix an arrangement for another night, yet invited her now when there was no time for anything other than sex. Was that all he wanted? On the other hand, she could hardly blame him: she wanted to be in his bed every bit as much as, it would appear, he wanted her to be there. She reminded herself that this was exciting, a midnight assignation with her lover.

She thought back to when she had last doubted him, remembering the restored bicycle. She had been naïve then in assuming that because he didn't call straight away it was over, never going to happen. But it wasn't. And two or three times since then they'd taken their bikes at weekends and pedalled to various places together: nowhere special, but it had been lovely to cover some distance yet cycle slowly enough to look at hedgerows and clouds, the immaculate *potagers* and sloping vineyards. One day, returning home, they had stopped at the gates to the local cemetery, set among fields of mown hay. Patrice dismounted and, holding out his hand, had led her to a simple headstone.

'My grandfather, Patrice Broyard,' he told her.

'Your grandmother, too,' Leonie had said, pointing out the other name, the newer letters below carved more sharply into the stone.

76

He sighed. 'I idolised his memory when I was a kid, but now I wonder what the true story was – about his death.'

Leonie had been surprised. 'Does it matter now?'

'Josette was always disappointed in me, as if I could never measure up to him. But then once, when she was really cross, I remember her shaking me, scolding that I was just like him.' With the toe of his shoe, he nudged the stone edging around the grave. 'I'd never seen her so full of spite, like I had something really bad and evil in me. So maybe he wasn't such a hero after all.'

'Grief makes people angry. Maybe it was just that. Nothing to do with you.'

He had shrugged and turned away. 'Maybe.'

There, surrounded by the sun-kissed fields, she had taken his arm to walk back to where they'd left their bikes, following his lead in talking of other things. Now, in her darkened car, she breathed more deeply. There was nothing bad in him. Whatever his demons, he was not trying to conceal them from her. She had doubted him before, and it had been all right: he had wanted her to have the bicycle so she could ride beside him. She must try not to let herself get into quite such a state. Patrice would surely have heard her car draw up and must be wondering by now why she hadn't come inside. If she wasn't going to turn around and go home, she must resolve to take what he offered at face value.

When Patrice opened the door, Leonie was touched to find that he seemed as nervous as she. Greeting her with little more than a peck on the cheek, he made for the kitchen, asking if she wanted coffee. It occurred to her how, once he'd made his phone call, he'd had to wait alone for her arrival. Maybe he'd been having similar doubts about the interpretation of his impulsive action. The insight empowered her, and she stopped on the threshold. 'I've had my dinner, thanks.'

She cast her gaze provocatively up the stairs, but he gave a short laugh, deflecting her, and said, 'I guess maybe I need a drink.'

Determined to enjoy this erotic adventure, she leant stagily against the door jamb. 'And I'd like a kiss.'

Still edgy, he came to her. She was beginning to understand how, despite his passion, he nevertheless sought to evade responsibility, to repudiate the role of seducer. She wondered if maybe he feared repeating whatever erotic decision or mistake had led to the end of his marriage. And so she chose to be reassuring, slow, seductive, and in the almost frantic sex that followed allowed herself to forget all about having no contraception.

Although she resolved never to take such a stupid risk again, the few days of uncertainty and forbidden hope that followed opened a door on her thorniest sorrows – that she was thirty-four and desperately wanted to be a mother, and that it was her desperation to have a child that had driven Greg away.

III

Leonie's period arrived bang on time a fortnight later. The familiar stomach cramps made her shift around in the car seat as she drove to pick up Stella from the airport. She had taken a couple of days' holiday herself so they could spend time together. Although fewer of Gaby's rental properties were occupied in mid-October, there was still plenty of work to do. Inventories had to be checked, repairs organised, recalcitrant owners persuaded to refurbish. Photographs and other details on the website needed to be updated and costings revised, all before the new booking season opened for the following year.

The autumn colours of the landscape chimed with her dragging sense of regret, of life passing too quickly. She couldn't wait to set eyes on Stella, the one person in whom she could confide. Leonie had to admit that she was exhausted, strung out. Life was full of intensity and novelty, which was wonderful, but there were too many nights when she and Patrice didn't sleep until after midnight, when his bed was ridiculously narrow for the two of them.

79

Too many nights when, alone in the more spacious bed in her own apartment, she stayed awake, hoping past all reasonableness that he'd call. She had imagined she would feel more settled by now, more entitled to his consideration, though she wasn't sure she would care to admit that even to Stella. Besides, this obscure dejection must surely just be hormones. She should buck up and make the most of her friend's brief weekend visit.

'Lennie!' Stella, a big, graceful woman wearing untidy clothes, hugged her fiercely. 'I can feel your ribs. I hope you're eating!'

'I'm absolutely fine. But oh, I've missed you!' Finding relief in the effortless expression of a simple emotion, Leonie bit back the insidious reminder of how she still felt the need to be guarded with Patrice: neither had yet used the L-word, for example, though sometimes it hung in the air between them.

'Well, I can't tell you how good it is to be here. I'm shattered.' Stella surrendered possession of her carry-on case and let Leonie lead the way out of the terminal.

'But you're still glad you took the job?'

'Oh yes. The more I get into it, the more fascinating it is. I'll fill you in, don't worry! But first, how soon do I get to meet the man?'

'Tomorrow probably.' Waiting for the automatic doors to open, Leonie avoided Stella's glance. 'He's not a great one for arrangements,' she added, making light of Patrice's rather trying and, if she was honest, hurtful refusal to be nailed down on when he'd come over to meet her oldest friend.

The women postponed the big topics until they were on the road to Riberac. 'If I tell you all about work now, then it's out of the way and I can forget about it 'til I go home,' said Stella. 'But I am so pleased I made the change.'

Stella's previous job had been to match children in care to optimistic couples who tended to have little idea of the problems they were taking on, and who, despite her best efforts, seldom wanted to be told. Stella had watched helplessly as some adoptions broke down under the stress of extreme behaviour which comprehensively trashed both parties' dreams of happy family life. Leonie could only admire Stella's pragmatism and fortitude when she'd had to step in and send already damaged children back to inadequate children's homes or temporary foster families, and she'd seen how Stella's close involvement in such guilt and disappointment took its toll. She had hoped her friend's new role would carry less emotional attrition; now Stella assured her that it did, as well as teaching her unexpected detective skills in tracing birth parents and other lost family members. Not every story ended well, Stella explained, but she spoke enthusiastically about the rewards of negotiating the boundaries of first reunions, and the joy and relief to which she was often witness.

'It's so great, what you're doing.' Leonie was hotly proud of her. 'Makes me question what the hell I'm up to being a glorified holiday rep.'

'Is that all it's turned out to be?' asked Stella, disappointed for her.

'No. Actually I love it. Much more than I expected.'

'Really?' Stella sounded sceptical.

'Yes,' answered Leonie robustly. 'I like being out and about, and it's great having to use French so spontaneously. And what more innocent pleasure than ensuring people enjoy their holiday?'

'Think you'll stay another season?'

'Perhaps.'

'Burying yourself out here . . . is any man worth that?'

Leonie ran through several attempts before formulating her answer. 'It's not just Patrice. I like the rural life. Even if I came back to England, I'm not sure I could face living in London again, especially not in the winter.' She kept her eyes on the road, but couldn't escape awareness of Stella's steady gaze.

'If you stay away too long, it'll be tough getting back in.'

'Into what?'

'Publishing. Translation. Academic research. Jobs are scarce.'

Leonie shook her head. 'I don't miss any of it. Truly. I enjoy it here.' She caught Stella's doubtful look, and laughed. 'I won't throw myself away. Honest.'

'So go on. Tell me all about him.'

'He's like no one else I've ever met. So much going on beneath the surface, so much still to understand. Though no wonder Romeo and Juliet were teenagers. Once you get to our age, this stuff is exhausting!'

'You do look a bit haggard, I must say.'

'Oh, time of the month, that's all. I couldn't be happier. Honestly.' Leonie fought the urge to pull the car over and weep.

To Leonie's delight, Patrice rang that night to ask if he could join them the following evening. He arrived freshly shaved, with flowers and a bottle of wine. He had never given her flowers before, but she quickly replaced the disloyal idea that he had done so now in order to make a favourable impression on Stella with the conviction that, an undemonstrative man, he wanted to display his affection in front of her friend. Throughout the evening, he was charmingly solicitous of them both, encouraged them to reminisce, to talk about the subjects that flowed naturally between them, without seeking to insert himself unnecessarily into the conversation. After insisting gallantly on helping to clear up, showing himself to be at home in Leonie's kitchen, he took himself off, wishing Stella all the best for the remaining two days of her visit.

After a lingering farewell kiss, Leonie watched him cycle away then returned to grin at Stella. 'Well?'

'He's certainly intriguing. And very beautiful – I can understand why you're so hooked!'

Leonie waited for more. Stella licked her lips. 'He's pretty self-possessed, isn't he?'

'He knows his own mind,' she agreed. 'It's one of the things I love about him. If he doesn't want to do something, he doesn't do it. You always know exactly where you are with him.'

'Off on your bikes together?' Stella teased.

'It's fun!'

'Making vegetarian food?'

'He's very principled. I still eat meat.'

'And since when did you start buying into homeopathy?'

'I'm not saying it's serious science, but I reckon there's a role for it. Even if it is just a placebo effect.'

'You're really besotted, aren't you?'

Leonie tried to laugh but she couldn't help being offended by Stella's lack of faith. 'Patrice is a good man. He helps people because of who he is, not necessarily because of what he does. That's what alternative medicine is all about, isn't it? Treating the whole person, not only the disease.'

'But why does that mean he has to denounce hospital medicine? What's "allopathy" when it's at home?' Stella saw she'd gone too far. 'Sorry, Lennie.' She went to give her a hug, which Leonie halfheartedly returned. 'Go on, fill me in. What's the rest of his story?'

'I told you. He spent quite a bit of his childhood here, and came back when his grandmother died, after his marriage broke up.'

'He's a Euro-brat, right? If his folks were multinationals.'

'Yes, I suppose he is.'

'What about his other exes?'

'He's only mentioned his ex-wife.'

'But there must have been other relationships. He hasn't been on his own all this time, surely?'

'He's never really said.' Leonie blanked Stella's look of disbelief.

'So what happened to the marriage?'

'I think there was someone else. Didn't last long, anyhow.'

'You've Googled him, obviously.'

'No! Why would I?'

'You're kidding? Come on, let's do it now.' Stella went and lifted the lid of Leonie's laptop, sitting down in front of it.

Leonie didn't move. 'Don't, Stella. Please. It'd be like I don't trust him or something.'

'No, it's not. Everybody does it.' Stella was already typing in Patrice's name. 'We're not hacking into his private stuff. Just a little innocent cyber-stalking, that's all. I've got good at this in the new job.'

'Please don't.'

'What's wrong with it? You do trust him, don't you?'

'He'd hate it.' Leonie tried to make a joke of it. 'He's hardly going to be on Facebook, is he?'

Stella looked at her seriously. 'Lennie, if you're afraid you'll find something, that's all the more reason to look.'

Leonie relaxed. She had no fear of any terrible secret being revealed, and she could accept that her friend was merely looking out for her. 'I'm not afraid of anything. I'd just rather he told me about himself in his own way, in his own time, that's all. I don't need to have read every line of his CV to understand who he is.'

Stella remained sceptical. 'How much does he ask about you? I mean, I don't care whether or not he's curious about me, but I imagined he might've been a bit more interested because through me he finds out about you.'

Leonie conceded: 'Okay. I did mind at first that he didn't ask more questions, but now I like it this way. He's very instinctive, and there's no rush. I know where I am with him. And it's good sometimes not to have to dredge up the past.'

'So long as he cares about you, cares about what you want.' Stella closed the computer unwillingly.

'He'll move at his own pace. My theory is that it's from when he was a kid, packed off to boarding school or to stay with his grandmother. She sounds like a real refrigerator type. Left him a bit closed up. If anyone gets what that must've been like for a child, you should.'

'Sure I do. And look what happened to some of the kids I had to deal with.'

'He needs to take his time, that's all.'

'Damaged goods aren't always happy ever after.'

'But what about those who do get past their fear of being abandoned again?'

'Well, okay . . .' Stella didn't hide her misgivings. 'But don't be *too* patient. Remember, you have your own stuff that'll come seeping out between the cracks the minute you really let yourself be vulnerable. You need someone capable of being there for you, too.'

'You're right, of course. And it *is* scary. But what's wrong with being scared? I'd rather feel too much, and risk getting hurt, than not feel anything.' She laughed at herself. 'Oh, Heathcliff! We were taught at school that love is bigger than any of us. And I swallowed it, hook, line and sinker.' When Stella remained concerned, she reassured her. 'Please don't worry about me. I'm over Greg, and I feel alive again. That's what counts, surely?'

Stella gave Leonie's arm an affectionate rub. 'I do like Patrice. What's not to like about a man who brings flowers?' she joked. 'And if anyone can nurture a rescue dog and be rewarded with loyalty and devotion, it'll be you!'

At the airport two days later, as they hugged goodbye, Stella whispered into Leonie's ear, 'I have no idea how you can bear to go through all that pain and ecstasy again, but I'm bloody envious!'

After Stella's departure, Leonie tried to explain to herself her weepy exhaustion; to rationalise the instant, wild compulsion to run after the retreating figure of her oldest friend, climb onto the plane with her and go home. Why this sudden powerful urge to turn her back on her full and pleasant life here, to run away from further entanglement with Patrice? He had done nothing to provoke such a need to escape. It must be, as Stella said, that falling in love had left her raw and exposed in a way she hadn't been for years – perhaps had never been, given how young and unformed she was when she met Greg. Maybe it was that Stella had brought with her some fleeting sense of comfort and safety that had disappeared again the moment she went through passport control.

With a jolt, Leonie asked herself whether this meant that she had no such sense of comfort or safety with Patrice? In answer to the question, she had reluctantly to admit that she did not. But, she told herself, they were still new to one another. And besides, there must surely be mutual trust, or how could they be so wonderfully physically intimate? No; all that was actually at risk was her familiar comfort zone, and that she'd gladly lose. After all, if she was too much of a coward to dive into uncharted waters, what was the point of living? She might as well give up now.

When Leonie returned to the office after her long weekend break, Gaby repeated an invitation to bring Patrice to dinner. It was an idea Gaby had floated several times before, but she had always tactfully retreated when Leonie made vague excuses. This time Leonie accepted. She had let herself become too accommodating to Patrice's foibles: if she was to regain her equilibrium, she must be a little more pro-active about winkling him out of his shell.

She resolved to ask him to Gaby's dinner face to face, rather than on the phone. To fortify her confidence and calm her agitation, she showered, washed her hair and dressed with care before going over to his house. Even then she waited until they sat down with plates of steaming pasta puttanesca before telling him of her employer's invitation.

'Would I like her?' he asked. 'You said no one moves around here without Gaby knowing, right?'

'I've told you lots about her,' protested Leonie.

'Doesn't sound my type, I have to say.' Though he spoke lightly, she glimpsed in his eyes the bright blue implacability behind his words.

'It would mean a lot to me if you came.'

'I'm no good at dinner parties.'

Leonie perceived that this was a hurdle that would have to be jumped if she were to escape getting somehow mired into a submissiveness she did not believe he truly intended. It was a test for both of them. She had to be sure that, in respecting his reticence, she didn't deny him opportunities to do things for the sole reason that they mattered to her, that she mattered to him.

'Well, if you won't come, then don't go asking me to slink over here into bed with you afterwards,' she said, aiming to sound light-hearted.

He laughed a little guiltily. Normally she would have backed straight off rather than discomfit him, but she kept her promise to herself and persevered. 'Please come. For me?'

He looked at her in surprise, but picked up the pleading

in her eyes. 'Okay. So long as it doesn't become a regular fixture.'

Reassured and emboldened by this success, once they had turned out the lights and gone upstairs she tackled him about the other change she wished to make.

'Wouldn't it be more sensible for us to move into a room with a bigger bed?'

'I couldn't sleep in Josette's bed. Way too spooky.'

'Doesn't have to be hers, but this is far too small for the two of us. The one in the spare room is twice the size.'

'A slight exaggeration.' He had his back to her, unbuttoning his shirt.

'I could help you renovate one of the other bedrooms.'

'Finishing the hall will take a while yet.'

'Yes, but— '

'Come here.'

He turned to her, cupped her face in both his hands, fastened his lips on hers, and walked her backwards onto the bed. He was tender and thoughtful, his mouth roving her skin, but though she surrendered, the rebellious notion persisted that this sensuous kissing and stroking was to stop her asking anything else of him. Was to shut her up.

Leonie had butterflies about Gaby's dinner all day. Patrice had made it plain soon afterwards that he regretted his acceptance, and dropped heavy hints that he expected Leonie to let him off the hook. With an effort, she had resisted. Then there was the issue of how to get there. Gaby and Thierry lived a few miles outside the centre of town and Leonie had no intention of cycling there and back in the dark this late in the year, especially not when all dressed up for an evening out. But Patrice refused, as she expected, to go in her car. She couldn't help being annoyed that they would have to arrive separately: how could it hurt the planet if, for once, he were a passenger in a car that was making the journey anyway? But there was no point arguing against his ecological integrity, he was too stubborn. And so, aware of the awkwardness if he were to get there before her, not knowing anyone, she would have to make sure she arrived first – and then have the anxiety of wondering whether he'd find the house, how edgy he'd be when he did turn up, whether he'd come at all . . .

A woman as overtly prying and curious as Gaby was easy to misjudge: from the moment Leonie entered the Duvals' house, her boss was full of discreet solicitude and encouragement, and Leonie blessed her for her kindness and tact. Leonie was fond of Thierry, too, a small, wiry man, every bit as shrewd as his wife and full of an energy that was generally, and instinctively, directed at assisting others. Leonie greeted his sister Sylviane and her husband, Jean-Paul, whom she had met before, but her heart sank when Gaby introduced Sylviane's school friend Catherine and her husband Philippe, reminding her that it was Catherine who had for a long time remained in touch with Patrice's mother, Agnès Hinde.

'Gaby told me she has Alzheimer's,' said Catherine. 'So

very sad. All the same, it'll be good to hear news of her. I hadn't realised Patrice was living here again until Sylviane explained who he was.'

The door bell chimed. 'That'll be him,' announced Gaby. Leonie made haste to follow Thierry out to the hall so she could make the introductions between Patrice and his host, and perhaps manage a private word to warn Patrice about Catherine's link to his mother. Only now did she realise, too late, how it would be sickeningly revealed that she and Gaby had been discussing him behind his back. As Thierry took Patrice's coat and turned away to hang it in the hall closet, she held his arm. He looked down at her. 'No need to look so scared. I said I'd come!'

She had no chance to say anything before Thierry ushered them into the drawing room, made the necessary introductions and gave Patrice a drink. As everyone sat down on low grey sofas around a glass coffee table, Sylviane helped herself to a morsel of Melba toast dotted with foie gras.

'Mmm, delicious. What a treat!' She pushed the plate towards Patrice.

Leonie had forewarned Gaby that Patrice was vegetarian, and now sharp-eyed Gaby was there before her, proffering a dish of olives so that he could decide for himself whether to declare his principles. With a conspiratorial smile at his hostess, he silently accepted an olive. Leonie saw from Gaby's response that, far from scrutinising him for potential flaws, Gaby was ready to be charmed by his courteous reserve. Relaxing enough to pay attention, Leonie noted that Patrice had dressed with care, and was lankily elegant in black jeans with a black linen jacket and a soft green shirt he had not worn before. She began to feel a little less discouraged about the evening.

'So you're Agnès' son,' Catherine addressed him. 'You won't remember me, but I knew you as a little boy. Sylviane and I were both at school with your mother.'

'Though she and I lost touch long ago,' added Sylviane.

'But I do remember,' laughed Patrice. 'I taught your son to play cricket, which, as I recall, he turned out to be rather too good at. And you used to feed us bread with delicious home-made plum jam.'

Catherine was delighted. 'Fancy you remembering that! I'd completely forgotten, though I still make jam. I must give you a jar.'

'Please do!'

'Now, tell me, how is your mother?' asked Catherine.

Leonie silently thanked her for not blundering in with illicitly obtained information and reminded herself to have greater confidence in these women's social finesse, essential to the maintenance of harmony over lifetimes in a small provincial town.

'I saw her at your grandmother's funeral, but since then—' Catherine ended with a polite Gallic shrug.

'She's not been well, I'm afraid,' answered Patrice. 'They say it's not Alzheimer's, but ... did you see much of her in recent years?' His expression as he awaited the reply held a curious watchfulness.

'Yes. Whenever she visited her mother, we'd meet. Except the summer just before Madame Broyard's death she didn't come – or didn't tell me if she did, anyway – and the year before that, I was away; my daughter was unwell and I had to look after the children.'

Patrice nodded. 'Then you're aware of how anxious she could become,' he said quietly. 'Now it's overwhelmed her, I'm afraid.'

Leonie thought he looked as sad and bleak as she had ever seen him, and her heart went out to him.

'I'm sorry to hear that,' said Catherine. 'We always wrote, and sent birthday and Christmas cards. But these last years, nothing. You must give me her address. I'd hate Agnès to think I'd forgotten her.'

'She's in a nursing home. I'll write it down for you.'

'That would be kind.'

'She's unlikely to reply, I'm afraid. It's a while since she was able to write a letter.'

'All the same. Such a sweet woman. I've always been very fond of her.'

'Yes,' said Patrice. 'Very loving. She tried so hard to be brave. And who knows, hearing from you may bring back happier times.'

'Tough on your father, too, I imagine,' put in Philippe.

'Well, of course,' agreed Sylviane. 'Both your parents are still young. Only sixty-five, the same as us.' She made a little *moue* at Patrice and Leonie. 'Though that might not appear so young to you!'

Patrice laughed chivalrously.

'Agnès usually came alone to visit her mother,' Catherine probed, clearly hoping he might shed light upon his parents' marriage.

Patrice responded with a fixed smile – from which Leonie concluded he had been quizzed on this topic more often than he liked – before saying, 'Dad never had an easy time. I suppose poor Maman was nervous right from the womb. Josette was eight months pregnant when her husband was shot dead, remember?'

'Oh, too far back for me!' laughed Catherine. 'But in recent years, I think I only saw Geoffrey when he came for the funeral.'

'He gets along as best he can.' Patrice was sitting upright on the low sofa, his hands flexed and rigid on his thighs. 'It's not his fault. Nothing is his fault.'

'Leonie, I hope you've not had any more trouble from that strange client?' Thierry diverted the conversation. Even as Leonie turned away to answer, she could still detect Patrice's heart hammering in his chest. Whatever had happened in the past was still very much with him now.

'Actually, another postcard arrived yesterday,' she told Thierry.

'At the office? He doesn't have your home address?' He was sharp with concern.

'No, no. Though he did his best to trap me into revealing it.'

'Well, we'll never accept another booking from him,'

said Gaby. 'And I've requested other agencies that cover the area to do the same.'

'Good.'

'What happened?' asked Jean-Paul.

'A client got rather obsessed with Leonie,' explained Gaby. 'Turned into a bit of a stalker. Father of five, wife a dowdy little mouse.'

'Horrid for you!' said Catherine.

'Just a sad little man. It's fine.'

'It's the pathetic ones you need to watch,' warned Philippe.

'You didn't tell me,' protested Patrice to Leonie.

'I did mention the postcards. And I'm sure he's harmless.'

'You should take it seriously, Patrice,' admonished Philippe. 'Nothing more dangerous than an inadequate man.'

Patrice glared at Leonie's self-appointed champion before turning to her. 'These were the views of the Lake District?' he demanded.

She nodded, rather flattered by Patrice's prickliness. 'He sends two or three cards a week. Quotes bits of Wordsworth, or Wainwright. Could hardly be less sinister. And he's safely back in Yorkshire now.'

'Mid-life crisis,' decided Sylviane, and all the women agreed.

'Let's eat!' announced Gaby.

As they all rose to go through to the dining room, Leonie

linked her arm through Patrice's. She could feel his muscles clenched and hard through the sleeve of his jacket, and he looked straight ahead, avoiding any physical contact with Philippe as they went through the door. It struck Leonie that, like an angry, fearful dog, its hair bristling along its back, he too expressed his vulnerability physically.

Gaby served smoked fish as an *hors d'oeuvre*, then roast partridge: Thierry, Leonie knew, regarded any meal without meat as a snack. Without comment, Gaby handed Patrice a dish of large and succulent *cèpes* in place of the game, passing him the other vegetables in turn. Philippe leant forward across the table to peer at Patrice's plate, then turned away with a dismissive laugh, saying nothing. Leonie saw Patrice's jaw tighten. She had not met Philippe before this evening, and she was beginning to dislike him intensely. She looked around the table. Thierry, Jean-Paul and Philippe were discussing the wine, a good Crozes-Hermitage purchased on a past tasting trip to the region – evidently a regular event shared and enjoyed by the three men. They made no attempt to include Patrice, who in any case was listening sympathetically to Sylviane's tale of her granddaughter's eczema, and suggesting she bring the girl to him for a homeopathic consultation.

As Leonie agreed idly with Gaby and Catherine's complaints about new parking restrictions around the market square, she found herself speculating about the three couples. She looked at Thierry, Jean-Paul and Philippe, noting the dry grey hairs sprouting from their ears and nostrils, their balding skulls and the sagging skin of their necks, and couldn't imagine any one of them making love to their wives. Granted they were all a generation older, but she pitied them their passionless existences. Sunk in their companionable habits, she doubted whether they had ever comprehended the knife-like ecstasies that awaited her and Patrice later that night. At that very second, Patrice caught her eye, and she had to stop herself laughing aloud.

As if he read her mind, his eyes narrowed as they did when he was aroused, and involuntarily she inhaled sharply. Distracted from her conversation, Gaby glanced over to check she was all right, and Leonie had to nod reassuringly and sip at her water to disguise the erotic images writhing inside her head. She caught a glimpse of Patrice over the glass, but he was talking once again with Sylviane. Leonie watched the older woman warming in unconscious response to his raised level of desire, and thought to herself hilariously, 'If you only knew!' She glowed with satisfaction at being the woman who – alive, full, trusted – Patrice had chosen as his lover, taking pleasure in the possession of such an identity.

Over the cheese, Leonie overheard Catherine talking to Patrice again about his grandmother, and endeavoured to listen in as Catherine asked what his childhood with Josette had been like.

'It didn't help that my mother had abandoned her by

marrying a foreigner,' he replied. 'And Agnès giving me her dead father's name was a reminder of Josette's earlier loss, as well.'

'Yes, that was hard. And of course it all meant that Agnès was far too close to her mother, growing up.'

Patrice nodded. 'I expect that's partly why Josette could never allow herself any real affection for me – in case she lost me, too. Which of course meant I never offered her any.'

'Such a shame.'

'Yes. She could be rather cold, but I do believe it wasn't really a lack of emotion, just that she'd battened it all down so tightly. She can't have been entirely without feeling.'

'Not much comfort to you!'

'She wasn't able to offer a child much in the way of sympathy, but at least she was consistent. I appreciated that.' He toyed with the crumbled cheese biscuit on his plate. 'My parents moved around a lot.'

Patrice's arm rested on the table, his fingers touching the stem of his glass. Catherine reached out to pat his hand in friendly concern. Surprised by her touch, he jerked, knocking over the glass and spilling the wine. In the small commotion that followed – apologies, mopping up, refilling his glass – he looked over at Leonie, casting his eyes to heaven and shaking his head in self-mockery. She hoped her return gaze was eloquent of the love she felt for him, and was glad when he smiled back and, his shoulders dropping, seemed to relax a little.

Suddenly the door-handle rattled and a child's voice

called out from the hallway. Gaby looked indulgently to Thierry, who got to his feet and went to open the door.

'Our grandson. He's sleeping here tonight to save our daughter a babysitter,' Gaby explained. 'He's learnt how to climb over the side-bar we put up.'

Thierry came back with the little boy cradled in his arms.

'Didier! You should be asleep!' Gaby reached up and tickled her fingers against the toddler's rounded, sleepy body. Didier nestled down further into his grandfather's embrace while covertly surveying the up-turned faces, shrewdly judging the limits of their fondness.

'You have a son, don't you?'

Leonie looked around in confusion, then perceived with amazement that Catherine had addressed Patrice. 'Me?' He was wide-eyed, taken aback.

'I was sure Agnès had written to tell me you'd had a baby, a little boy.'

'I have no children.' Patrice's eyes flickered wildly towards the door.

'Oh, my mistake. Excuse me. All our friends are so busy acquiring grandchildren these days, that I probably muddled up the messages in the Christmas cards.'

'You don't want to leave it too late,' murmured Philippe. Though Leonie assumed that Philippe meant well, Patrice stared at him murderously.

Didier held out his arms for Gaby, and Thierry set him down carefully on his feet. The pyjama-clad little figure lurched towards his grandmother, but landed up beside

Patrice where, to keep his balance, he gripped Patrice's thigh and held on tight, looking up into his face. Patrice froze, his nostrils flaring in distress, but everyone was concentrating on the child, laughing as Thierry scooped him back up.

'Come along, little man, you don't belong here,' he joked. Didier, recognising defeat, put his thumb in his mouth, drawing exclamations from the women on his adorableness. 'Let's get you out of here right now!'

Only then did Leonie notice how pale and clammy Patrice had become. He blanked her look, concentrating on getting his breathing back under control. She felt horribly afraid, but of what she couldn't say.

As Thierry went off with Didier, the party took the opportunity to break up. For the next ten minutes, the guests clustered in the hall waiting for Thierry to come downstairs so they could say goodnight to their host. As the women fetched handbags, wraps and coats, the men dug in their pockets for car keys, and thanks, kisses and promises to meet again soon were exchanged. Patrice managed to evade all eye-contact. Leonie worked her way around to stand beside him. Gingerly she stroked his arm. He turned to her and she was shocked by how his eyes were exhausted, drained, the eyes of a dead man.

Outside in the dark, she was glad to find that her car had been blocked in by the other two. As if by tacit agreement, Patrice lingered beside her, going to retrieve his bike only once the others had driven off.

'Are you sure you don't want to come with me?' she asked gently. 'You don't look well.'

He shook his head, made sure his lights were working, and mounted the saddle.

'You'll come to my apartment?'

'I don't want you to have to wait up.'

'I don't mind.'

'If you're sure you want me.'

He looked so lost and dejected that she summoned up all her courage. 'Patrice, do you have a son?'

He was leaning forward, fiddling with the flickering front light, and she couldn't make out whether he had heard her or not.

'You don't have children, do you?' she repeated.

He straightened up, and shook his head. 'Before we married, Belinda always said she didn't want to give up her work.' He met her gaze quite calmly. 'She's a musician. It means a lot to her.'

Leonie was flooded with relief. Her fear earlier at the table, that he had failed to tell her something so important, her terror that she might not know this man at all, melted away. He leant over and touched his lips to hers.

'See you later.'

He cycled away, and when her headlights picked him up later on the road, he raised a hand and waved as she drove past.

It was five o'clock the following afternoon before she

heard from him. He rang to say that he'd had a puncture and by the time he'd managed to mend it in the dark it had been too late to come to her apartment. He was tired, he said, and would see her later in the week.

IV

Leonie approached the office on Monday morning well aware that Gaby would be anticipating a full debrief on Saturday's party. Even full-throttle, Gaby was seldom malicious, and in the past, whenever Leonie had socialised with her employer, she had thoroughly enjoyed these after-sessions. While part of her dreaded hearing Gaby's observations on Patrice, she was also much in need of illumination. His failure to turn up, or even to call until so late on Sunday, had left her hurt and on edge, and she desperately wanted a trusted opinion to contribute answers to her questions about his behaviour.

Usually in late October, with the new booking season open, there was not much leisure to chat, but this morning Gaby arrived ten minutes late bearing *pains au chocolat*, a sure sign that they would relax over their first coffee of the day. Gaby's immediate verdict on Patrice was positive: 'Gorgeous! Rather unusual, and I imagine pretty strong-minded, but a very beguiling man.'

Leonie was relieved; reassured that, fundamentally, Gaby approved, she could afford to reveal some of her own current reservations. 'What did Thierry make of him?' she asked. 'I realised on Saturday night how I'd never really seen Patrice in male company before.'

'Nothing wrong with not being a man's man. After all, a lot of men don't actually like women. Certainly don't always understand them! Can't say I'd want Philippe as a husband, would you?' she laughed. 'Allows for why Catherine was so taken with Patrice! Much better to find a man who enjoys women.'

Leonie relaxed a little more. 'Patrice seemed to get on well with Sylviane, too.'

'Yes. She's taking little Lily to see him. Terrible eczema. Sylviane is convinced it's food-related. So what did he say about all of us?'

'Delighted by the evening. He's sending you a note.'

'Oh, I do like a man who writes his own thank-you letters! And maybe we'll see more of him, now that he's broken the ice.'

'Mmm.' Leonie wasn't ready to face the leaden realisation that Patrice was unlikely ever again to accompany her socially. Wanting to escape having to explain her solitary Sunday, she ate the last of her pastry, reached for the plates and carried them through to the kitchenette. Safely out of Gaby's line of sight, she called through the door, 'Did Catherine say anything else?'

'She did, sweetie.'

Rinsing the plates, Leonie expected Gaby to continue as soon as she had turned off the noisy tap, but Gaby waited for her to come back and sit down. Their desks faced one another, computer screens back-to-back, and Leonie couldn't avoid her serious expression.

Gaby licked her lips before continuing. 'Sweetie, Catherine says she really is pretty sure that Agnès did write to say that Patrice was married and had a son. Must have been a year or so before Madame Broyard's death.'

Leonie breathed again. 'Oh, no. I asked him about that, and he never had children. Said his wife didn't want them.'

'But Catherine couldn't fathom how else she'd have known he'd been married.'

'Just because he *was* married doesn't necessarily mean that Catherine *knew* he was married, if you get what I mean. She could still have muddled up the messages in her Christmas cards. I bet she gets loads.'

Gaby nodded, but didn't try to hide her lingering concern.

'Why should he lie about having a son?' persisted Leonie, laughing. 'If he were going to lie about something, surely it would be about having an ex-wife? And he's never tried to make a secret of that.'

Gaby was still not convinced. 'People lie for the most trivial reasons. Maybe it was an acrimonious divorce, and he doesn't get to see the boy. Hurt pride.'

'But look how freely he talked about his parents, and Josette. He's always been perfectly candid about his past. Just—' As Leonie searched for the appropriate word, she

106

caught an uncomfortable glint of scrutiny in Gaby's expression. 'He's private. And shy. That's all.'

Gaby shook her head, but backed off a little. 'Well, I have to say that Thierry wasn't a hundred per cent sure about him, either. But then any man who refuses to eat meat is always going to be a bit suspect in Thierry's book!'

Leonie was disappointed. She had wanted to discover whether Gaby had noticed Patrice's odd reaction to little Didier's appearance at the end of the evening and, if so, what she'd made of it. But Gaby's residual resistance – her perhaps understandable solidarity with her own circle of friends – left Leonie unable to raise the subject. She decided to let it go. She had probably been a bit overwrought and imagined Patrice's extreme tension. No one else appeared to have witnessed it and, for all she knew, it had been indigestion, and she was merely being over-sensitive about his attitude to children because she so wanted a child herself. She had asked him outright if he had a son, and he'd told her the truth, of that she was certain. Reminding herself to be more careful about projecting her own issues onto other people, she settled down to work.

By the middle of the week, Patrice had still not phoned. At first Leonie took an almost warped pleasure in the novelty of being irritated by his wilfulness. It was a luxury to have a man to grumble about; it proved that their relationship was sufficiently taken for granted between them to admit the existence of minor faults. But as another evening passed in silence, and then another, her bravado trickled away. Late on Friday she called Stella.

'Oh, Lennie. No one's such a sensitive flower that they can't go to a simple dinner party without freaking out,' said Stella. 'And Gaby's so nice, I can't believe she can have done anything dreadful to upset him.'

'No, I know.'

'Did anything happen?'

'No, not really.'

'So why put up with this kind of behaviour? Is it worth it?'

'Yes.'

'Sure?'

'Yes!'

'Okay, so what's going on with him?'

'I was thinking . . . about his grandfather.'

'His grandfather! Oh, for chrissakes, Lennie, there are many reasons a man fails to call, but a grandfather he never even knew is not one of them!'

'No, listen. Because we're English, we forget that the war was different here. This is a small community. The Duvals and their friends all grew up here, most of their grand-parents, too.'

'So?'

'So what if Josette had known or suspected who it was in Riberac who shot her husband? Maybe that's why she wouldn't let Patrice play with other kids; or give his mother much freedom either, by all accounts.'

'You're suggesting Patrice might believe that some relation of Gaby's was a collaborator who shot his grandfather for being in the Resistance?'

'I don't necessarily mean someone in Gaby's family, but someone in the town. Or maybe the shooting was revenge for something else, a settling of old scores. But Patrice definitely seems to think there was some mystery.'

'If that were so, then why would Josette have chosen to stay put?'

'What would've been different in the next town? Plus she was heavily pregnant.'

'No reason why Patrice had to return to live and work there, though.'

'True.' Leonie fell silent.

'And even if the past was that complicated, it all happened years ago, so why couldn't he talk about it at dinner?'

'I just thought maybe it would explain why he was so antsy that night, why he doesn't mix.'

'Okay, let's say you're right,' said Stella even-handedly. 'France was in chaos at the end of the Occupation, and all kinds of private vendettas must've been played out. Makes a great story but that's not what's going on here, is it?'

Leonie sighed. 'No. I guess not.' The silence filled itself as Stella waited for her to say what was on her mind. 'What if he seriously doesn't like kids?'

'Then that's a tough one. Bit of a deal-breaker for you, I imagine.'

'Gaby's grandson came in while we were eating, and Patrice's reaction was really strange. I'm afraid it's a major part of why he's not called me yet.'

'Explain.'

'Nothing to tell. He just – didn't want to be there. But he said it was his wife who never wanted children.'

'So maybe it's something else. Maybe she had an abortion? Maybe that's what split them up? That she denied him a child?' suggested Stella.

'Maybe. But he told me before that he let her down. What would that mean?'

'How would I know?'

'I wonder if there was another woman involved.'

'Someone he's not told you about?'

'Maybe. Or his wife got pregnant by another man.'

'Jesus, Lennie! Stop groping about in the dark and ask him!' When Leonie didn't reply, Stella went on. 'This is crazy. You have to sort this stuff out before your imagination spirals out of control altogether.'

'How? I can't just ask, please can I have your babies one day? It's way too soon for that conversation.'

'Well, you must have talked about contraception at least. How relaxed is he about that?'

'It's no secret I use a cap.'

'Why can't you just ask him why he reacted so weirdly?' Leonie had no answer.

'Look. Call him. Right now. See him this weekend, and

ask him a few questions. Nothing heavy, but get a few things straight in your own mind.'

Leonie dared not voice her worst fear, that she wouldn't see Patrice this weekend.

'Call him,' repeated Stella kindly. 'If the boat's on fire, you're not going to put out the flames by doing nothing.'

'No, I know,' said Leonie humbly.

'Call me straight back, okay?'

'Okay. Thanks. Bye.'

Taking a deep breath and instructing herself not to be ridiculous, Leonie pressed in Patrice's number. He answered after a couple of rings.

'Hello. How are you?' He sounded guarded, but nonetheless pleased to hear from her.

'Oh, had a busy week. Wondered how you are.'

'Rushed off my feet. Your friend Sylviane came to see me. She's a nice woman. Brought her granddaughter Lily.'

'I've only met Sylviane a few times, but yes, she is nice. You know she's Thierry's sister?' When he didn't answer, she took the plunge and pressed on. 'I was afraid you hadn't enjoyed the evening at Gaby's.'

'I told you I'm no good at dinner parties.'

Forcing down a rising sensation of panic, Leonie refused to acknowledge how false his cheeriness sounded. 'Look, I was just running a bath,' he went on. 'Don't want it to overflow, but see you soon.' And he was gone.

Rather than call Stella back, and hear her friend suggest that the burning boat might be sinking with all hands on deck, she texted her to say that she'd been unable to get hold of Patrice – a fib that would give her time tonight to sob privately into her pillow.

On Monday morning, Gaby took one look at Leonie's wan expression. 'Are you all right, sweetie?'

Leonie nodded. 'Patrice is being a bit unavailable, that's all.'

Gaby frowned, shaking her head. 'Men can be such cowards!'

'Oh, no. I'm sure there'll be some good reason. Last time I thought I might not hear from him again, everything turned out absolutely fine.'

Gaby pursed her lips, but said no more. Inwardly, the dull monologue that had tormented Leonie all weekend went on beating its sombre drum: what if it was over, and it was her fault? She should never have made him go to Gaby's dinner. There had been no need to shove him out of his comfort zone. It was too soon. He wasn't ready. She had taken too much for granted. She should never have driven off afterwards like that and left him to cycle back alone. She should have gone with him. It could have been fun, bundled up against the cold, pedalling along in the dark together. No wonder he felt separated and apart. Whatever demons had been unleashed in him that evening, she had made it worse by abandoning him yet again, shutting him out like so many other people in his past.

She cursed Josette for the toll her malign legacy was taking on Patrice; and, like a contagious disease, on her. What the hell had gone on in that family to make such a kind, sweet-natured man so evasive, so tightly hidden inside himself? Was it to do with his parents? His grandparents? What was it that he couldn't speak to her about? How she longed to lead him out into the sunshine where he could be his best and fullest self, for she was intuitively sure it was what Patrice himself most wanted, however deeply buried that wish might be right now.

A second week went by, and still he did not call. Almost as a penance, Leonie took to using her bicycle. Although it was often inconvenient not to drive, the physical exercise calmed her and she felt somehow closer to him whilst riding it. She barely admitted to herself the illicit hope that their paths might cross, that if he happened to spy her riding past then her use of the bicycle he'd refurbished would signal her fidelity. As the days passed, her estimation of the hurt and damage with which this good and endearing man must be grappling increased. She did not believe that his continuing silence was bad faith towards her. The image of the wild creature, fearful of human contact, came to her repeatedly.

It was easy for Gaby or even Stella to advise her to walk away and abandon him, but they couldn't see how Patrice was struggling. She took on board Stella's wisdom about those adopted children for whom no amount of love and attention was ever enough to undo the abuse they had suffered, and heard Gaby's well-intentioned warnings about why loners might be friendless, but she comprehended the difficulties of love; however hopeless their bond might look right now, she was still prepared to go the distance. She understood his need to test how far she would tolerate the necessity for caution, to be sure that he could trust her to wait patiently, and intended that, when he felt ready and able to contact her again, she would be there, as serenely as she knew how.

At lunchtimes, saying she wanted to stretch her legs, she would refuse Gaby's offer of hot soup and buy a baguette to eat while sitting well wrapped up on the chilly bench by the church. Rather than depressing her, the contrast of the early November vista to that July day when Patrice had first brought her here gave her courage. Love has its seasons, she reminded herself, forcing herself to swallow the crusty bread despite feeling no hunger. Regeneration is painful. Winter has to come first, a time of inwardness and hibernation. All would be well. These nearly leafless trees would measure her love while she waited for spring. July would come and they would sit here or walk by the river again. But first she had to allow him time to heal. Even to herself she sounded silly and over-romantic, but there had to be more to existence than the stuff in which Gaby and her friends around the dinner table apparently found contentment. These brief months with Patrice had made her fully human, and she refused now to settle for less than the bliss that she was lucky enough to have glimpsed with him.

Then one day Leonie skidded on wet leaves and came off the bike, tumbling painfully and twisting her ankle in a vain attempt to prevent her face smashing into the greasy stone of the square. Her knee, hand and cheekbone were grazed and bleeding, and, unable to put any weight on her ankle, she could just about hop. People came running, solicitous and unbearably kind. Someone retrieved the bike and another person her bag and other possessions, while a woman her own age helped her into the brightly lit pharmacy where the assistant in her spotless white tunic pulled out a chair for her. Leonie wasn't aware of crying, but the assistant handed her a box of tissues to dry her face.

They patched her up and phoned Gaby, who came straight over and drove her to her house, where she insisted Leonie spend the night with them. In a borrowed dressing gown, her face bruised and swollen, her bandaged ankle up on a stool, Leonie felt foolish and humiliated. She felt even worse when Thierry returned home, and, through the open doorway to the hall, Leonie overheard an exchange between husband and wife.

'What was she doing on a bike in such weather? Is there a problem with the car?' he wanted to know.

'No, the car's fine.' Gaby lowered her voice. 'He gave her the bike. Patrice Hinde. She's still yearning after him.'

Leonie heard Thierry's exasperated exclamation. 'Surely she realises she can do better than that? All that self-dramatising he goes in for, being vegetarian and making out it's romantic to hide away in that dilapidated old house the way he does. Just attention-seeking. Afraid he won't shape up in the real world.'

It brought a lump to Leonie's throat to hear herself so championed, and she couldn't help appreciating the unasked-for support.

'Afraid of being ordinary, if you ask me,' Thierry went on, evidently ignoring Gaby's attempts to shush him. 'Selfish, expecting everyone else to fit in around him and his faddy ideas.'

Leonie felt a sneaking disloyalty and quickly reassured herself that even Gaby had admitted that Thierry, dear though he was, would never understand a man like Patrice.

There was some further murmured conversation, then Thierry came into the sitting room, where, studying her with manifest concern, he greeted her fondly.

'Been in the wars, I see.'

''Fraid so.'

'Well, you stay here with us as long as you like.'

She did her best to smile her thanks.

'Let someone take proper care of you for a change. Time to put yourself first.'

Try as she might, Leonie couldn't stop the rising emotion. She began to sob and could not stop. Thierry sat beside her, his arm around her shoulders, drawing her to him as he must have done many times with his own grown-up daughters. He allowed her to weep against his chest, damping his cashmere pullover with her tears. 'There, there,' he said. 'There, there.'

*

After two nights with the Duvals, Leonie insisted she would manage fine with her twisted ankle back at her own apartment. Brooking no argument, Gaby went first to the supermarket for her to stock up on provisions, then announced that until such time as Leonie could drive again she would come every morning to pick her up for work. It was on Leonie's second evening alone at home that she answered the ringing phone expecting it to be Gaby keeping tabs on her and heard Patrice's voice.

'Hello, it's me. I heard you'd had an accident. Sylviane told me you've been staying with Gaby.'

'Yes. It was stupid. I fell off the bike.'

'Did something go wrong? A loose pedal? A brake pad come unstuck?'

'No, I don't think so. I haven't checked. It was wet and I slipped over, that's all.'

'Are you all right? I couldn't bear it if you were hurt and it was my fault.'

She laughed, experiencing a rush of gaiety as a weight slid off her shoulders. 'I look a sight, but I'm not badly hurt,' she promised him. 'Honestly. A twisted ankle, bit of a black eye. I'll mend.'

'Thank goodness.' She could hear the rush of relief in his voice. So he did care about her! She had been right to be patient! 'May I come and see you?' he asked.

'Oh, please!'

Patrice arrived twenty-five minutes later, bringing in the autumn chill on his clothes, and sporting a bedraggled bunch of chrysanthemums and a bottle of red wine. They greeted one another lightly with a kiss on the lips, laughing as she hopped about trying to hold the flowers while closing the door behind him. They went into the tiny kitchen, where she sat at the counter so he could open the wine, remembering without hesitation where to find the glasses and corkscrew.

Rather shyly he also produced several small phials which he placed in front of her. 'I've brought some remedies for you. Arnica, obviously, though you should really have had that straight away. And Calendula cream. This is Bellis Perennis, and also Hypericum, though they may not be necessary.'

Leonie was touched. 'Thank you. I'm sure they'll help, since they come from you.' She leant over and tugged his sleeve, pulling him to her to offer a thank-you kiss. He came diligently, without resistance, but barely returned the kiss.

'Put the Calendula on your grazes,' he said, lightly touching the side of her nose. 'Hypericum is in case any nerves were squashed or compressed, but you may not need it. And Bellis Perennis will help the muscles and deep tissues. Though Arnica is really the best, even for your ankle. I couldn't be sure what to prescribe 'til I'd seen you.'

As he spoke, she only half-listened; all she really wanted was to drink in his familiar presence, to gaze at his beloved features – his rather too-thin lips, the lines around his eyes, the soft skin of his neck above the shirt collar and the smooth forearms and square, capable hands revealed by his rolled-back sleeves – hands that had touched and held her with such delight.

'Looking at you, I think maybe just Arnica and Calendula,' he finished earnestly.

She smiled gratefully, floating on the cloud of his concern. 'I've missed you,' was all she said.

He nodded, serious, not meeting her eyes. 'I'm glad the bike wasn't at fault. I'll check it over before you ride it again.'

Again she smiled her thanks, asking, 'Have you been all right?'

He bit at his lip, but seemed reassured by what he read in her tone. 'I needed a bit of time to myself.'

'Doesn't matter.' She laughed happily.

'You can ask me anything,' he said in a rush. 'If there's anything you want to know about me, I will tell you.'

Leonie was slightly taken aback. His breathing was shallow, his expression sincere. In his face she read an appeal for forgiveness that made little sense to her. 'I will,' she answered. 'Though I can't imagine there's anything vital I need to ask right now. Is there?'

He stepped closer, took her bruised face between his hands and kissed her. It was wonderful to feel his lips again, to have his hands touch her skin, his tongue search out hers. She slipped off the kitchen stool and, balancing on one foot, pressed herself against him. He groaned, and, his mouth still on hers, bent himself away from her so he could reach to unfasten her jeans. Awkwardly, she tried to unzip him, but fell against him, laughing.

Patrice had never been so urgent in pursuit, as if he could not wait for the feel of his flesh and bones against hers. He made love to her with a trance-like, slow insistence, pausing to gaze at her breasts, her limbs, even her toes, on and on throughout the night, as if he had returned from a long journey and could not believe that he was here beside her once more. Leonie was entranced, more in love than she had ever felt it possible to be. At last they rolled apart and fell seamlessly into sleep.

She awoke in darkness and confusion. Patrice was struggling with the sheets, calling, beseeching, wailing. As her own dream world dropped away, she realised he was having a nightmare. She shook him awake, and the dreadful keening sound he was making stopped, though it was several minutes before he became aware of his real surroundings. He refused her offer of a hot drink, didn't want her to turn on the light, or read a book to him for a little while. Instead, turning his back on her, he curled into a ball, his head in his hands, and pretended to be asleep. She lay mutely beside him, stroking his hunched shoulder, wishing she knew what could cause him such distress.

Patrice went off in the morning, jaunty and crowing, apparently with no memory whatsoever of her waking him from a nightmare. Later, when Leonie was at the office, absently stirring a mug of coffee while secretly savouring the still lingering physical sensations of the night before, she recalled with a pang of guilt – accompanied by soaring hope – that she had never given a moment's thought to any contraceptive precautions.

V

Leonie felt her conscience scratching as she rang Stella to let her know that she wouldn't be coming to England for Christmas as they had planned. 'It's Patrice's fortieth birthday a couple of weeks beforehand,' she explained. 'I'm trying to persuade him to celebrate, so, if we have a party, maybe you'll come over here instead?'

'Possibly,' said Stella, a little stiffly. 'Though it's not easy to get the extra time off around Christmas. We get a wee bit busy, with everyone's dreams of reuniting long-lost family.'

'Well, he's yet to give in and agree to anything, so I'll keep you posted.'

'Okay.'

'You don't really mind, do you, if I don't come to London?'

There was an infinitesimal pause. 'I guess I can make other plans.'

'I'm sorry to let you down. But do see if you can get the time off to come here. You know how much I'd love to see you.'

'You sound happy,' said Stella neutrally.

'I am. Things have really shifted between us. He seems, I don't know, lighter, somehow. We're clearing one of the other bedrooms, getting a new mattress for the bed in there.' Leonie chatted on, instinctively offering Stella time to recover from, and forgive, her offence. 'He's said he wants us to spend Christmas together. He's had the chimney swept in the salon and we've started having log fires.'

'How nauseating.'

'Jealous?'

Stella laughed more naturally. 'You bet!'

Leonie was relieved. 'Good! Speak soon.'

'Bye. Oh, Lennie?'

'Yes?'

'I really am happy for you. You know that.'

Leonie hung up the phone, smiling to herself – she had never known Stella be ungenerous or unfair – and went to empty the washing machine. It was one of her increasingly rare evenings at home in her apartment. Over the past two or three weeks she had spent four or five nights a week at Patrice's house. It had begun with him wanting to take care of her while her ankle was still sore, and had now slipped into a routine.

Though he remained stubborn about all sorts of things – probably always would – their relationship had become far more teasing and pliable, and she felt more relaxed in his company. He continued to resist her hints about throwing a birthday party, however small, but, unprompted, he revived her suggestion of colonising a spare bedroom to give themselves more space, and ordered the new mattress after discovering that long-dead mice had nested in the existing one.

Sometimes, retrieving forgotten objects from book-shelves or cupboards, he told her snippets about his child-hood. Taking him at his word, she asked many more questions about the past, which he was usually happy to answer, and eventually she confessed how she'd questioned Gaby and Thierry about anything they'd heard as children that might shed more light on the fate of Patrice's grand-father. Far from minding, Patrice had been curious to know more about a subject which, as he told her, his mother had rarely discussed and in any case appeared to know as little about as he did.

'Do you think your grandmother knew who shot your grandfather?' she asked cautiously, one Sunday morning as they drank tea in bed.

'No idea,' he answered. 'Josette was always pretty tight-lipped about him. I idolised him when I was a kid. Used to read every wartime adventure story I could lay my hands on, and I imagined him sending radio signals to secret agents or going off with the *Maquis* to blow up railway lines. Used to pester her for stories about him . . . must've driven her nuts.'

'Except that Thierry reckons local resistance was fairly passive,' explained Leonie. 'Not much derring-do. If your grandfather was a *résistant*, it was probably more a matter of passing around a few clandestine leaflets.'

'Makes sense,' agreed Patrice.

'But then why was he shot?'

'Being shot doesn't automatically make him a hero.'

'I don't understand.'

'Well, in retrospect, I'm not sure how much of a hero he really was. I mean, he could even have been a collaborator himself, for all we know.' Patrice made the suggestion with apparent nonchalance, pummelling his pillow to make himself more comfortable. 'Not a *résistant* at all.'

'That's a bit of a jump!'

'It crossed my mind recently, that's all. Looking back and trying to make sense of why Josette seemed so unforgiving about his memory. The real hatred in her face that time she told me I was just like him.' His mouth pinched tight and he spoke reluctantly. 'She didn't speak to me for a week afterwards.'

'What?'

'It was her way of punishing me. I had no one to play with, and she wouldn't speak. I'd go for days without a word to anyone.'

'My God!'

'Her way of dealing with things.'

'How old were you?'

'Don't remember. Eight or nine, maybe.'

'That's horrible. I mean, okay, I can imagine her shock at being left a widow, eight months pregnant, the whole world in chaos around her. But why take it out on a kid?'

'Maman should never have given me his name.' He shook his head with a wry look. 'Having a scandal to keep quiet about would go a long way to explain my mother's anxiety. Secrets perpetuate destructive miasms.'

'But if he was shot for being a Nazi sympathiser, surely it could never have been kept under wraps in a place like this?'

'You'd be surprised.'

'But he'd have to have done something terrible to warrant being shot,' argued Leonie. 'I mean, most people just went along with the Occupation, didn't they? I think very few probably dared voice open dissent, so most resistance was just quiet defiance. Didn't make them collaborators. Silence doesn't make people culpable.'

'Doesn't it?' asked Patrice, looking at her strangely. 'I hope that's true.'

'Besides, people round here would never have stood for Josette claiming he was a hero if he wasn't!'

'Maybe she didn't. Maybe she just never contradicted Maman's childish belief that he was. Anyway,' Patrice sighed wearily, 'what does it matter? It's how it goes, isn't it? Maybe he was simply murdered by some jilted lover of Josette's. Or, in a provincial town like this, by the son of the man from whom my great-grandfather stole some land. Maybe it was the father of the girl to whom my great-great-grandfather sold a horse that threw and crippled her. It goes back and back. Generations of unforgiven deeds. Whatever it was, I inherit all the injuries that were done.'

Patrice looked so white and sick that Leonie placed her mug on the bedside cabinet and took his free hand between both of hers as if to draw off his sorrow. 'All families hang onto past injuries,' she argued. 'Bad karma. We're all the same.'

He gave her a twisted smile and nodded assent, then withdrew his hand, swung his feet to the floor and sat with his back to her, his head down.

Leonie felt a flare of alarm. 'What else happened to you in this house, Patrice?'

He didn't seem to hear at first; when he turned to look at her, he looked drained and exhausted. 'Here?' he asked. 'I've told you. Nothing.'

'Then with your parents, or at boarding school. What was done to you?'

'Nothing.'

'Was it when you were very little? Did something happen to you when you were Didier's age?'

'Didier?'

'Gaby's grandson.'

His eyes widened in alarm, and Leonie felt that same sense of fear she'd experienced at dinner.

'Why ask about him?' he said, his voice sharp with distress.

'Because you were so upset. Please tell me what was wrong that night.'

127

Patrice said nothing, but she pressed on: 'Why didn't you come for your grandmother's funeral?'

'Who told you I didn't?' His face was filled with sudden anger.

'No one,' Leonie defended herself. 'Just local talk.'

'What did they say?' he demanded.

'That there was a disagreement over the will or something,' she conceded.

'Is that all?' He asked fiercely, scanning her face.

'Yes. Why?'

His expression relaxed, and he shook his head. 'Josette's will was perfectly straightforward.'

'Then why? Why do you care what they said? What else did Josette do to you? Patrice, tell me.'

He shrugged. 'Those remedies I gave you are dilutions,' he began. 'Pure distilled water that carries the memory of an original active substance. People are like that. We remain susceptible to predispositions we inherit at birth. I was never starved or beaten or locked in a cellar. No one set out to be cruel. Josette and my parents loved me in their way, but I inherited their susceptibilities. I repeat past damage.' Patrice turned away again, sitting with his hands gripping the edge of the mattress, hunched against her.

Part of Leonie sensed his real distress and felt deep concern; another part recalled Thierry's overheard comments: 'All that self-dramatising he goes in for. Afraid he won't shape up in the real world.' She felt confused – disloyal, selfish and resentful that he should be able to hijack her emotions in this way. All she wanted was a tranquil Sunday morning in bed. But, she reminded herself, she had asked him what was wrong, had sought to understand. She couldn't now reject him when he tried to explain himself, took the risk of revealing himself to her. Leonie shifted across the bed and pressed her lips against his bare shoulder.

'I'm sorry,' he said, reaching over to pull her hand around to his mouth, kissed it and held on tight. 'I warned you I'm not a good bet.'

'I just wish I understood. Wish you could be happier with yourself.'

'You must be fed up with me,' he said sweetly. 'But don't leave me. I don't think I can be alone with myself again.'

'I won't,' she promised passionately. 'Never, never.'

She half-expected that he would turn, roll over onto her, lose himself in making love to her. But he patted her hand, let go and stood up.

'I thought I might dig over some of the vegetable patch today, if it stays dry.' He smiled down at her, then reached for a robe and his old mules and disappeared downstairs.

When Patrice re-appeared from the garden, he was his usual self. They spent the rest of the day in the salon with a bright fire burning, reading newspapers and listening to music, closing the shutters early against the wintry gloom. If few of Leonie's questions were answered, nonetheless it seemed that their strange conversation of the morning had brought them closer, and she treasured his avowal that he needed her. He didn't refer again to the past and she decided not to probe further, at least for the time being. Besides, she had thoroughly disliked her own traitorous suspicion that he chose to make a big deal out of ordinary suffering. His isolated childhood can't have been much fun, but really he'd just got into a habit of introspection through living here alone for so long.

Leonie decided that, instead of dwelling on old wounds, from now on they would look forward and have jolly times together. Hankering after being more normal – it was the only word for it – as a couple, and longing for them to knit themselves tighter into the social fabric of the town, she made a point of continuing to see her friends. On one of the few occasions when she prevailed upon Patrice to accompany her, she caught herself thinking that, sitting in a bar with other people, they were like two actors in a play, each striving to be what they imagined the other wanted them to be. She rapidly dismissed the idea, sure that such doubts stemmed only from her own stupid insecurity about not daring to believe that she deserved to be so happy.

At the end of November, Patrice asked if, instead of a party for his fortieth birthday, she would like the idea of going away together for the weekend.

'Where?' she asked, her pleasure at his romantic wish to celebrate his birthday with her alone dousing any disappointment she might have felt at relinquishing the chance to gather together Gaby, Thierry and other friends such as Audra and Martine for a bigger celebration.

'Provence? Or the seaside? Let's go to the Riviera!'

'In December?'

'Sure, why not?'

She laughed, and left it to him to make the arrangements.

Ten days later, they took the bus to the station in Bergerac, arriving in Bordeaux in time to catch the sleeper to Nice. Disembarking early, they lingered over coffee and croissants in a seafront café, glad to shelter behind the thick plate glass, then walked up to their small hotel above the harbour, carrying their weekend bags. Their room had a view of the sea, but was small and stuffy, and Patrice was jittery and nervous. But he soon explained that, although the trip was his suggestion, it was a long time since he had left the Dordogne, or made an occasion of any anniversary let alone a fortieth birthday – a daunting enough age for anyone.

Leonie readily forgave him. In truth, she had her own preoccupations. It was now nearly a month since Patrice had come to her apartment and they had made love without contraceptive precautions. Her period had not arrived, and lately he had remarked approvingly on how full her breasts were. If she *was* pregnant (and she was pretty certain she must be), then she would be overjoyed. It had felt far too public to go into either of the pharmacies in Riberac to buy a testing kit, or even to risk the transaction going unobserved at the Carrefour. Had this weekend not been arranged, she would have driven to Bergerac or Angoulème to make her purchase anonymously, but now she planned to grab an opportunity in Nice to buy one when Patrice wasn't around to notice.

Before going out for dinner that night she lay in the hotel bath contemplating her flat belly: her desire, after so many years of feeling girlish and barren, to watch it swell and grow was accompanied by an inescapable foreboding about Patrice's reaction. She reassured herself that she had not set out to trap him, had not intentionally allowed it to happen. She hadn't expected him to come over that evening and had no reason, after his long silence, to assume they'd end up in bed. And when they had, she'd been so glad to have him back in her arms that she had genuinely forgotten the risk. Nor, she assumed, had he considered it, either. If she was pregnant then, she reassured herself, the responsibility was shared equally between them.

She ran in more hot water and began to soap herself. She must calm down, or she would blurt out the truth without thinking! Were she sure of his reaction, she would present the news as a birthday gift, but deep within her lay a terror that he would reject any idea of a baby. She couldn't help recalling the harrowing arguments she'd had with Greg over her longing for a child, a longing which had led to their break-up. She would soon be thirty-five: she might not have many more chances. All she wanted was for Patrice to be content. He didn't have to marry her or change anything about their relationship, just be accepting of her having his child. But she was unable to shake loose the memory of Gaby's grandson clinging to Patrice's thigh and the look of horror on his face, as if the child's hands were dead things clutching at him from beneath dark waters.

Now she was becoming hysterical, she told herself, pulling the plug and stepping out of the bath. She towelled herself dry with a briskness designed to chase away ridiculous fears. The door opened and Patrice came in.

'Oh,' he said, looking past her. 'I thought I'd share your bath.'

'Too late,' she laughed. 'You'll just have to enjoy having fresh water all to yourself.'

'You could have two baths,' he teased.

She smiled and shook her head, feeling too brittle to respond erotically. 'I'll turn into a prune,' she protested. Seeing his shrug of disappointment, she regretted her mood, but, needing to clear her head, went out, closing the door on him.

As she dressed, Leonie marvelled that they had never before got ready to set off out like this for an occasion together. Patrice's birthday was the following day; before they left home he'd told her that, although happy to splash out and have fun on the weekend, he didn't want a fuss made of the day itself, didn't enjoy being the centre of attention. Accordingly, Leonie had done some online research and booked a table for this evening at a seafood restaurant recommended for its *bouillabaisse*, a dish she knew he specially liked. Taking his arm as they exited the hotel lift, she gleamed at the reception staff and took pleasure in his holding the door open for her. He held her close as they walked down into the city centre.

While Patrice derived little satisfaction from the traditionally attired waiters, linen tablecloths and abundant glass and silverware, he was curious about the menu, and touched that Leonie had pre-ordered a bottle of champagne that the maître d' opened and poured while they read it and discussed what they would order. She was relieved when Patrice failed to notice, after the waiter topped up their glasses, that she barely drank from hers. Their starters arrived and, as they ate, he told her stories about his first homeopathic patients and the embarrassing mistakes he'd made. Then he listened happily as she chattered about her old life in London, visits to her mother and step-family in Toronto, about the days when she and Stella had first met and become friends. The *bouillabaisse* was delicious, and after drinking the lion's share of the champagne he began to speculate ridiculously about a stolid couple across the room who were assiduously tackling enormous lobsters while all the time jealously eyeing up every dish that passed them en route to other tables.

'Don't you envy greedy people?' he laughed. 'It must be wonderful to be so guiltless about self-indulgence.'

'Like us!' she said, as the waiter removed their dishes.

'People who are always controlling themselves, always hyper-vigilant, can be so exhausting.'

'You mean worrying all the time about how strangers might judge them?'

'Not so much that. I suppose I was thinking of my parents. With them, it's more their own unspoken prohibitions.'

Leonie held her breath: Patrice so seldom talked about Agnès and Geoffrey that she was avid to learn more. 'Give me an example,' she asked casually.

'Oh, they had all sorts of rituals. An evening like this would've been a minefield.'

'Is that why you don't like dinner parties?'

He laughed. 'Probably. My folks found it hard to relax. And they made each other worse. Maman on her own could sometimes let her hair down a bit, but Dad always had to stay in charge. He'd wind himself up so tight anticipating any tiny thing that might destabilise Maman, that she stood no chance of forgetting to be anxious.' He caught Leonie looking at him, and smiled wryly. 'Anxiety is highly contagious.'

She nodded. 'Horrid. Affects everyone close to it, I imagine.'

In reply, he gave her the same strange look he had when they had discussed whether his grandfather was a collaborator, though she still couldn't work out quite what it signified. 'I'm talking too much,' he said. 'I don't think I can manage another morsel. Shall we just have coffee?'

They waited for it to be brought, and during the sudden

and disappointing silence that followed, Leonie was struck by a powerful sense of Patrice's withdrawal. What she felt was not that he had disappeared into an intense and fully occupied inner space of his own in which, perhaps, he had returned to scenes of his youthful self in a European restaurant somewhere with his parents. She wasn't sure how to put into words what she was picking up from him. It seemed like a dislocation from himself, a disengagement, an emptying out. It had the effect of making her anxious and fearful – the contagious emotion he had that very moment described. What right did he have to take himself away from her like that, close himself off and leave her there alone! Just when she wanted to be close, to be able to confide in him and trust him to support her. This absence made her want to walk out, go back to the hotel by herself – she'd take a taxi, if only to spite him! – then refuse to speak to him when he returned to their anonymous room. Or even, as she watched him glance from his coffee cup to the emptying tables around them, go straight to the station and run away altogether.

She forced herself to calm down but, however irrational it was to be so influenced by his simple choice to remain silent for a few moments at the end of a long day, she was not imagining the porous effect on her: she did feel as if she were perched dizzyingly on the edge of a potentially annihilating drop into the abyss.

The bill paid, they left the restaurant and Patrice sobered

up in the icy wind blowing off the sea, shaking off his odd mood. Taking her arm, he looked down at her as they rounded a corner. 'Are you all right?' he asked. 'We're okay, aren't we?'

Leonie nodded, forcing a smile, but, in truth, she felt unaccountably tired.

They came out onto the Promenade des Anglais and turned to walk along to their hotel. The freezing wind swept at them off the dark sea, tasting of salt, and Patrice laughed. 'I love this biting cold, don't you?' When she didn't reply, he asked again: 'We're all right, aren't we?'

She pressed his arm close against her side. 'Of course we are!'

They did not make love that night, for which Leonie held herself to account. In the morning, determined to throw off her pique, she delighted in Patrice's pleasure at the birthday gifts she had chosen with such care. Audra had found them for her – proper Belle Epoque brass stair rods for the hallway, something Leonie knew he had been searching for, and an old Moroccan fruit bowl glazed in soft greens and browns. Unable to drag them on the train, she had photographed the rods laid out in a pattern around the bowl, then printed out the images to place inside his card. Eager to escape their slightly too cramped, slightly too hot hotel room, they went out, walked on the blustery beach, then spent hours chatting about nothing over the kind of brunch they never dreamt of eating at home, complete with a celebratory chocolate *gâteau* which they were unable to finish.

Afterwards, the plummeting temperature and paltry light left little to do until their train left that evening except return to their hotel room where, enervated by the long winter afternoon, they lay side by side reading their books, inhibited from initiating sex by the strange bed and thin walls. Later, tucked up in their banquettes on the train, they held hands and dozed companionably as if they had indeed successfully accomplished the perfect weekend away.

They arrived back in Riberac around Monday lunchtime. Making the excuse that she wanted to fetch his gifts, Leonie went straight to her apartment. In fact she could wait no longer to try the pregnancy kit that she had managed to buy while Patrice had been occupied choosing a newspaper.

She locked herself in the bathroom, despite there being no one to spy on her, took the predictor stick out of its box and sat on the loo to pee. Then she counted off the seconds of two extraordinary minutes, staring sightlessly into the basin's plug-hole. Taking a deep breath, she dared to look: it was positive! The dream of many years. A child. A child with a man she loved more tenderly than she had ever imagined possible. She gazed at the stick. Life was growing inside her right now, a life they had created together. She grinned at herself in the mirror, mocking her own cliché-ridden thoughts, then danced through to her bedroom to change her clothes. Nothing wrong with clichés, she told herself, not when they were so joyously, amazingly, miraculously true!

Distracted, she almost forgot to take Patrice's presents with her when she drove to his house. She rang the bell and stood in the gathering darkness, certain she would be incapable now of keeping her news to herself. Besides, she reasoned, what difference would it make *when* she told him? There was no such thing as the 'right moment'. Okay, so it wasn't meant to happen now, so soon, but it had, and it had happened to both of them. When Patrice opened the door, she threw her free arm around his neck, kissed him, and presented his gifts. Back on familiar ground, he too was more composed and contented. He unwrapped and admired the glazed bowl, carried it through to the kitchen table, then returned to lay out some of the stair rods: they fitted precisely, enhancing the imposing hallway in just the way he wanted.

'Thank you!' he kissed her. 'They're perfect. Come and have a drink. Omelette okay? There's not much else in the fridge.'

'Plenty! But actually I won't have any wine. Just water.' She followed him into the kitchen. 'I've got something to tell you.'

When she did not enlarge, he turned from rinsing a tumbler at the sink to look at her. She grinned idiotically. 'Can't you guess?'

He shook his head, a polite smile masking his thoughts.

139

Leonie took a deep breath. 'You remember the night I twisted my ankle and you came over?'

He handed her the glass of water. 'Yes.'

'Well, I wasn't expecting you.' She paused. He still didn't get it. 'I didn't use my cap that night.'

He went very still. She saw his eyes lock down. But she was getting used to that now and refused to let it alarm her. Besides, almost as soon as she had registered it, the blankness was gone. 'Wow,' he said, breathing again. 'Go on, tell me.'

'Oh, Patrice, I'm pregnant!'

'You've known this all weekend?'

'No. I only just did the test. I wasn't sure before. Just hoped,' she said, offering him a lead on her state of unambivalent happiness. 'Though it is the reason I was a bit jumpy in Nice. Sorry about that!'

'Gosh.'

He sat down at the table and ran his finger round the roughened edge of the Moroccan bowl. She waited in trepidation, watching him closely, but his face was in shadow. He lifted his head and looked once around the black-and-white-tiled kitchen as if committing it to memory one final time before his life changed for ever. He took a shuddering breath, then she saw his shoulders drop and he smiled up at her, his eyes clear: he had decided. He got to his feet and folded her in his arms.

In the morning Leonie had to leave early for work. The previous night had been the closest and sweetest they had ever spent together. Patrice had been both tender and demanding, murmuring endearments he had never voiced before. She thought she had woken in the night to him thrashing and wailing in the grip of another nightmare, but her memory was hazy, lost in the depths of unconsciousness. Now they were in a weekday morning rush, both running late. Kissing him farewell at the door, she teased him: 'I won't hear from you for days now, will I?'

'Don't be silly. I'll call tonight.'

'We'll see about that!' she joked, and went off as happy and carefree as she had been in years.

'Bye for now,' he called after her.

Gaby looked over the top of her computer screen when Leonie walked in. 'How was Nice? Good weekend?'

'Magical!'

'I'm so glad. I want to hear all about it over lunch.'

Leonie knew she could not yet say anything to Gaby, her employer, about the future: she was barely a few weeks into her pregnancy, and it was tempting fate to announce it too early. Not that her mind wasn't already leaping ahead to the contingency plans they would have to make in the office for next summer when the baby would be born. Meanwhile, she let her boss assume that her inability to concentrate was due to her romantic weekend away, and was rewarded by Gaby's evident pleasure in hearing about the windswept Promenade des Anglais, welcome proof that the older woman's attitude to Patrice was softening.

Leonie couldn't wait to get back to her apartment at the end of the day, bursting to ring Stella.

'You're kidding? That's spectacular news!' was Stella's instant reaction. 'Can I be godmother?'

'Who else?'

'How did Patrice take it?'

'Pretty well, considering. Really well, actually. I suspect he's rather pleased. He was – we were together last night, and he was— Oh, Stella, I am ecstatic.'

'Some Christmas you're going to have! I'm so happy for you, Lennie. If anybody deserves their dream-come-true, it's you.'

'Thank you,' said Leonie humbly. 'I still can't believe it's happening.'

'So your weekend went well, obviously?'

'I was in a bit of a state. Hardly surprising. But it was fine. I didn't tell him 'til we got home.'

'I guess you'll have to start negotiating moving in together.'

'Don't! I'm already fantasising about turning his old bedroom into a nursery. We'll have to do something to modernise the bathroom, too.'

'And Patrice is truly on board with all this?'

'Yes, I think so . . . after last night.' Leonie glowed at the warm memory. 'Don't worry, I'm not going to railroad him. There's plenty of time.'

'Good.'

'Frankly, I won't be surprised if he wobbles. That's what

he's like. But he's said he'll be there for me, and however much he drifts off sometimes, he keeps his promises.'

'Well, I want regular updates, okay?'

'You'll get them. Bye, Stella.'

'Bye, Lennie. Look after yourself.'

After she hung up, Leonie could hardly contain herself. She wanted literally to jump up and down with joy, but there was no one else to share her news with, not yet. Her family had grown too distant, other friends in London not close enough, and friends here, like Audra and Martine, while they would be thrilled for her, might spread the word before she and Patrice were ready for it to be common knowledge. Half of her wished he would ring and be unable not to see her tonight, but the other half knew him well enough to warn her that this was fairy-tale thinking. He wasn't about to change overnight. Her news was a shock, no two ways about it, and he would need time alone to digest and process this potentially seismic shift in his life. But she luxuriated in the certainty that he would call tomorrow. Or even the day after. It didn't matter in the great scheme of things. Time and parenthood would gradually alter his habitual reserve. She had only to be patient and to wait.

By Wednesday night she was cross and irritated. He wouldn't be able to go on being quite so self-absorbed once he had a child to look after! At some point he would have to learn to take other people's feelings into account. Around ten, before she went to bed, she called him. He didn't pick up, but he often ran a bath at this time and might not have heard the phone. At lunchtime the next day she called his office, but got the answering machine – he never employed a receptionist – and decided there was little point leaving a message. When she got home that evening she called his house again, where the phone rang and rang. She tried his mobile, but it was turned off. The first cold fear that this was going to be a more serious wobble than she had anticipated began to creep into her mind, but she rejected it robustly. She had been here before, and all had been well in the end. She just had to allow him to absorb the bombshell in his own peculiar way.

On Friday at the office the ringing phones all day were torture; she prayed each time she picked up that the caller would be Patrice. As she put the key in the lock of her apartment door at the end of the week, panic began to set in. How could she be so foolish as to let herself imagine so easily that, at forty, he would welcome the prospect of fatherhood with a woman he had known for a mere few months, had not even yet lived with? To what depths of self-delusion was she letting herself sink? She could hardly blame him for avoiding her! But while she braced herself for a dose of reality, she also knew that time was on her side. The baby was not due until August. Even if, as after Gaby's dinner party, it was a few weeks before he came back to her, did it honestly matter? He was a decent man who would never turn his back on her, of that she was sure. She pushed from her mind all memory of Didier.

After she'd climbed wearily into bed, another buried recollection surfaced and clutched at her: when she'd rung his office number the previous day, she'd not listened attentively to the out-going message. Now, certain that out of hours no one would be there, she dialled it again: she was right, the message he'd left had been changed from the usual one. Patrice's voice sounded neutral, bland, but announced that he wasn't booking any new appointments at present. If the matter was urgent, he recommended a colleague in a nearby town. She pushed down her infernal misgivings. It would soon be Christmas. He probably wanted to delay all new appointments until after the New Year, that was all. Make some time for himself. Maybe create more free time to spend with her, for all she knew. She must not over-react, not allow hormonal changes to drive her to panic. And even if he had cleared the decks so he could think things through in peace on his own for a little while, he'd be back in touch eventually.

All that night she fought the urge to get up and dressed and drive over to his house. How ridiculous she would look if she turned up, dishevelled and maddened with anxiety, and then found him calmly reading beside a cosy log fire in the salon. But in the morning she showered and dressed with care and went over there, determined not to upbraid him, to act as if five days' silence from the father of her child were the most natural thing in the world.

As she turned off the ignition outside his house and opened her car door she took in the unusual fact that all the shutters were closed. Trembling in the winter cold, she went to the front door and rang the bell. She could hear it pealing in the empty hallway but there was no sound of his approaching footsteps. She went around to the side door, but found the garden gate padlocked. The padlock was brand new. She stared at it, uncomprehending. The gate was never locked. Full of dread, she returned to the front door. Every window was shuttered, she could not see in, and there was no answer to her increasingly frantic ringing of the bell.

VI

It took Gaby and Thierry some time to chip away at Leonie's disbelief. She had driven straight to their house and burst in on them as they were reading the Saturday newspapers. In complete shock, she told them everything. Failing to notice Gaby's disappointed shake of the head at the unhindered revelation of her pregnancy, she castigated herself soundly. How could she have been so naïve, so self-obsessed, so carried away with her own fantasies? Patrice was a dear, beautiful man, trying to recover from past difficulties, and she had just barged into his life, trampling over his most delicate feelings, considering only herself and what she wanted, and expected him to adjust instantly to the idea of parenthood. Hardly surprising he'd felt suffocated, unable to explain himself, in need of some space! It was all her fault.

The Duvals exchanged concerned looks over Leonie's slumped shoulders and shook their heads.

'Sweetie, nothing's ever as one-sided as that. I'm sure he's more than capable of speaking for himself,' said Gaby, making a huge effort to restrain her indignation. 'Maybe he does need a bit of time to adjust, like you say. Probably just gone off somewhere neutral to think things over for a day or two, that's all. Doesn't want to face you until he's ready.' Gaby looked up at her husband, but found him unwilling to fall into line.

'There are other ways to extricate himself from the situation without turning tail,' said Thierry roundly. 'Strikes me he's taking the easy way out, looking after number one.' Gaby shot him a look. 'Unless there's some other simple explanation, of course,' he amended. 'He could have padlocked the gate because of kids breaking in and making a mess, or something.'

Faced with Leonie's beseeching look, Thierry excused himself. 'I'm going to make some calls,' he said. 'See what there is to find out. Anyone want more coffee first?'

Leonie shook her head, but Gaby gave instructions. 'Good idea. And bring Leonie some of that apple cake. She needs to eat.'

'No, really, I'm not hungry. Thanks.'

'You'll eat something.' Gaby patted Leonie's cold hands. 'You've got more than just yourself to take into account now, remember?' She shifted close, holding onto Leonie's hands. 'Sweetie, do you think it's to do with his having another child?'

'What other child?' Leonie asked, bewildered.

'Catherine's convinced she's right, that Agnès Hinde did say she'd had a grandson.'

'No, no.'

'Well, whatever the truth, he'll probably be back soon,' Gaby resumed a brighter tone. 'And with the biggest bunch of flowers you've ever seen!'

'Poor Patrice,' mourned Leonie. 'What have I done to him?'

'You're the one who needs consolation, sweetie. Not him.' Gaby looked up at her husband as he returned with coffee and cake and widened her eyes in warning.

'He'd never have done this unless he had to, unless it was all too much and he couldn't cope,' Leonie went on.

Thierry shook his head. 'All that should matter is making sure you don't harm anyone you love.'

'But surely the way he's behaved shows how deeply damaged he must be?' she appealed to them both.

'A wounded animal is often the most dangerous,' observed Thierry.

'My friend Stella, she learnt from the kids she used to work with. The worst behaved were always the ones with the worst histories,' insisted Leonie. 'They can't help it.'

But Thierry shook his head, having none of it. 'Why is it that women always have to make allowances for their men?' he asked. 'Any scoundrel offers a plausible enough excuse and everything's forgiven.'

'We forgive our children,' said Gaby simply.

'He's not a child,' snapped Thierry. Gaby failed to shush him, and even nodded in agreement as Thierry declared, 'He's a coward. And Leonie deserves better!'

*

Embarrassed and exhausted, Leonie refused the Duvals' kindly invitations to stay on for lunch, or even the weekend, and took herself back home. Her apartment seemed smaller and more makeshift than ever. It would be Christmas in a fortnight's time. The cashmere scarf she had so carefully chosen for Patrice lay in its bag in her bedroom cupboard, waiting to be festively wrapped. Thierry's calls had thrown no light as yet on Patrice's unoccupied and shuttered house, but a voice at the back of her mind warned her he had gone for good. She couldn't rationalise it, knew it made no sense for him to give up his life here, but was utterly convinced.

She thought back to last Monday night, when she had taken his birthday presents over to his house. She hadn't noticed any cards or gifts other than her own. Had there really been nothing at all? Patrice had grown up in this town, spent half his childhood here, then returned to work here four years ago. He was a charming man who gained deep satisfaction from helping people, and his patients liked him. How had it been possible not to accumulate friends and acquaintances who knew him well enough at least to acknowledge his fortieth birthday? Why had he never made a social life for himself, however small and tight-knit? Why would anyone willingly tolerate such isolation? But then, maybe he had an existence of which she remained completely ignorant. Maybe he had women all over town, or each kept in separate compartments of his life. Her icy terror at the idea made her laugh: she couldn't imagine him juggling different women, lying to each of them. He was too sincere, his feelings too transparent. No, he was not that type of man at all!

Leonie recollected how Stella had wanted to Google him – she must call Stella, but not yet. She wished now she had not gone to Gaby's house. What if Thierry were right, and there was some simple explanation and Patrice was about to call any moment? It was stupid of her to have over-reacted. Patrice would quite rightly not be pleased that she had told her boss about the pregnancy without consulting him first. She would delay calling Stella about this latest development. No need to go overboard until the worst was confirmed, until she knew for certain that Patrice had walked out on her.

But of course, argued the voice in Leonie's head, abandonment was what Patrice knew best. It was what he had grown up with: all those lonely childhood summers with Josette, cut off from his parents, punished with days of silence and rejection. Escape into himself was for him the natural way to react under pressure, she knew that. She had experienced the impact of his brief withdrawal that night in the restaurant in Nice, but the next day he had been fine again.

Gaby was right; he needed time to adjust. She must keep believing in him, not lose faith. Once he had thought things through, he would return. She would set herself a limit. Let him disappear for Christmas – always a holiday fraught with too much expectation – and then start fresh in the New Year.

She dug out her next year's diary and pencilled in a mark at the first weekend. If she had heard nothing from him by then she would accept that Thierry's harsher view was justified, but until then Patrice would remain the man she knew and loved. She was carrying his child. She was going to bear and raise his son or daughter. She must not set out on that adventure with bitterness in her heart. Saturday, the eighth of January: she repeated the date to herself. However difficult, she would somehow keep the faith until then.

Stella arrived at dawn on Christmas morning. She had queued at Folkestone for a last-minute cancellation on the Shuttle then driven through the night. She didn't like how Leonie had sounded on the phone and wasn't going to be fobbed off with silly evasions, so came to see for herself what on earth was going on. She found her friend looking gaunt and strained, with nothing in her fridge but houmous and eggs.

'Lucky I brought provisions, then,' she said, unpacking the supermarket bags she'd carried up from her car. 'Not exactly turkey with all the trimmings, but at least we can cobble together a square meal. Looks like you haven't eaten properly in days.'

'Bless you. Really. The thought of Christmas Day on my own, I couldn't have faced it.'

'What friends are for. So where's Patrice?'

'Still don't know. Not a word.'

'He's coming back?'

'No idea. He's locked up his house, cancelled all his patients and gone.'

'For chrissakes, why didn't you tell me it was as bad as this?' demanded Stella.

'Hoped he'd be back by now.' Leonie sat down wearily at the kitchen counter. 'Or at least have been in touch. I convinced myself he would, tried to believe it. Don't think I can keep it together much longer, though.'

'Oh, Lennie.' Stella hugged her, but Leonie pushed her feebly away.

'Don't be too sympathetic, or I'll fall apart.'

'Okay. But, Jesus, I'd like to throttle him!' Stella tried to shake off her incredulity. 'I know I only met him briefly, but I liked the guy! I certainly never imagined ...' She trailed off, sighing at the diminished spectacle of her friend. 'You'd better bring me up to speed. Properly, this time,' she warned.

'After I told him about the baby, I half expected him not to call. But then, when he never answered my calls, I went round to his house. It's all shuttered and padlocked.' Leonie tried to block out Stella's reaction, striving to relate events as levelly as she could. 'Sylviane told Gaby he'd cancelled her granddaughter's appointment saying he wasn't able to re-schedule it, but giving no explanation. Apparently the pharmacist has had lots of people asking when he's coming back. Nobody knows.'

'Have you been to the police?'

'Why? He left everything in order. Thierry found out he's given notice on the office he rented. Left instructions for any post to go to the bank. I suppose some patients still owe him money.'

'You don't reckon he's . . . You know . . .'

'Topped himself?' Leonie shrugged. 'I don't think so. But frankly your guess is as good as mine.'

'I was actually thinking there might be someone else.'

'Another woman?'

'Or back to his wife?'

'Who knows? My one solid fact is that I've no way to be certain of anything.'

'Do you suppose he was planning to scarper even before you told him you were pregnant?' asked Stella. 'I mean, what if this has nothing to do with you.' She caught the look of desolation on Leonie's face. 'I don't mean that you don't matter to him,' she corrected herself. 'Only that there's something else going on. Money, or some legal thing with a patient or something?'

Leonie shook her head in consternation. 'Three weeks ago I'd've sworn blind nothing like that was possible, but I have no idea any more who he is or what he's capable of.'

'I never imagined a person's silence could be so callous,' mourned Stella.

'Did I tell you his grandmother's way of punishing him was not to speak to him?'

'For how long?'

'Days, I think.'

'That's not good. That counts as quite serious emotional abuse.'

Leonie fell silent.

'You've no clue as to where he might have gone?' Stella persisted.

'Believe me, I've worked through every possible permutation. Right now, if someone told me he'd been abducted by aliens, I'd simply be relieved to have the truth at last.'

'Sorry, I'll shut up.'

'No, no.' Leonie gave Stella a watery smile. 'It's better than getting paranoid in the middle of the night, deciphering the runes, clutching at straws.'

Stella looked sorrowfully at her friend, her expression failing to hide her contempt for what Patrice had left behind.

Stella and Leonie ate sausages and roast potatoes for their Christmas dinner, during which Leonie asked dutifully about Stella's work and life in London. Afterwards, exhausted by the effort, she went to lie down and fell fast asleep. Stella took out Leonie's laptop and Googled Patrice's name, but brought up nothing she hadn't found before, nothing that would go any way towards explaining his disappearance or shed light on where he might have gone. There were other methods she could apply, search facilities for tracing people that would be available through her office network, but she was unable to access those accounts from Leonie's computer. It would have to wait until she went home. Deprived of sleep after her long night-time drive, Stella dozed off herself.

Leonie, sitting down beside her, woke her an hour or so later.

'I dreamt I was breaking into Patrice's house.'

Stella struggled awake. 'Really?'

'My dream-self was magically skilled at picking locks. I could observe everything from about two feet above my normal eye-line. It's all neat and tidy. A coffee cup washed up by the side of the sink. A newspaper from the day I last saw him left on the kitchen table, his mobile next to it. Yet the milk in the fridge is fresh and the ash in the fireplace is still warm, as if he's only just gone. I'm quite calm until I float up the stairs and reach the bedroom door, where I'm so overcome by what I know is inside that I daren't even turn the handle. That's when I woke up.'

'Oh, Lennie.' Stella grasped Leonie's hand and held it tight.

'In my dream, I'm convinced I'm going to find the key to all this. That I'd notice some object lying on the table, discarded by his chair. I'd pick it up, have a moment of revelation and everything would magically fit into place, miraculously come right again.'

Stella squeezed her hand.

'I keep hoping I'm going to wake up and find it all spun into gold, like in a fairy tale. Spun into a coherent story that I can understand and be done with, instead of it going round and round in my head.'

'How about some tea?' was all Stella could find to say. Leonie nodded and followed her to the kitchen, where she leant against the counter in a stupor as Stella filled the kettle and rinsed out mugs.

'I found it endearing that he wouldn't tell me stuff,' Leonie went on, watching vacantly as Stella threw away an empty box and searched for more teabags. 'But it wasn't. It's scary.'

Stella couldn't help agreeing.

'Part of what I loved about Patrice was how he was so elusive,' she continued. 'It drew me in, hooked me. But it meant I let him get away with not actually telling me anything, while I was so impressed by how honest he is, how he never lies. Why didn't I ask?' she wailed. 'I honestly believed he was telling me about himself. But he didn't.'

Stella handed her a mug of hot tea. 'Don't keep beating yourself up, Lennie. Don't make it worse than it is.'

'For all I know, he's been totally cold-hearted and calculating all this time,' Leonie went on. 'I'm having his child, yet have no idea who the hell he is.' She cradled the comforting warmth between her hands. 'How could I be so stupid?'

'You're not. This isn't your fault.'

'It is! I was stupid! Why else did I just assume that he'd go along with happy ever after?'

'You were in love, Lennie. That's what love does. Besides,'

Stella went on, 'it's a romantic dream to expect to know anyone entirely. Everyone keeps some little part of themselves private. And he may have lied as much to himself as to you. If not more.'

Leonie nodded obediently, but went on lecturing herself for so willingly letting herself be duped.

Stella comforted her as best she could, but their Christmas Day ended in misery. As they went to bed, Stella took a deep breath, obviously making up her mind to say something: 'I know you're not ready to hear this, but Patrice has not behaved honourably. Even if he comes back, and even though he's the baby's father, you shouldn't forget that.'

Leonie nodded, too sore to speak. Stella looked at her wretchedly, clearly wishing she could do more to relieve her pain, but all she could do was hug her tight. 'Sleep well, Lennie. Happy Christmas.'

But the nights were the worst. The moment Leonie closed her eyes, she was swept away on a wave of longing and regret for all she had lost. She felt his physical absence like a homesickness. Along with the craving for his smell, his touch, the warmth of his body next to her in the bed, came renewed anguish to be released from the ache of not knowing what had happened. Where was he? What were his thoughts? Did he still love her? For all his lack of candour, she could not believe that what he had told her instinctively with his hands, his mouth, his body, had been a lie. It was so easy in the dark to imagine him back beside her; she had only to roll over to imagine she felt his warm back press against hers. The memory of his touch was sharp and real even while her body felt butchered and toxic. Never before had she experienced the duality of mind and body so forcibly. It drove her mad, stopped her sleeping. Her body, the source of such joy and pleasure, felt old and weary. So far, the new life inside her was still only a concept, a blue mark on a plastic stick; meanwhile every heartbeat was a reminder of her mortality.

The memory of the last night they had spent at his house was the hardest. She tried to avoid the probability that their final hours together had been so close and sweet not because he loved her and was happy they were to have a child but because he already knew that he was leaving. Ignorant, she had actually watched him make his silent decision as he sat at the kitchen table, looking around the room as if for the last time; had observed him relax because, with his valediction clear before him, he had felt safe with her, perhaps the only time he ever did. All the tenderness and love he had expressed that night, those murmured endearments, were in reality regret, apology, sorrow at the chain of events he had determined to set in motion in the morning. Their love-making had been his guilty Judas kiss, the worst lie of all, something monstrous, as if, somewhere deep in him, the reality of her had already ceased to exist. Reviling his betrayal, yet yearning to hear him say all those wonderful words again, she fell asleep.

The following morning dawned dry and clear. Stella suggested a walk and Leonie chose the path beside the river. While Stella buttoned up against the chill rising from the dark, fast-flowing water, Leonie seemed oblivious, her mind going round and round on its now sickeningly familiar loop.

'Do you know anything about the Way of St James?' she asked Stella abruptly.

'It's part of the pilgrimage to Santiago de Compostela, isn't it?'

Leonie had no idea.

'I'm sure it is,' Stella went on. 'Why?'

'He said once that he walked here, followed part of the Way of St James.'

'Walked from where?' Stella asked.

'I don't know. I assumed it was like a vacation. I wasn't really paying attention, but what if he's done this before?'

'Left other women the same way, you mean? Just walked away?'

'Literally walked out on his whole life. Arrived here on foot, with what he could carry.'

'There are people who do that,' agreed Stella. 'Simply go off with no warning, no plan of what they're doing. People who go missing because they've forgotten who they are.'

'Except that he was heading for his grandmother's house when he came here, wasn't he? So when he set off, he knew his destination.'

'He refuses to drive, doesn't he?'

Leonie nodded.

'So what's all that about?' mused Stella. 'When you first told me, I wondered if maybe he'd been responsible for some dreadful smash-up.'

'If so, then it didn't leave a mark on him.' Leonie realised she was becoming confused by her own tangle of suspicions. 'Oh, nothing makes sense!' She linked her arm in Stella's.

'Lennie, this will pass. You will get over him.'

'I don't want to get over him! I want him here!' Her voice cracked. 'Even if I never see him again, I need to know that he did love me.'

Stella stopped on the path to hug her friend. 'Shush now. It'll all come good. You're going to be fine.'

Leonie stood crying, not even raising her hands to wipe away her tears. Stella began seriously to fear for her friend. 'Listen to me,' she said, shaking Leonie's shoulders, trying to get her to concentrate. 'You have to start thinking about yourself. You're fabulous. A much better person than him.'

'But I don't feel whole without him,' Leonie wept. 'Being me's not enough any more.'

'I hate leaving you,' said Stella two days later. It was a damp, misty morning. She had loaded up her car and now stood beside it with Leonie shivering in the cold. 'Are you going to be all right?'

'I have to be, don't I?'

'Oh, Lennie, I had such faith that this would turn out well. I still can't believe it hasn't.'

'It was never going to work. It's been in him all the time to do this. And part of me always knew it.'

'Then you're better off without him.'

Leonie nodded, unable yet to conceptualise any notion of a viable future.

'Take care of yourself. Call me if you need me.'

'I will. Promise. And thanks, Stella. For everything.'

The two women embraced, and Leonie stood and waved as Stella, fighting back tears, drove off. As Leonie went back indoors alone, she couldn't help feeling relieved. The constant effort of emerging from her thick fog of sadness to pay proper attention to another person had sapped what little energy she had. Now she was free to return undisturbed to her own relentless thoughts. Disappointment, she was learning, was a very under-rated emotion. It was not that she felt betrayed at being left to have their child alone: she had never made Patrice aware of her avid hunger for a child, of her sense of time running out. On that subject, as she had to acknowledge in her most self-lacerating moments, it was she who had tricked and misled him. No, her grief now was for the loss of an imagined future, of all the cherished illusions and daydreams she'd allowed herself to believe could indeed come true because they loved each other. The unfairness of placing such a burden upon him did not prevent her feeling its loss. The final wrench – like pulling a barbed arrow out of her heart – would be to let go of all those dreams, and that she could not accomplish because to do so must surely kill her.

All the while, a fierce and insidious internal voice kept whispering eagerly that it wasn't over, it couldn't be, not something so precious and special. She knew this was fantasy, but the idea of returning to a life without even the potential for such bliss was unbearable. Without the ecstasy she believed she and Patrice had shared, then her life stretched ahead cold and meaningless: she did not want it, not even now that it held the child for which she had yearned. Such comfortless thoughts frightened her. What kind of mother would she be if she couldn't stop such despair intruding on her view of the future – her child's future? She had to find some new way to live with herself, to fall out of love. She reminded herself that she had done so before, after Greg, when she had first come to France, and for a second she saw that it might be possible to survive this dreadful pain, to forgive herself for being so undeserving of Patrice's love.

But she knew she had never loved Greg with the same visceral attachment, never felt her own identity as obliterated by the loss of his love for her. She had been younger and more hopeful and had chosen to leave. And even though she no longer really cared, she still heard through Stella where Greg was and some news of what he was up to. Patrice's exit was a rebuke to everything she thought she'd known and understood, to her very existence. She could no longer comprehend anything about a world where this could happen.

The week after New Year Gaby re-opened the office and Leonie went back to work. She also made an appointment to see a doctor about her pregnancy, something she had postponed before Christmas in the vain hope that Patrice would return and be there to accompany her. Gaby immediately reported that neither she nor Thierry had gleaned any new information, though Leonie guessed that, whatever talk there was in the town about Patrice's continuing absence, Gaby chose not to repeat it. She was grateful that the older woman's loyalty and discretion overruled any relish she may once have had for gossip on the subject. Leonie recalled guiltily how dismissive she had been of the Duvals' life together when she had taken Patrice to their house for dinner. How had she permitted herself to belittle such warmth and kindness? Was it merely because she had been, as Stella had dubbed it, too loved-up to see what really mattered? If so, she had learnt a hard lesson.

That first day back at her desk Leonie found it impossible to concentrate, but gradually the mundane details of taking bookings, mailing confirmations, arranging repairs and sending out brochures cleared her mind. For a whole half-hour she forgot her troubles. Through such small, welcome glimpses of returning normality she began to gain some insight into just how obsessed and disordered her mind had become.

When she arrived home that evening, there was a letter. On recognising the handwriting, she staggered as if propelled against the wall by her surge of joy. Smiling idiotically, she stroked the envelope that still bore traces of his touch. She was right: he hadn't abandoned her! She fetched a knife from the kitchen drawer and, almost reluctant to expose the reality of its contents, carefully slit open the envelope and extricated a single sheet. Seeing the brevity of the writing, she tried in vain to check her disappointment.

She unfolded the paper and read the few lines. 'Dear Leonie,' he had written, 'you will be very angry with me, and I don't expect you to forgive me. But I am sorry. I didn't know what else to do for the best. Your loving Patrice.' There was no address or date; the envelope bore a French stamp, but the postmark was blurred and useless. Leonie rested her hands on the counter, her arms like stone. Was this all he had to say to her?

Her emotions swung swiftly to the opposite extreme. Here finally was the proof she had so longed for that he *did* think of her, was aware of the pain he had inflicted, did feel for her. And her heart went out to him that he could ever imagine that she would be unforgiving: did he honestly not realise how much she loved him? At this evidence of his misapprehension, his lack of faith, she yearned to hold and comfort and reassure him. Yet, at the same time, the leaden weight of her limbs told her that after such intimacy this inadequate explanation was a devastating annihilation. It showed how little he truly cared, how worthless she must be to him. With trembling fingers, she put the sheet back into the envelope, climbed on a chair in her bedroom and slid the letter underneath some boxes on the top shelf of a cupboard.

Half a dozen times that evening, even after she had gone to bed, she put on the light and dragged over the chair to climb up and re-read the letter, hoping that, as if by magic, a longer, as yet invisible, message would appear, or some revelatory meaning be vouchsafed. Each time she handled the paper, she felt its physical association with him fade beneath her fingers. It was both a comfort and a torment; she was simultaneously gladdened by it and despairing that these were not the words she had craved to hear. By the time she set off for work in the morning, she had persuaded herself that, since he had written once, he would write again. She must trust him and be patient. She tried hard to cling to that belief over the course of the week, but gradually common sense overcame what she knew deep down to be the delusion of hope.

By Saturday, the date she had set herself as the point at which, if Patrice had not returned, she would have to accept that he was gone for good, she acknowledged that his letter had, if anything, deepened the quality of his silence. It was no longer a neutral absence. While writing it, he had considered what to say and deliberately chosen not to offer her any shred of hope. Much as she longed to forgive him, she saw now that his silence was intentional, and therefore cruel.

On Sunday, a bleak and colourless January morning, she steeled herself to drive across to his house. Although she had expected to find it just as grimly shuttered and padlocked as it had been on that other morning a month ago, it still came as a shock to read once more the brutality of his departure written on the surface of the building. A few winter leaves lay unswept on the path to the front door, and the stem of a rose that grew against the railings of the tiny front garden had snapped. They were normal winter depredations, yet, aware that she was not far off hallucinating with grief, she observed herself regarding them as omens of ruination. She did not linger, but returned alone to her apartment where, numbed almost to indifference for half an hour or so, she relinquished the last thread of conviction that Patrice would ever phone or write more fully to explain himself. She was certain now that nothing lay beyond the onslaught of his continuing silence.

All that he had not written resonated, she was convinced, with all that he had purposefully left unsaid during the months they were together. True, she had rushed to colour in the gaps herself, but he had permitted her to do so, confident that she would concoct a story for herself that would be satisfactorily wide of the mark. Then, his lacunae had been untruthful enough, but now it seemed to her as if they had joined together, ousting all emotional interests but his own and rejecting any claim she might make on his compassion. Such a withdrawal required effort, and she berated herself for failing to perceive that the strength she had admired in him had been that of the survivor, where every last shred was needed for himself; where not an ounce of pity could be wasted on another human being. Had she really loved such a man?

Leonie entered a new phase of mourning. Going about her everyday life, she walked beside the abyss that had opened at her feet. She knew it was there, and it became an act of will not to look down and risk slipping into its depths. She visited the doctor, who smiled briskly, told her she was physically fit, and booked her into the local hospital for a foetal scan.

This provided a new horizon on which to focus. If she could get through the days before her appointment, then the on-screen image of her child moving within her must surely chase away the terrors conjured up by her perception of Patrice's emptiness. She made more effort about shopping and cooking, ensuring that she ate as healthily as possible, though the few wintry stalls in the market held little appeal; she began to compose a letter explaining to her mother the circumstances in which she was due to make her a grandmother and proposing a visit in early spring; and informed the letting agent that she wouldn't renew her lease on this cramped apartment, asking instead to be informed of any two-bedroom apartments, especially those with small gardens attached.

Stella rang while she was making a batch of vegetable soup to take to the office for lunch.

'I've just sent you an email.' Stella's voice sounded strange. 'I've been doing some digging. It's not much, all I could find, and from a while back, but I've sent you the link.'

'What is it?'

'Prepare yourself. It's unthinkable. I can't begin to explain. Take a look and call me back.' Stella ended the call.

Leonie turned off the stove and went to her laptop. Stella's email was waiting to be opened. Various sickening possibilities of further betrayal paraded before her, clenching at her guts. Her hand shaky, she clicked on the emailed link. It was to the Brighton *Argus*. The header for the piece, a short side column in a local newspaper, contained the word 'tragedy' but Leonie was already reading down. She exclaimed in sorrow and with her fingertip traced the name 'Patrick Hinde' where it appeared on the screen. 'Oh,' she breathed, 'you poor, dear man.' She leant forwards, cradling the laptop.

PART THREE

Sussex 2005

I

The July sun was bright against Patrick's eyes, blinding him, as he followed the fireman up the alleyway and into the yard behind his Ditchling office. He saw at once that the windows of his Renault had been smashed and that men in boots and fluorescent jackets were leaning in, kneeling over something in the back seat. He felt baffled as to what it could be. The fireman had asked him to bring his car keys, and now turned to snatch them out of his hand. Then an ambulance arrived, backing up through the narrow alley, though Patrick didn't understand why one should be required.

The paramedics pushed him aside, heading for his car. He watched them, suddenly certain that he did know what he was about to see, though he couldn't understand how it could be, how this could be happening. The fire crew drew back respectfully, making way for the paramedics. One of the men turned to look at Patrick with contempt, another with pity, as the paramedics lifted out Daniel's inert body and rushed with it to the ambulance. Patrick

173

froze. It was an incomprehensible effort just to blink his eyes or turn his head. Someone, a woman in police uniform, was speaking to him, but he couldn't make out what she was saying. She took his arm and pulled him towards the ambulance. He didn't want to go, but she pushed him up the steps while a paramedic leant down and grasped his arm to haul him into the vehicle before clambering out past him to go around to the driver's door. The other paramedic was busy over something on a stretcher. Daniel was so small that all Patrick could see of him was a naked foot, the heel soft and unworn.

The horror was too much, and Patrick vomited half-digested tea into his cupped hands. The police officer, who had climbed up behind him, handed over some rough green paper towels, sat him on a flip-down seat and clipped a seat-belt around his waist as the ambulance started to move, its siren wailing.

The paramedic stood back from the stretcher, bracing one hand against the interior side of the wagon as it sped through the Sussex lanes. 'How long was he in the car?' he asked.

Patrick couldn't speak. He wanted to say that surely he had dropped Daniel at the childminder? That was what he'd meant to do, had somehow imagined he had done. But he couldn't move the necessary muscles to say the words.

'What time did you leave him there?'

Patrick stared at him, preoccupied with the desperate attempt to recall what Christine must have said to him this morning as she took Daniel from him, but his mind was blank.

'He is your child?'

Patrick managed to nod his head.

'I'm very sorry,' said the paramedic. 'It was already too late by the time we got to him. We're unable to revive him.'

Patrick reached out and held his son's lifeless foot in his hand. A ragged toenail softly snagged his thumb. He closed his eyes, waiting for the pain of what he had done to begin, the torment of what he had somehow allowed to happen to his child, to Daniel, his son, his baby. He deserved the pain, welcomed it, wanted no respite from it, ever. But it didn't come; only nauseous waves of shock, horror and dread.

At the hospital, the woman police officer remained by his side while the paramedics disappeared with the trolley onto which they had fixed the stretcher. A nurse came out from where Daniel's body had been taken, and spoke to a colleague, but Patrick remained oblivious to the curious, wondering glances they directed at him. A serious-looking young doctor came and stood in front of him, asking if Daniel had any health problems or had been seen recently by a doctor. Patrick shook his head to all the questions.

The doctor and the police officer spoke together before leading Patrick to a small waiting room where the doctor gave him a piece of paper, explaining something or other. Patrick put it blindly in his pocket.

'Is there anyone we should inform? Your wife, your partner?' asked the police officer gently. Patrick nodded. 'We have your name and address from the car registration, Mr Hinde. I just need a name. An officer will go and break the news.'

When he stared at her, still speechless, she held out her notebook and a pen. He took them from her with stiffened fingers. It was an effort to bring the letters of his wife's name to mind, but eventually he succeeded in writing them down. The officer stood outside the door while she spoke into her phone, passing the information on to someone at the station. At the thought of Belinda, Patrick's heart broke and he began to weep.

Half an hour later, a more senior police officer arrived, a clear-eyed, overworked man in his early forties. After a quiet word with the uniformed constable, he came to introduce himself.

'Mr Hinde, I'm Detective Inspector Cutler.' He looked down into Patrick's face, which was soaked with tears. 'My condolences for your loss. I'm very sorry to have to intrude on your grief, but I'm sure you'll understand that we need to ask you a few questions, to establish what happened today.'

'I forgot him.'

Cutler held up a hand. 'I must caution you that you do not have to say anything. But it may harm your defence if you do not mention when questioned something which you later rely on in court. Anything you do say may be given in evidence.'

Patrick felt the first inkling of potential relief: he was
to be punished! The future was to be taken out of his
hands, and he would now be arrested and tried and locked
up. He smiled to signify that he understood.

'It would be easier if you came to the station.' Cutler
paused uneasily. 'It's your choice. You're not under arrest,
but your wife is on her way here. In the circumstances, it
might be better if you came with us now? There's nothing
more to be done here.'

'Can I see Daniel?'

'I'm afraid not.'

'I can't leave him here alone.'

The detective looked weary of this world. 'I do understand, Mr Hinde. But until we establish what happened,
I'm afraid it's not possible for you to have any further physical contact with your son. Arrangements can probably be
made for you to spend time with him later.'

Patrick nodded and got to his feet. He half-expected,
hoped almost, to be handcuffed and led out of A&E in
ignominy and shame, but Cutler shepherded him towards
the exit with the woman officer following mutely behind.
Patrick would never retain any memory of her name and,
once they reached the station, never saw her again.

He baulked when he saw the waiting car, but it was
clear he had no choice but to get in. He cowered on the
back seat beside Cutler, fighting an intolerable, panic-
inducing claustrophobia. He had heard the locks click automatically and knew he could not escape by throwing

himself out. No one spoke, and he simply endured, with a rock-like, vegetable endurance, until the brief journey ended.

DI Cutler and a younger colleague interviewed him formally in a small, windowless room painted in calming, institutional pastels. Like all the officers who dealt with him, they remained professionally sympathetic and scrupulously polite, keeping any private feelings well hidden.

'Who found Daniel?' Patrick wanted to know.

'Someone's dog ran in there. The owner called 999.'

Ordinary stuff. Someone walking their dog. Like him checking unpaid accounts, eating an apple, listening to Meghan and his other patients. Ordinary daily activities. All those hours and he never gave a thought to Daniel. Was that correct? It wasn't that Daniel had somehow ceased to exist, it was that he had never thought of Daniel as being in the car. How could he have driven away from his front door with his child strapped in his chair on the back seat and then simply forgotten that he was there? Daniel had probably fallen asleep, but even so, it wasn't possible. Yet that, inconceivably, is what he had, lethally, done.

'Mr Hinde?' Cutler's firm voice brought him back to the present, and he struggled to concentrate.

'You confirmed to Dr Prasad that, so far as you're aware, Daniel had no underlying health problems.'

'Nothing.'

'There were messages left on your office phone. Why hadn't you listened to them?'

'I was busy.' A terrible cry ripped from him at the banal reality of being too busy to prevent his son baking to death yards away from where he had sat drinking tea. 'I'm sorry,' he sobbed. 'Daniel, I'm so sorry.'

Cutler waited, pushing across a standard-issue box of tissues, as Patrick forced himself to be calm and helpful. 'Two messages were from Christine Dawson, Daniel's child-minder. You were supposed to drop him at her house on your way to your office. What happened?'

'I don't know.' Patrick was genuinely bewildered. 'I thought I had. I wish I understood, but I don't.'

'Did anything unusual happen as you left home this morning?'

'No. My parents were staying, but that's all.' Patrick's mind went back to a conversation with his father about the best route to the M23, and stuck there on a seemingly endless loop.

'Or on the way?'

'No, nothing. But I don't remember. I don't remember driving. I never do. It's routine. The same journey every time.'

'Mrs Dawson says Daniel didn't go to her on a Monday.'

'No. My wife has him at home on a Monday.'

'Did you mistake the day? Assume it was Monday today?'

'I don't think so. I don't know, I can't explain. I have no explanation.'

179

'Okay. Go back, talk us through your morning routine.'

Patrick, forlorn, stared at him absently.

'Bath or shower?' the detective continued. 'Wet or dry shave? What did you have for breakfast?'

'I see. Let me think. Belinda got Daniel up, got him changed, while I had a shower and dressed. I took him downstairs, gave him his juice and fingers of toast.' Patrick fought back the animal cry that rose at the physical memory of wiping his son's sticky fingers, his skin, his hair, kissing the top of his head. He made himself answer the inspector's question. 'I had coffee, muesli, a piece of toast. Then we got in the car.'

'Nothing else?'

Patrick shook his head, trying to clear the fog in his head.

'What did you chat to your wife about over breakfast? Maybe you made arrangements for later? You said your parents were there.'

Patrick stared at him uncomprehendingly. Cutler asked again: 'Your parents were staying?'

'Yes. They were. But I don't remember. The best way to get to the M23.'

'Okay. How's your work? Any problems there?'

'No. It's fine. Going well.'

'Did you leave your office during the day?'

'No. I was booked solid.'

Cutler nodded. 'We'll be talking to your patients. Tell me, what sort of relationship do you and your wife have?'

'Lovely.' Patrick stopped as the realisation hit him that his existence would now be forever divided in half and that he could never go back to the life he had lived yesterday. 'Then,' he corrected himself. 'This morning. Not now. Not any more. Never again.'

'Did you like being a father?'

'Yes.'

'Was Daniel an easy child? Some kids, you know, they cry, keep you awake, interfere between you and your wife, stop you having time to yourselves.'

'No, he was a joy.'

'We all get fed up sometimes, however much we love 'em. Wish to hell they weren't there. Even if only for five minutes. Is that what happened?'

Patrick shook his head dumbly like an injured beast. 'No,' he groaned. 'No. He was the best thing ever to happen to me.'

'Kid gets on your nerves, you think you'll teach him a lesson. Leave him in the car for a bit. Grab a moment for yourself.'

'I didn't realise he was there. I thought – oh I don't know what I thought.'

'You leave him in the car for five minutes. You're enjoying the peace and quiet. Makes a nice change, after all the racket, all the demands. Then you get busy and forget about him. Is that what happened?'

'No. I wouldn't have left him there on his own, not even for a second. Never. I realise it makes no sense, but I didn't know he was in the car. Didn't remember he was there. He must have been asleep. It's no excuse, but I was sure I'd dropped him at Christine's.'

'Do you take drugs, Mr Hinde? Prescription or otherwise?'

'No. I'm a homeopath.'

'Alcohol?'

'Sometimes. I don't think I blacked out or anything. I just forgot. I forgot my son was there.' Patrick again fought the urge to scream and go on screaming until he ceased to exist.

'Is there anything else you'd like to bring to our attention?'

Patrick shook his head, not trusting himself to open his mouth.

'For the record, please, Mr Hinde.'

'No,' he whispered.

'Very well. We'll be making further enquiries. Meanwhile, you can go home. I imagine you'll want to see your wife.'

'You're not keeping me here?' Patrick was shocked. He had expected to be locked in a cell for the night. He wasn't sure he could cope with freedom.

'Don't go away anywhere without informing us.'

'You're not charging me with anything?' Patrick couldn't disguise his disappointment.

'That'll be up to the Crown Prosecution Service. And there'll be an inquest. It'll all be explained at another time, unless you have any questions you'd like to ask now?'

Patrick shook his head, and DI Cutler got to his feet, leaving his colleague to deal with the recording machine. His tone softened and he touched Patrick lightly on the shoulder: 'Might be an idea to talk to your priest or whatever.'

Patrick smiled politely – the idea of any kind of future in which he might do such a thing was as yet totally impenetrable – and followed Cutler down the corridor. The custody sergeant offered to call him a mini-cab. The thought of the interior of a car repelled him, but he refused courteously enough, aware that all he had to cling to at this moment was the carapace of good manners.

Patrick headed down to the seafront, still relatively busy with summer visitors at this hour. He heard, smelt and sensed the movement of the sea rather than saw it in the growing darkness. He wanted to be near it, at one with its vast instability, close to the danger that constantly girdled the everyday world of people and bars and takeaways and houses and roads and cars. How had he ever taken for granted the assumption that the world was a safe place?

He went down the steps onto the beach, his feet sliding on the hard pebbles as he threaded his way between revellers and courting couples to where the waves rolled and broke along a line of glistening shingle. The pier to his left was brightly lit, but straight ahead of him lay the bulky water, shifting and dark. The whole world was not worth the loss of Daniel. There was nothing contained in the existence that lay behind him on the promenade, that went on gaudily up on the pier, that he could ever imagine wanting as much as he wanted the feel of Daniel now in his arms, against his chest. Nor was there any place for him except to atone for what he had done; and the rest of his life would not be enough for that. He had forfeited even the right to swim out to sea and quietly drown.

After a while, disturbed by youths nearby drunkenly yelling and cheering over the business of chucking pebbles into the sea, he made his way back up to the road, and began to walk. Once free of the crowds he gathered pace, finding physical comfort in the contact of his feet with the pavement, in the regularity of his steps; he found himself counting them, counting to sixty, seventy, before a lapse of concentration made him start again. Thus eventually he found himself in front of his house. The gravel area where usually he would park his car was empty, a fact he registered without further association. A light was on upstairs. He stared at it, trying to remember who was there.

Patrick felt automatically in his jacket pocket for his keys, which had been returned to him at the police station. He drew them out and looked at them, as if trying to divine their purpose. There was something about them that he needed to remember, but couldn't. He selected the correct one and opened his front door. The house was quiet, the hall and stairs in darkness. He hesitated on the threshold: to enter felt like a violation, yet he knew he must not run away. He closed the door behind him and stood, his head cocked, listening for some clue as to what to do next. As his sight adjusted to the dim light, he made out the bundle of coats hanging on hooks alongside the kitchen door. Overlapping the adult garments was a little anorak, the padded sleeves standing out like sausages, colourless in the darkness, though Patrick knew it to be green. The pain made him stagger, took the strength from his legs. He lowered himself onto the bottom stair, his head in his hands, trying to breathe through the successive piercing shafts that threatened to stop his heart.

He felt movement behind him. Light spilled from an open door upstairs. Belinda came and sat several stairs above him, her bare feet just visible out of the corner of his eye. He did not turn around. He could not begin to imagine how she must feel towards him. After a few minutes, she got up and retreated. The bedroom door closed again. He sat on for an hour or more, increasingly numbed and cold, until, barely awake, he stumbled up the stairs, almost on hands and knees. An instinct to be near his son drew him into Daniel's room. Fully clothed, he climbed into the little bed; eyes closed, knees drawn up to his chest, breathing in Daniel's scent with every breath, he concentrated on drawing as deeply into his own body as he could this final precious essence of his child.

II

Patrick awoke with the light: the blind in Daniel's room had not been lowered. At first he assumed he was not in his own bed because, as sometimes happened, Daniel hadn't settled and so Belinda had taken him into their bed, exchanging him for Patrick. But on those occasions, too big for Daniel's child bed, he slept in the guest room. Patrick then also realised that he was dressed, had not even removed his shoes. He sat up, puzzled. Then the blade twisted in his guts, his heart, his brain. He knew he had to move, had to function, or he would be turned to stone.

He instructed himself to concentrate on each first step, to recall what he would usually do. The bathroom. He must go to the bathroom. Pee. Brush his teeth. Get out of these stale clothes and have a shower. Don't think beyond that. Just do it. One foot in front of the other. The effort was enormous, as if he had been extremely ill, or was getting out of bed for the first time after major surgery. But he focused on standing up, walking through the door, lifting the lavatory seat. In the shower, he had a moment of absence; he returned to himself with no idea of how long he had stood immobile under the streaming water. It was an act of sheer will to stretch out his hand for the soap.

Patrick put on the robe that hung on the back of the bathroom door and went down to the kitchen. He couldn't remember when he'd last eaten, and did not think that he was hungry, though he assumed he must be. His body no longer seemed capable of anything except guarding the toxic shock that had invaded his very sense of himself: should the brimming pain spill or overflow, he knew with utter certainty that he would not survive.

Carefully he went through the ordinary motions of making breakfast, then forced himself to eat and drink. Following this same impulse, when Belinda did not appear, he made a mug of coffee for her. He tried to imagine what she would want. If their roles were reversed, what would he expect of her? But his thought processes rejected even the possibility of such imaginings. The coffee had gone cold by the time he made up his mind. He made a fresh mug and took it up to her, although he knocked gently on the door before going in, something he had never done before. She was curled up in their double bed, her tangled hair spread across the pillow and her eyes open, staring sightlessly in his direction. She sat up abruptly, as if startled, and held out her hands automatically for the mug. She looked half her age, a fourteen-year-old woken after a late-night party. Patrick handed her the coffee then returned to the kitchen. Hearing the shower a little later, he went back up to the bedroom, took out clean clothes and dressed hurriedly, careful to leave the room again before she finished in the bathroom. He did not seek to evade her, merely to show courtesy to her feelings. He knew of nothing else he could do for her now.

Belinda soon joined him in the kitchen, sitting across from him at the table, but not looking at him directly.

'More coffee?' he asked humbly. 'Can I get you something to eat?'

She shook her head.

'I'll go, if you want me to,' he offered. 'Move out. I don't want to, but I'll do whatever you wish.'

Belinda shook her head again. For a moment, she stretched out her hands, regarding them as if she had never seen them before, then continued to sit, one hand cupped over the other, like in a pew in church. 'I can't speak,' she said at last. 'Just don't expect me to.'

Patrick nodded, and they sat together in silence, hardly moving, until, some time later, the telephone rang, taking their breath away. Patrick got to his feet but, reaching for the handset, was unable to imagine lifting and speaking into it. He noticed that the message light was already flashing: two missed calls. Whatever they were, it could hardly matter now. The ringing eventually stopped, and he watched the display change and show three missed calls.

Belinda stood up. 'I'd better tell the school I won't be coming in.' She took the handset and went out, closing the door.

Patrick tried to think about the patients who were booked to see him that day. He ought to ring them, apologise, cancel all his appointments. But his mind slid sideways, couldn't keep hold of his patients' reality. They belonged in some faraway foreign country where he had once lived, too distant now to require any action from him. He heard Belinda come out of the sitting room and walk slowly upstairs, registered the sound of the bedroom door closing. He realised he was expecting that his life would now be taken over by officialdom, be dealt with by some external machinery responsible for disasters. And so he simply sat, waiting to be told what to do.

After a long while, the blinking message light seemed to summon him. He reached over to press the button and listened. The first voice was Agnès, saying thanks for such a lovely visit. The second was Geoffrey, also offering perfunctory thanks and confirming that they had got safely back to the hotel in Weybridge where they were putting up while looking at houses. Both messages had been left the previous evening. The latest call was from Geoffrey again, slightly irritable this time, wondering where everyone was, why no one had yet rung them back. Patrick was aware that he was probably supposed to tell them that Daniel was dead, but it made no sense, and he felt no urgency about doing so.

Stupefied, he remained motionless at the kitchen table. For whole moments he was able to forget why he was there, sitting at home on a weekday morning listening to distant traffic noises. Each time, when awareness rushed

189

back in, the waves of grief and guilt were bigger, stronger, more overwhelming. And yet, though he knew it to be true, that he had abandoned his son to die in a car on a hot July day, he still was not yet able fully to believe what he knew, let alone to inform his parents of it.

Belinda's younger sister Grace arrived an hour or so later, after hurrying down from London. Belinda let her in, and they disappeared upstairs together. When Patrick encountered her in the kitchen at lunchtime, he saw her hands shaking as she tried to cut up some fruit. She stared at him, a stockier, sharper-featured version of Belinda; her eyes were red and swollen from crying, but her face was white with fury.

'What have you done to her?' she demanded. 'How can you even look at her, after what you've done?'

Patrick had no answer.

DI Cutler arrived in the early afternoon, accompanied by a mournful, overweight woman in her forties. Patrick failed to retain her surname, and she anyhow suggested they call her Beverley. Belinda joined them in the sitting room, choosing to sit with Patrick on the sofa, a small act of loyalty for which he was insanely grateful. Beverley explained in painstaking detail how she was responsible for safeguarding local children and would have to review Daniel's death. Apart from offering them a booklet with a photograph of a flower on the cover to clarify any concerns they might have, and taking notes of the conversation, she then remained largely silent.

190

Cutler reminded Patrick that he remained under caution until they had received the preliminary report from Daniel's post-mortem, which, he informed them as gently as possible, was taking place that day. He said that their GP had confirmed that Daniel had appeared to be a perfectly healthy little boy. Cutler also told them that the police had been able to confirm Patrick's journey time thanks to Automatic Number Plate Recognition cameras on part of his route, and had checked that he had not used his mobile phone; his drive to work appeared to have been entirely uneventful. He asked if Patrick could now recall more detail of what had happened before he left home the previous morning.

'I'm sorry. I've tried, but I can't come up with any conscious memory of before I started work.'

'What about your father?' asked Belinda in disbelief.

'Well, they were here, I'm aware of that.'

'But the way he behaved!'

When Belinda stared at him, he turned to Cutler. 'Dad can be a bit abrasive,' he said with a shrug. 'Probably why he never got where he wanted in life.'

'How could you forget it?' cried Belinda.

'What?' Patrick was genuinely puzzled

'Him telling you to get rid of Daniel!'

Patrick saw Cutler glance involuntarily at Beverley, who immediately wrote something in her large notebook. He felt clammy and sick.

'Let's just go back a bit first, shall we, Mrs Hinde?' said

191

Cutler. 'Your parents-in-law had been staying the weekend?'

'Yes,' answered Belinda. 'We had a nice enough time with them.' She glanced sideways at Patrick, who was staring at the floor. 'I have Monday off,' she continued, 'so they spent the day with me. They went off yesterday when we both left for work. Agnès got distressed when she realised that' – Belinda took a steadying breath – 'realised that Daniel went to a childminder.'

'Agnès is your mother?' Cutler asked Patrick. 'Mr Hinde?' he prompted when Patrick appeared not to have heard.

Patrick nodded.

'And she was unaware of your childcare arrangements? Why was that? Were they deliberately kept from her?'

When Patrick made no move to answer, Belinda explained. 'No. They live in Geneva, so we don't see much of them. But now Geoffrey's retiring, and they're over here house-hunting.'

'Where were you both when your father-in-law said these words?' Cutler asked.

'I was in the hallway, putting on Daniel's shoes,' Belinda answered promptly.

'And you, Mr Hinde?'

'I'm not certain.'

'You're not able to recall the moment?'

Patrick shook his head miserably. 'Not really.'

'Then would you mind going on, Mrs Hinde? How were your in-laws travelling? By car?'

'Yes. They were all packed, ready to go.'

'But Agnès became upset?'

'She's a very anxious soul. Obsessive compulsive. That's right, isn't it?' Belinda turned to Patrick, who was staring wildly at the door. He dragged his gaze back to the watching faces and managed to nod. 'Geoffrey can't stand it when she gets like that. I haven't spent a great deal of time with them, but when she starts to obsess about something, he just loses it.'

'So what happened?'

'She didn't want us to leave Daniel with the childminder; a stranger, she said. Then Geoffrey just grabbed Daniel, shoved him at Patrick, and told Patrick to get rid of him.'

'Is what your wife says correct, Mr Hinde?'

Shamefaced, Patrick nodded. 'It must be.'

'And what did you do?'

'I remember hugging him. Holding him, waiting for them to go.'

'You didn't mention this yesterday.'

'I'd forgotten it.'

'But you remember it now?'

'I remember being a bit upset.'

'Angry?'

'Sure.'

'At Daniel?'

Patrick was uncomprehending. 'Daniel? No, *never*. At—' Patrick stopped, defeated. 'Oh what's the point? He can't help it. It's not his fault.'

'Not whose fault?'

'Dad. There's no use getting angry at him. It's not going to change anything. You just have to go along with it until you can escape.' He shook his head wearily. 'I just wanted them to go away.'

'But surely this is the heart of it?' Belinda appealed to Cutler and Beverley. 'It's stuck in my head all night, going round and round, Geoffrey telling Patrick, get rid of him!' She turned to Patrick, who shrank back into his chair. 'He said get rid of him. That's why this happened!'

'No,' groaned Patrick. 'No, it's not their fault. It's nothing to do with them. Don't start that. Don't. Please. Don't bring them into it. It's my fault. I'm the only one responsible. There's no one to blame but me.'

'But—'

Cutler held up a hand and Belinda, accepting his authority, held back her words. Heavy tears began to run down her cheeks, and she wiped them aside as if they were some irritation unconnected with her. 'We will need to talk to your parents.' Cutler ignored Patrick's cry of protest. 'If you could write down their contact details and where they're staying.'

'Have they been told?' asked Belinda, looking to Patrick.

He took a deep breath. 'Not yet.' There was silence as everyone looked at him. 'They're in Weybridge.' He thought for a moment. 'There'll be a train, I suppose.'

'We'd like you to be interviewed by a forensic psychologist, Mr Hinde. I'll get in touch as soon as we can set up an appointment.'

Cutler and the social worker got to their feet. Cutler assured Belinda that she could call him at any time if there was anything she wanted to ask; that they would keep her informed of everything that was happening; and that, probably the day after the post-mortem, they would be able to spend time with Daniel if they so wished, and could make funeral arrangements as soon as his body had been released by the coroner. Patrick sat on, immobile, an image of his mother's face turning to him in distress playing repeatedly in his head.

As the others prepared to leave, he finally found a voice. 'I can't do it. You don't understand. It's impossible to speak to them.'

When Patrick raised his head, he saw the three of them regarding him with varying degrees of baffled pity. Suddenly he was a small boy again, at the start of the summer holidays, alone at his bedroom window, one hand clutching the dusty linen of the *toile de Jouy* curtains as he looked out at his mother's taxi driving away.

Patrick sat down beside Agnès, tolerating the wait while Geoffrey made a business out of ordering him a soft drink. It had been a short walk from Weybridge station to the hotel, which he found to be just the kind of place he'd expect his father to select; once presumably a coaching inn, it was now trying too hard to appear modern. He was glad he had been able to prepare himself for this task alone. Immediately after Cutler's visit, Grace had come downstairs carrying Belinda's overnight bag, and soon after-wards had taken Belinda away to stay with her. Now he had found his parents in the small lounge area. Allowing himself the cowardice of a contained public space in which to release such news he had chosen not to suggest that they go upstairs or out for a walk. Taking his mother's hand, he began his explanation.

'Maman, Dad, there's no other way to tell you. Something's happened to Daniel.' Agnès' manicured nails dug into the flesh of his palm. 'He's gone,' Patrick said quietly. 'He died.'

'Is that why you didn't call us back?' demanded Geoffrey. Patrick closed his eyes. When he opened them again, he could see that Geoffrey regretted his words but had no clue as to how he might recover himself. Patrick leant across and patted his father's arm.

'It's all right, Dad. I guess you've been worrying. I'm sorry.'

Geoffrey nodded like some Chinese mandarin toy, trying gruffly to compose himself. Patrick turned to his mother, ready to soothe and reassure. Yet, though her eyes had widened in alarm, they remained clear: always anticipating catastrophe, now it had struck, maybe she would not after all lose control. 'My poor boy,' she said, and Patrick realised with a terrible inward collapse of resolve that she meant him, her own son. '*Mon pauvre* Patrice. To lose your little one. I understand how you must feel. But you must tell us the rest when you are able.'

His mother's sympathy, so seldom available to him throughout his life, was sad and disorienting. He forced himself to stick to the words he had rehearsed during his journey in the tawdry, litter-strewn train. 'I have to tell you now, Maman. There are other people who will want to speak to you.'

'Why? What happened?' Geoffrey's voice was harsh.

'You'll have to decide for yourselves. I left Daniel in the car. I forgot he was there.' He ignored Agnès' cry and ploughed on. 'The cause of death was heatstroke and dehydration. I am solely responsible.'

Geoffrey sagged into the plush hotel armchair, looking suddenly old and frail. 'We're due back in Geneva next week,' he said.

'Yes, I know.'

'So what about the funeral?' Geoffrey persisted.

'Apparently there has to be an inquest or something first.' Patrick heard his own words as squalid and sordid, but kept going. 'We were warned it might be weeks. Or even longer.'

Geoffrey stared at him aggressively, and Patrick recognised this as a symptom of shock. Agnès rose uneasily to her feet, her expression bleak. 'We don't need to discuss this now, do we?' she asked her husband, who nodded his agreement with apparent indifference. 'Not here, like this.' Unused to following his mother's lead, Patrick rose too, and she gave him a short, fierce hug, the kindness of which made him tremble.

'Who is it we have to see?' asked Geoffrey, levering himself out of his chair with unaccustomed difficulty.

'A Detective Inspector Cutler. He's been very decent.'

'When is that likely to be? We'll need to be told if we're to change our travel arrangements.'

'Soon, I suppose. I'll let him know your plans.'

'We'll be ready.' Geoffrey drew himself up, and Patrick could picture his father preparing himself, brushing the jacket of his good suit, straightening his silk tie, pulling out his shirt-cuffs, doing all he could, thought Patrick poignantly, to save his train wreck of a son.

'Go now,' said Agnès, pushing Patrick from her. He was amazed that the expected collapse had not materialised. He glanced across at his father who, thinking himself unobserved, was shaking his head in despair. 'You'll be tired,' Agnès went on. 'I understand the tiredness. Go now, Patrice. Look after yourself, and Belinda.'

Geoffrey mumbled his farewells, his gaze fixed on the carpet. Ashamed at preferring this resigned fatalism to one of his father's impotent rages, Patrick made his way out of the hotel. He walked back to the station with his shoulders bent stiffly forwards, shielding his heart, afraid to straighten his spine in case he jarred the brimming pain.

Belinda came back unannounced from her sister's the following day. The principal at the school where she taught had assured her that, with so few days of the summer term remaining, there was no reason for her to return before September. She had offered to take it on herself to cancel Belinda's private lessons, if she so wished.

At home, Belinda and Patrick moved around one other in as diplomatic and courteous a way as possible; while she had been in London, he had moved all he needed into the spare room, which she accepted without comment. They continued by tacit consent to share mundane tasks, staring like zombies into the fridge or putting clothes into a washing machine whose simple controls had morphed into indecipherable hieroglyphics. Only their inability to comprehend fully the finality of their bereavement got them through the empty days together. Belinda overheard his instructions to the local garage to pick up their Renault as soon as the police released it, to repair the broken windows and then drop it off for sale at a car auction, but said nothing, just as she wordlessly absorbed his unspoken resolve not to get in a car even as a passenger, although she remained willing to take a taxi or accept a lift from friends.

Patrick did not care to investigate whether his gratitude was for her absence of comment or because she accepted his avoidance. The one comfort he allowed himself was to take long baths, sometimes two or three a day. He would lie, relieved of all effort of will, watching his naked limbs float in the tepid undemanding water as he tried – and failed – to submerge his consciousness in the featureless element.

Although friends arrived unannounced to drop off home-cooked meals, averting their gaze and hurrying away, eventually Belinda and Patrick had to draw up a list for the supermarket. They struggled to imagine future needs; once there and faced with a plethora of choices, they stared helplessly at the packed shelves, not knowing if they wanted all of it or none. As they moved along the aisles, they crafted their faces to hide their confusion from those pushing trolleys alongside them, people who seemed to feel no absurdity in belonging here, in making precise choices among varieties of crispness, flavour or scented-ness. Patrick marvelled how he had ever viewed this neon-lit, air-conditioned realm as mundane. Their mutual bewilderment bonded them, gave them something to share, and they sat beside one another on the bus home, embracing bags of fruit, milk and loo rolls on their laps, feeling the comradeship of strangers in a strange land.

When his nightmares began, they were not about Daniel. The hours of darkness when he was able to bring Daniel back, could re-live his intoxicating smell, his laugh, his sturdy limbs, the absolute trust with which his son had allowed himself to be carried in his father's arms – those nights provided fleeting moments of serenity, almost of happiness. He knew they were just dreams, waking reveries, but he didn't care. So long as he didn't open his eyes and could imagine Daniel's warm breathing presence beside him, then some vital morsel of his soul felt less bereft. The nightmares came when he was most deeply asleep.

Though he was often awoken by his own screaming, he was certain that they were not about the discovery of Daniel's body – he re-lived those minutes in the yard behind his office every single day when awake. All he could recall was how appalled his inner sleeping self had been by the ravages of destruction unleashed by his despotic nightmare self, but the task of delving further into his subconscious seemed insurmountable.

Privately he celebrated the terror they inspired. He deserved to suffer; until he was told what his punishment was to be, he yearned to be shunned, cast out, banished. He could not bear it when people were kind to him. He had been amazed by the polite tolerance of relative strangers, how they would tiptoe around, mouthing well-meant platitudes when he would not have blamed them for showing all the disgust he was convinced they must feel. He secretly cherished Grace's open condemnation, and was sure that sometimes he caught Belinda, too, looking at him as if trying to divine what truly lay concealed inside him. He shrank from her inspection before admonishing himself that he had no right to consider himself. Believing that his own feelings no longer mattered, he did his best to hide evidence of his grief from her, as she mostly did from him. If, on entering a room, he came upon her weeping noisily, her mouth ugly and twisted, her eyes blind and swollen, oblivious to his existence, he would quietly close the door and go away, believing that because he was the cause of her agony, he had no right to offer comfort.

They agreed they must visit Daniel's childminder, Christine, and walked there together. She showed them into her small front room, which looked threadbare without the usual run-around mess of busy children, and, as if she had been waiting for a signal, almost immediately broke down. 'I should have realised something was wrong,' she wept. 'That you would have rung me if there'd been some glitch. I should have done something. Not just assumed. Got hold of Belinda at work. Something.'

Convinced that Christine could only recoil from his pariah's touch, Patrick withheld the healer's impulse to reach out to her. She looked at him tearfully. 'If only I'd done more. I'm so sorry. I hope you forgive me,' she said with dignity.

Her innocent sorrow almost made him swoon, but, bracing himself against his own emotion, he spoke firmly. 'Christine, you must never think like that. You left messages for me. I am solely to blame for what happened. You did all you could.'

Belinda gave a small nod of assent – he had done the right thing. Christine looked at him doubtfully, but he could see, as he had often observed with his patients, that she was ready to accept absolution.

'Daniel loved coming here,' he told her.

'He was such a cutie-pie,' she agreed.

They sat awkwardly, with little else to say. As they got up to go, Belinda handed over an envelope containing some money Christine was owed. 'It helps no one for you to be out of pocket,' Belinda murmured, pressing it into her hands. 'And there's a photo in there I thought you might like to keep,' she added, making it gracefully impossible for Christine to do anything but accept with thanks.

'Did you notice,' Belinda remarked as they left the house together, 'that she'd tidied away every single toy? Trying to save our feelings, probably.'

Before they walked away, she looked back wistfully, and Patrick guessed her thoughts: despite the intimate connections between Daniel and this house, they had no reason ever to come here again. Indeed, if truth be told, they were likely to be unwanted visitors, trailing with them as they now did such unwelcome knowledge of the world.

As they wound their way home through the Edwardian terraced streets, they passed several women pushing children in buggies or unlocking front doors with shopping bags at their feet and a child balanced on one hip. Patrick's gaze ran over them without interest: none of them was Daniel.

'There's something I need to understand,' said Belinda suddenly. 'About Geoffrey, when he told you to get rid of Daniel.'

'He didn't mean any harm,' said Patrick automatically.

'I need you to explain why it doesn't make you angry.'

He sighed. 'I'm used to him, I suppose.'

'I wanted to strike him down for it.'

'It's his anxiety. He can't bear it when Maman gets anxious, that's all. He's worse than her.'

'But it must make you feel *something*?'

'You can't blame Dad, Belinda.'

'I'm not. I'm trying to make sense of what happened to you. Was it about Geoffrey?'

'I don't know. I don't know that it was about anything.'

'There has to be a reason.'

'Maybe there isn't. I've gone over and over and over. I wish I could tell you some reason, but I can't.'

'I have to understand what went on inside you that morning. You would never have just left Daniel. There is an explanation, some key to this, I know there is.'

Patrick focused on the distant glitter of sea between the houses, fighting the urge to run.

'Help me, Patrick. If I can't make some sense of it, I'm lost.'

It took every bit of strength he possessed, but he stopped and placed his hands lightly on her shoulders. It was the first time he had touched her since he had driven away that morning, a mere few days earlier, but she did not flinch.

'Just give me time,' he beseeched her. 'I'll try, I promise. I'll do anything you want. I'll do my best to help you. I will. But right now I don't understand anything.'

Her answering look was unfathomable, and he suddenly realised that, though he loved her dearly, there were aspects of his wife that he barely knew; that, despite the ways in which he understood his patients and their troubles, there were aspects of other people he would never know.

*

'When will you start seeing patients again?' Belinda asked that evening as, without appetite, they picked diligently at the supper Patrick had made. Evenings were difficult, each feeling Daniel's loss delineated by the absence of the familiar routines of his supper, bath and bedtime. There was no reason to stay in alone, yet neither of them could imagine wanting or enjoying those activities – a meal out, a movie, a drink with friends – previously restricted by parenthood. 'We're going to need the money soon. My salary's not enough,' Belinda went on. 'You can't afford to put it off too long,' she added carefully. 'There might be some people who won't come back.'

Patrick wondered, but didn't say, if *any* patients would choose to see him again. Though the police had so far kept the tragedy from the local media, word had obviously spread among Patrick and Belinda's colleagues and professional contacts, and beyond. Patrick had not told Belinda that he had already received two anonymous letters calling him a monster, a murderer, unfit to be anywhere near a child ever again. When, unsuspecting, he had opened the first, his reaction had been to laugh in horror and agree with the writer's sentiments, since his judgement of himself was much the same. When the second envelope bearing unfamiliar handwriting appeared on the mat, he had initially been tempted to destroy it unread. But he'd torn it open and scanned its contents. It had taken a slightly different tack, accusing him of resenting his son so much that he sadistically inflicted horrible suffering on him, treating him worse than a dog on such a sweltering July day. Even though both letters had been addressed to him, he was careful now always to vet the post before she could reach it.

Patrick had been depressed by the despairing lives that must surely have lain behind the mailing of such spite. Wasn't there enough cruelty in the world without taking the trouble to manufacture yet more? Such evidence of random hate made him chary of returning to work. Trust was essential between a homeopath and his patients, and if he himself was riven with doubt about how people now regarded him, then the bond necessary to healing might be impossible. But he couldn't explain any of this to Belinda.

'You're right,' he told her. 'I'm seeing the police psychologist on Monday. Maybe I can discuss it with her.'

She seemed content with this, and said no more. Patrick collected their plates and went to fill the sink with hot water – a reversal of their domestic convention, which was that whoever had cooked did not also wash up.

Belinda elbowed him aside. 'I'll do them.'

'Don't worry. It's fine.'

'You made the pasta.'

'So? Let me do it.'

'Stop it!' she exploded. 'For God's sake, act normally!'

'I'm only trying to—'

'Well don't!' She pushed him roughly out of the way. 'Stop trying! Just let me do the fucking washing up!'

'I have to do *something*.'

'No, you don't.' She grabbed wildly for the plastic brush. 'There's *nothing* you can do. That's just it. That's what you have to live with. There is nothing now that you can do. It's all too fucking late.'

She flung the brush into the soapy water and slammed out of the kitchen. Then, from the sitting room, for the first time since Daniel's death ten days before, Patrick heard the sound of her violin. Her playing was awful, jerky and off-key, reflecting the way she drew breath in jabbing bursts. After a while, during which he finished the dishes, her breathing eased and the melody began to flow after a fashion. The music was hardly her best effort, but clearly marked some moment of transition and release. Patrick took it as a sign that Belinda might yet survive this tragedy. His instinct was to leave her alone but, remembering what she had just yelled at him, decided he must simply enter the room and sit listening until she finished playing, just as he would have done 'normally'. As he crossed the hallway he was struck by how absurd it was no longer to possess a natural unconsciousness about how to act. That too was forfeit.

Belinda ignored his entrance. She turned the pages on the music stand and began playing the piece again from the beginning, as she always did after a poor performance. Patrick sat on the sofa and listened, but his mind wandered as it began to dawn on him that the true damnation of what he had done lay in the simple repetition of days that lay ahead.

He remembered a tale he had once heard about animals

207

trained to lead others calmly into the slaughterhouse. A Judas goat had no choice but to go on living amidst the flock, the only one to hold the secret of what the future held for its fellows, and alone with the knowledge that, to secure its own survival, it must repeat its betrayal. How did such an animal live out its days? Patrick still hoped for legal punishment, though he knew that his wish, like the temptation of suicide, was selfish. Belinda had given no sign that his imprisonment would relieve her in any way, and, however much a gaol sentence might assuage some tiny part of his own guilt, he couldn't wish for something that would inevitably further complicate her life. He struggled not to dramatise his predicament, not to concentrate on himself, but he wished he knew how to go on living. He had never imagined the answer to such a simple question could be so impenetrable.

III

Patrick arrived early for his first meeting with Amanda Skipton, the police-appointed forensic psychologist. The tattered magazines and random signage about disabled access, toilets and abusive behaviour towards staff all seemed faintly derelict, yet the waiting area smelt incongruously of fresh paint. He was rather surprised to discover that he was almost eager to relate again to a stranger the events preceding Daniel's death – events he already turned over constantly in his mind – longing to believe that speaking his endless questions aloud might grant him some momentary peace. Amanda came to summon him from the reception area. She was younger than he had pictured her. As she led the way to her small office under the eaves, he caught one of her sidelong glances and suspected she would turn out to be a shrewd listener.

'Do sit down, Mr Hinde.' She gestured to the chair opposite her own on the other side of a low table and regarded him pleasantly. 'Do you mind if I use your first name?'

'Not at all.'

'Good.' She gave a neat smile, observing him with a frankness that was neither judgemental nor falsely sympathetic. There was nothing in the narrow room to give any clue to her personality or home life, which Patrick knew to be a professional strategy – his own office was the same. 'You're here at the request of the police. Although what we do and say here won't be like a police interview, you do understand that it's not therapy? What is said here does not remain confidential?'

'Yes, I realise that,' Patrick answered.

'That's good. I'll probably see you two or three times, and then write an assessment of how your thoughts and feelings and mental state contributed to what occurred. Are there any questions that you'd like to ask me?'

'No, I don't think so.' He rubbed his hands on his jeans.

'Well, please feel free to do so at any time.'

Patrick nodded obediently, as though he were about to take an exam. He cleared his mind of extraneous thoughts, just as he did when preparing himself to see his own patients.

'I'd like to begin with your family history. Where you were born, your parents, siblings, grandparents, that sort of thing. Anything you'd like to tell me, really.'

Patrick waited for Amanda to ask a question, but when she merely observed him encouragingly he realised she expected him just to pitch in.

'My mother's French, my father British. I was born here but lived in various places. Dad worked for a couple of big multinationals. I'm an only child.'

'So did you go to school abroad?'

Patrick nodded. 'To start with. Then I boarded at a prep school in Hertfordshire.'

'How old were you?'

'Seven.'

She was making notes, not looking at him. When he did not continue, she looked up again interrogatively.

'It was fine,' he told her, well used to people expressing concern that he had been sent away so young. 'It seemed the best alternative.'

'Is that what your parents said?'

'Well, it was true.'

'You held that opinion at the time? When you were seven?'

Patrick shrugged. 'I just accepted it.'

'Can you remember how you felt?'

'Homesick, I suppose. Though they'd just moved from Holland to Belgium, so there wasn't really a home to miss.'

'What about your parents?'

'I don't understand.'

'Did you miss them?'

'Of course.'

'What did you miss most?' When Patrick regarded her in puzzlement, she smiled. 'It's not a trick question. I just wondered if you could remember anything special that you missed? Things you did together. Bedtime routines. Food. Jokes. Smells.'

'Routines,' Patrick answered ironically. 'Maman had a lot of routines.'

Amanda nodded sympathetically and scribbled a note. 'Did you make friends easily at school?'

'Sure. The other boys were all right. A decent bunch.'

'Any special friends?'

'At the next school, when I was older, a couple of guys. One I'm still in touch with. The others met up in the holidays, which could be a hassle for me. But I was never bullied or anything like that. I was fine.'

'Have you talked to your friends about what's happened?'

Patrick was taken aback. 'No.'

She nodded matter-of-factly, making no further remark. 'How were you academically?'

'Did well enough to scrape into university.'

'Languages, I suppose?' asked Amanda, smiling. 'You must have a facility, after living in so many countries?'

'My French is fluent,' Patrick agreed. 'Thanks to my grandmother. But I liked human biology. Found it interesting.'

'Were your parents proud of you, going to university?'

'Well, it wasn't Oxbridge. Only Sheffield.'

'What about romantic relationships?' she asked next.

'I hardly got near a girl before I left school. But my first term there, a girl I sat next to in lectures asked me out. Annie.' He glanced at Amanda shyly, looking away as he enlarged. 'She'd had boyfriends before, at school, so I just went along with what she wanted. Seemed to go okay.'

'You don't find sexual relationships difficult?'

Patrick blushed. 'No.'

212

'How long have your relationships generally lasted?'

'A few months. I was never into one-night stands.'

'Nothing longer?'

'Not until I met Belinda. Then she fell pregnant.'

'Do you think you'd have stayed together if she hadn't?'

'I'd like to think so. She wasn't even that keen on having a baby to begin with. Her music's very important to her. One thing led to another, I suppose.' Patrick grew sombre. 'She should've steered well clear,' he said quietly. 'She deserves better.'

'Up until now, would you say you've made Belinda happy?'

Patrick considered the question. 'Yes. We made each other happy.'

'After you graduated, what did you do?'

'I did a year of further training, then dropped out. Kind of drifted for a while.'

'Tell me about that.'

'Nothing much to tell.'

She looked at him, waiting, and Patrick, embarrassed, nonetheless saw that he had to offer more. 'I got into the whole New Age thing. Raves, eco-protests, tribes. All that stuff.'

'What was the further training in?'

Patrick heaved a sigh: he always hated making this admission, the explanations that inevitably had to follow. No one could ever seem to believe that he simply hadn't wanted to be a doctor. 'Medicine.'

Amanda's eyes widened. 'At what point did you drop out?'

213

'I qualified. Just never applied for any jobs. Walked away.'

'After what, five years of training?'

'I wasn't the type. Too many hoops to jump through, a lot of stress. I only did it to please other people.'

'Then it must have taken guts to disappoint them.'

Patrick snorted in derision. 'Dad's never hard to disappoint!'

'And your mother?'

'Maman tends to get wrapped up in the small stuff. That I'll go out in the cold without a scarf, not eat properly.'

'So what did you do after you dropped out? Where were you living? Were you working?'

'Bits of casual labour. Moved around. That whole grunge, traveller thing, remember?' Patrick was mildly surprised at how Amanda let his well-rehearsed answers pass without comment.

'You were a crustie?' Amanda looked amused.

'Well, I don't think I ever actually slept in a doorway. But you're right. It wasn't much fun.'

'Were you depressed?'

Once again, Patrick was taken aback. 'Never thought. I guess I was a bit lost, if I'm honest. Most of the people I hung out with then were.'

'How long did this go on?'

'A while,' he said curtly. 'Until I began training in homeopathy.'

'And that gave you direction?' She leant forward slightly, interested in what he would say.

'It was like I'd finally found what I wanted for myself,' he answered truthfully. 'Something I could do well.'

'And you've never been tempted to go back into medicine? Not even to call yourself a doctor?'

Patrick shook his head. 'Why would I? I'm a homeopath.'

'Okay. Tell me how you feel about your work. About yourself when you're working.'

'Good.'

'In what way?'

Patrick blushed again. 'Like a good person. Safe.'

'Safe from what?'

'No. Like I'm safe. Can't harm anyone.'

Amanda regarded him steadily, but Patrick resisted the sense that she was waiting for him to make some connection.

'You said it was easy to disappoint your father,' she went on after a moment. 'Could you imagine a time when your son might have disappointed you?'

'Never!'

'Did you fuss over him, like your mother did over you?'

'No. Poor Maman, her fears are irrational. An illness. Growing up with that, I've never let things get to me.'

'How do you do that?'

Patrick shrugged. 'Dunno.'

'Ever think you're a little too laid back?'

'Hope not.'

'But you're able to block things out? Concentrate on what's before you – your patients, for instance?'

'Yes, when I need to.'

'Cut off, would you say?'

'Not really.' Patrick heard the slightly aggrieved tone in his voice and shifted in his chair as if to disown it.

'Forgetful?'

Patrick dropped his head and did not answer.

'I believe your GP is organising some neurological tests? To rule out any physical cause for your memory loss.'

Patrick nodded, miserable.

'You're still unable to remember your drive to work; parking the car and leaving Daniel?'

'It's like there's no memory there to be retrieved.'

'Do you think you might have emptied your mind in order to block something else out? Some uncomfortable feeling, perhaps?'

'I don't know.'

'Maybe you'd like to think about that for me.'

Patrick swallowed on nothing and stretched his lips into a smile. 'Okay.'

'Before this happened, how do you think you might have felt towards another parent who forgot his child, the same way you did?' Patrick stared at Amanda in surprise. 'It has happened to other people. You're not unique.' She nodded at him encouragingly. 'In America there are about twenty-five cases a year accounted for by parental memory lapse. I suspect such forgetfulness is fairly common here, too, but not often fatal, thanks to our climate. In France a few years ago two children died

in hot cars within a week of each other. Both had intelligent, diligent and devoted fathers, whose attention was
somehow fatally distracted. Just like you.' She watched
his reactions carefully. 'How does it make you feel,
knowing you're not alone?'

'Better. No.' Horrified, he corrected himself instantly.
'Not better, I don't mean that. There is no better. But – it
helps,' he ended lamely. 'Thank you.'

'How do you feel towards those other fathers?'

'I pity them.'

'Are you able to pity yourself?'

'No.'

'Would you forgive them?'

'Maybe. I know what you're going to say.' Patrick felt his
hostility to her rising into his throat. 'But it's not the
same,' he exclaimed. 'I'll never forgive myself. Never.
Daniel's dead. There's no excuse for what I did.'

'Well, I've read the police statements, Patrick. From your
wife, Daniel's childminder, people in the emergency serv-
ices who attended the scene, the patients you treated that
day. None voiced any suspicion that you intended to harm
your son.'

'I did harm Daniel.'

'Deliberately?'

'Of course not.'

'Then why should forgiveness not be possible? In time,
of course.'

'But it's obvious, isn't it? It's me. There's something in

217

me that harms people. I'm not safe.' At the back of his mind he heard a distant echo of Josette's voice.

Amanda sat back, saying nothing. The compassion Patrick could read on her face angered him. 'My son is dead because of me,' he told her coldly. 'It's not up to you or anyone else to forgive me. I allowed him to come to harm. I don't deserve forgiveness.'

An hour later Patrick sat down on a bench in a small park laid out in formal beds and paths around a war memorial. He felt as worn and exhausted as the dusty brown grass, as meaningless as the carved names of the long-ago dead. He could not picture what route had brought him here from Amanda's office. He couldn't face going home, going anywhere. All sorts of disconnected memories chased through his mind, of drab school dormitories, of listening late at night to his mother stealthily testing door handles and window locks in foreign apartments, of the way the light slanted in between the shutters as he sat on the floor at his grandmother's house, playing solitaire with an old wooden board and heavy citrus-coloured glass marbles. He wondered why he should think so vividly of that when he had barely mentioned Josette to Amanda. Josette had no bearing on any of this, and he pushed her out of his mind. He wondered what Amanda thought of him. He liked her, even though she had made him feel so gritty and irritable.

It occurred to Patrick that he had forgotten to discuss

his return to work, as he had promised Belinda he would. He recalled what Amanda had said about the supportive statements his patients had given to the police. The idea that it might after all prove possible to see patients again gave him his first unmistakable inkling of reprieve. This joined itself to the small and exquisitely painful spring of hope that had uncoiled inside him on hearing the simple fact that other men shared his guilt. The information that he was not uniquely capable of his act of lethal aberration released a tiny trickle of warmth that suddenly began to flow through his veins. But even such a minuscule sense of relief produced an overwhelming rushing sensation that made him panic. He leant forwards on the bench, bracing himself against the flood. He looked wildly around the little park, but saw he was alone. He tried to stand, to walk away, but his legs trembled and he sat back down on the hard bench, gasping for air.

He wondered if he were having a heart attack, and for a moment hoped he was. He felt no pain, but his head was swimming and he felt sick. His right hand gripped the edge of the wooden bench and, slowly, all his consciousness focused on the single sensation of touching its worn surface. His thumb began to circle rhythmically, and he recognised something to which he was accustomed in the dry grey dust working its way into the whorls of his fingerprint. Its familiarity began to calm him, and he was able to let his mind empty as his thumb continued to rub the desiccated wood, the feel of which reminded him more and more of aged, dusty linen. He remembered now that he knew all too well how to subdue hope, how to endure alone, to accept that he deserved no better. These things came to him more naturally than kindness, forgiveness or reprieve, and he welcomed the memory of how he had always survived before.

The next day, Geoffrey called and informed Belinda that the offer he and Agnès had made on a house in Esher had been accepted; meanwhile they would return to Switzerland until their lease in Geneva expired towards the end of September. Geoffrey attempted to sidestep Belinda's invitation to lunch, but she insisted, and they came over two days later. Patrick welcomed them. Geoffrey refused eye-contact, pushing past his son to present Belinda with a box of expensive chocolates. Agnès kissed his cheeks and clung to his arm, and he gathered her to him in a hug. In the sitting room Geoffrey requested a gin and tonic and launched into small talk about the house they'd found, garlanded with jovial asides about the estate agent and one or two totally unsuitable places that they'd also viewed. Agnès nodded and laughed at appropriate moments, her eyes never leaving her son.

Observing them both, Patrick felt despondent at how little real pleasure his parents had ever found in family life, and now never would. The old gloom of responsibility settled on his shoulders. Even as a boy he had never succeeded in lightening their spirits, never managed to work out where the insurmountable difficulty lay that prevented them from being happy. He felt a tearing wound of pity for the three of them.

Belinda called them to the table, where Geoffrey attempted to continue in the same vein. He talked randomly about their Channel crossing the next day and what route they would be taking through France, about farm shops and window cleaners, until Belinda cut across him, saying without preamble, 'Did Patrick tell you he's seeing a psychologist?'

Agnès' fingers flew to her earrings, but, when Patrick leant across to press her hand, she looked directly at him, signalling her support. Geoffrey stared at Belinda in incomprehension.

'Maybe, before you leave again for Geneva, you have things you'd like to say that might be helpful,' Belinda suggested, looking calmly at each of them in turn. 'Maybe now is the time to discuss things you don't generally talk about.'

Geoffrey looked petrified, but Agnès nodded cautiously, and Belinda waited for her to speak. 'Agnès?' she prompted.

'Patrice knows how much we love him,' she said, patting his hand.

'I'd like to understand more about why you sent him away when he was so young,' said Belinda blandly, though Patrick could detect how she struggled to keep her tone neutral. Such directness was unlike his wife but, he thought, looking at his father's drawn face and his mother's over-bright eyes, none of them were any longer like themselves. 'How you imagined he'd react to that,' she went on.

'You sent your boy to a childminder,' Geoffrey accused Belinda. Agnès reacted with immediate alarm.

'No one is criticising you, Dad,' cajoled Patrick. 'What matters now,' he appealed to Belinda, 'is to support one another.' But she returned his look with a resoluteness that was foreign to him.

'I don't hold with working mothers,' insisted Geoffrey. 'If you'd stayed at home with him, young lady, none of this would have happened.'

'Oh, no,' protested Agnès to her husband. 'Don't, dear. Don't.'

'See! Now you're upsetting your mother!'

'I don't believe Patrick forgot Daniel,' Belinda said passionately. 'It was you he was trying to get away from!'

Geoffrey rose to his feet, his chair scraping against the floor. 'Is this why you asked us here? So you could accuse us of – of something?'

'Sshh, Dad. Of course not. Sit down. Please.' Patrick appealed again to Belinda. 'We don't need to talk like this. Let's just enjoy our lunch.'

Still standing, Geoffrey jabbed his finger across the table at Patrick. 'You're to blame! No one else!'

'I know that, Dad,' Patrick agreed contritely, ignoring Belinda's flash of contempt. 'Please, sit down. This isn't helping.'

'It's not easy,' said Agnès. 'But we'll all try, won't we?'

'Well ...' Geoffrey cast around for some face-saving formula and held his attention on the bowl of fruit salad on the kitchen counter. 'Belinda's gone to a lot of trouble,' he conceded, sitting down. 'Your mother doesn't want to be ungrateful.'

'We're none of us ourselves,' said Agnès. 'How could we be?'

Belinda collected up their plates, rebuffing Patrick's offer of help, and prepared to serve the dessert, the stiff line of her mouth and uncoordinated movements betraying the futility of her fury.

'It was the same when your sister died,' said Agnès, handing a plate of fruit salad across the table to Patrick.

He looked at her in confusion. 'I never had a sister, Maman.'

Agnès turned to address Belinda. 'She was two days old. The doctors warned me when she was born that she was very poorly, not expected to live.'

Patrick stared at her in bewilderment. 'You never told me!' He caught Belinda's look of amazement. 'I had no idea,' he assured her.

'They said it was all for the best,' explained Agnès. 'Your father was away on business.' She glanced across at Geoffrey, a look of unexpected sympathy. 'He couldn't get back in time.' Geoffrey sat very still, his head bowed, making no sign that he was even listening. 'He never forgave himself.' Agnès reached out to clasp his hand, but he recoiled from her touch, pushing his chair back clumsily.

'Excuse me,' he cried, blundering to the door. They heard him rush up the stairs, then turn the lock in the bathroom door.

'Why did you never talk about this before, Maman?'

Agnès looked surprised. 'Your father doesn't like to. But it was never a secret.'

'You've never once spoken of it.'

'I feared it might upset you to talk of it. And you never asked, like other children, why you had no brother or sister.' The simplicity of her reasoning clearly made perfect sense to her.

'It never occured to me,' said Patrick, staring at her in perplexity, combing his memory for any evidence that he had known anything of this.

'How old was Patrick when she was born?' asked Belinda.

'Two. The doctors told us we should have another child right away. That's how people thought in those days. But it was too difficult.'

Patrick was astounded at his mother's demeanour. He had never seen her show such composure or resolve. He couldn't determine which was greater, his shock at her revelation or the strange shyness that overcame him faced with her novel air of quiet authority.

'Your father and I,' Agnès continued, 'we understand what it is to lose a child. Never forget that, *mon petit chéri*.'

Belinda's eyes filled with tears. Patrick sat still, trying to process his astonishment, until they all heard the sound of the bathroom door opening, then Geoffrey's reluctant tread as he descended the stairs. Patrick was not sure he could deal with his father any more today, but when Geoffrey re-appeared, Agnès reached for the jug of cream and offered it to him as if nothing exceptional had occurred. Geoffrey busied himself with his fruit salad; stunned, the others followed suit, making no attempt to break the exhausted silence. When, finally, Belinda suggested coffee, Geoffrey announced that Agnès had a headache, and ten minutes later, to everyone's relief, they had driven away. The next day they would be in Europe.

Patrick stood in limbo at his front door, able neither to re-enter the house nor to walk away. It took a moment for his mind to register the sound of Belinda sobbing behind him. With limbs of lead, he went to her. She sat at the kitchen table, her head in her hands, tears splashing onto the wood between her elbows. He sat next to her, not touching, and waited, not knowing what to say.

'I want Daniel back,' she wept finally. 'I miss him so much. I can't bear to think of him shut away in that hospital basement all alone.'

Patrick's heart clenched tight, stopping his blood. 'I know. I'd suffer every torment under the sun if I could only bring him back.'

Belinda's body shuddered. 'I keep thinking of him that day, all by himself in the car, frightened and crying. Wanting me. And I wasn't there.'

'I'm the one who should've been there.'

'And that made me think of you. It made me understand how you must have felt as a kid, what they did to you.'

'No. I was okay. It wasn't that bad. Look at them – you can't blame them.'

'All these secrets, things never spoken about. And you all play along.' Belinda stretched out her hand to him, the first time she had offered any physical sign of absolution. Patrick took it, the touch of her fingers jolting his every nerve. 'Did you really not know?' she pleaded, between gasping breaths. 'Did you not even remember your mum being pregnant?'

'No.' He shook his head. 'Though it makes sense. Especially about Dad not being there when it happened. No wonder the poor sod can't cope.'

'Your grandmother must've known.'

'I suppose so,' Patrick sighed. 'And I suppose I must've been aware at some level. I assumed it was just what grown-ups were like, not telling you stuff.'

'How could Agnès have sent you away after losing her baby? What sort of mother packs her child off at seven?'

'I upset her, made her anxious. She was ill.' He shook his head in wonderment. 'I can't believe she spoke of it now.'

'But think of you, alone at school, wanting your mum!' Belinda looked at him with terrible sadness. 'How come you never get angry at them? Always defend them?'

'Because I've caused all this, not them,' said Patrick. 'I'm the bad one here. The only one responsible.'

226

'No,' she wailed. 'Your dad's right. I'm just as much to blame as you are. I should have paid more attention to how seriously those two stress you out. I should've taken the day off. Kept Daniel at home with me that day.'

The horror that Belinda should feel contaminated by his guilt had never crossed his mind. It pressed down on him, an unforeseen and insupportable burden.

'I never looked at you properly before,' she went on, beginning to sob again. 'And I should. I should have seen what they're really like. What they do to you.'

'It wasn't that.'

'If I had, then he'd still be here, safe with us. It's my fault just as much as yours.'

'No!'

'I can't stop thinking,' she wept, 'if only I'd put his changing bag on the front seat, where you'd've seen it. If only I'd rung Christine.'

'No!' Patrick cried out in agony. 'It's not you.'

'It is. It's my fault. I left him there alone.'

'Don't say that. Don't think it.'

'Don't tell me how to feel,' she screamed at him. 'You have no idea how I feel. You never did!' Patrick recoiled from the hatred in her face. He sat in frozen penance while she choked and gasped through her tears.

Much later that night Patrick became aware of Belinda standing over him in the dark of the guest room, shaking his shoulder. 'You're having another nightmare,' she whispered. She slipped into bed beside him. Half-awake, he

227

rolled over automatically to make room for her and stretched out an arm to pull her closer. She lay still, and he fell back to sleep with his hand resting on her nightgowned hip. When he woke in the morning and found her there, he could not look at her for shame.

IV

Patrick walked. The rhythmic repetition of steps helped to limit and control his thoughts. He stared at the pavements, noting the York stone or modern aggregate paving, the asphalt repairs, Victorian coal-hole covers, crushed drink cans, old tissues, cigarette ends, dog turds and, already, a few turning autumnal leaves. His eyes and feet provided sufficient occupation to leave his mind empty. He was well aware of the matter he could not think about: Daniel's funeral. A date had been set for the inquest, after which the coroner would release his body for burial. Earlier this week Patrick and Belinda had had their first meeting with an undertaker, a man who seemed deft and intelligent, his sympathy apparently genuine. But they had left feeling bludgeoned by the obdurate reality of the choices and selections to be made. Until this point there had been no decisions about the future to discuss beyond a trip to the supermarket, and the change of focus had been raw and disorienting. Neither of them had any particular faith and Daniel had not been christened, so they had settled on a private cremation with some kind of memorial service to be arranged.

Later that day, after their appointment with the undertaker, Patrick had gone upstairs to find that Belinda had emptied the guest room of his belongings and re-made the bed he had been occupying. He had crossed the hall, pushed open the door to the marital bedroom and, with a fatalistic acceptance, seen all his things back in their original places. Since then, he had lacked the emotional energy to work out what he felt, so had adopted the routine of going upstairs after he heard Belinda finish in the bathroom and could see that the bedroom lights were off. Once in bed, they never exchanged a word, and lay curled up back to back, barely touching. The past few nights he had hardly slept, and was fairly sure that she had not, either.

But he could walk, his steps coming to resemble an incantation, the repetition of which drove out conscious thought. Patrick even found some perverse satisfaction in the notion of burning off energy. Despite their attempts to eat sensibly, both he and Belinda had lost weight, and he was aware that, with his long legs and dark clothes hanging loose, he was beginning to resemble a scarecrow. But he approved of his vanishing body. Now that the possibility of facing criminal charges of manslaughter or child neglect seemed increasingly unlikely, especially after he and Belinda had been interviewed by social workers who had determined that they remained fit people to care for any future children they might have, it seemed a small appeasement for his offence.

He was on his way to see Amanda Skipton. His wish to co-operate with the police and his lingering and ambivalent desire for external punishment made it easy for him to regard these sessions as something over which he had no control and to which he must passively submit. And so it was in a neutral frame of mind that he sat down opposite her again under the sloping ceiling of her narrow room, chastising himself for his ridiculous initial surprise that, at this second meeting, she should be wearing different clothes.

'When we met last week,' she began, 'I asked you to think about something for me.'

'Oh!'

'Did you?'

'No. I'm sorry. What was it you asked?'

'We suggested that it wasn't Daniel that you had wanted to forget, to put out of your mind.' Amanda paused, waiting for his agreement. When Patrick nodded cautiously, she went on, 'I asked you to think about what it might have been that you wanted to forget, what it was that you did block out.'

Patrick's mouth was dry, and he licked his lips. 'I didn't consciously block anything out,' he said.

'No. Not consciously. What were you feeling when you got into your car that morning?'

'I don't remember.'

231

'Before that, then. Before you left the house.'

'My parents always find partings difficult. Saying goodbye. Leaving. They get anxious.'

'And how does that make you feel?'

Patrick met her gaze, and knew that he had to make some effort to recover his feelings that morning. But so many similar occasions paraded across his memory – his school trunk, railway stations, airports, the decorative cast-iron railings that bordered Josette's front garden where Maman's taxi waited. He had done this so many times, coped so often with his parents' guilt and anxiety, his grandmother's blame and rejection, he was sick of it.

'I upset people,' he told her bitterly. 'I make them angry and miserable.'

Amanda's eyes opened wide in surprise. 'And how does that make you feel? To be responsible for upsetting people like that?'

'Tired. Fed up. I want them to leave me alone.'

'To get away from them?'

'Yes.'

'And how do you do that?'

He looked at her blankly. 'I don't know.'

'Don't you?'

He shook his head, dismayed.

'Do you think it might have anything to do with why you remember so little about the morning of the day when your son died?'

'I assumed maybe that was shock or something. Post-traumatic stress.'

'I'm sure it plays a part,' Amanda agreed. 'I imagine you have nightmares, too?'

'No,' he answered instantly. Amanda raised an eyebrow, but made no further comment.

'I wonder if you can think of any other occasion when you weren't able afterwards to remember some event, to account for some particular period of time?' she went on. 'Doesn't matter how trivial.'

Patrick thought hard. 'I forgot to go back to school once,' he told her, surprised at how readily the long-ago memory had jumped into his mind. 'My first year at public school. I'd gone to my English grandparents for half-term. I was supposed to go back on the Sunday afternoon, but went off on my bike instead and missed the train. Dad was there. He was furious.'

'Where did you go off to?'

'Oh, just some local wood, probably. It was twenty-odd years ago.'

'Can you try to remember?'

'I've no idea.' He met her gaze, smiling. 'Really, I don't.'

'Were you punished?'

'Hell, yes!'

'In what way?'

'Oh, the usual. I don't know. Loss of pocket-money, something like that. Not being taken somewhere I wanted to go. Sanctions, Dad believed in, not beatings.'

'What were your English grandparents like?'

'Grandpa Hinde had lost an arm. Nearly perished being evacuated from Dunkirk. Grandma Hinde was in charge. They both died while I was at school, but I was quite fond of them, even though Dad was always kind of thorny around them. He claimed they always favoured his younger sister, the post-war baby, bonny and blithe. Not like him.'

'Is that what your aunt's like?'

'She was good fun, yes. My cousins, too.' Patrick's recollections relieved some of his tension. 'She used to come and take me out from school sometimes.' Then his face clouded. 'I ought to write to her. Doubt Dad will have told her anything.'

'What sort of things did your parents tell you about yourself when you were growing up?'

'How do you mean?'

'Well, like your father told you that his parents preferred his younger sister. He must have got that belief from somewhere. I wonder what sort of beliefs you gained about yourself from your parents.'

Patrick stared at her, feeling a rising antagonism towards her. He knew it had nothing to do with her, but was nonetheless unable to subdue the stubborn anger and resentment that lodged in his chest. Amanda clearly sensed his change of mood, and, in return, regarded him steadily.

'They never wanted me,' he said at last. 'They wanted rid of me.' He recalled the bombshell Agnès had dropped the other day, about the infant sister he had never realised existed. He didn't think he could face explaining all that to Amanda. He sighed. 'I'm not stupid,' he told her instead. 'I realise it was to do with their problems, their inadequacies. Not me. Not really.'

'And if you had let them be upset, what's the worst that could happen? What were you afraid of?'

'This,' he said. 'This is what could happen. My son is dead.'

Amanda pulled a stapled bunch of papers out of the file on the table before her. She searched through the pages until she found the one she wanted. 'Here it is. That morning, before you left, your father picked Daniel up, handed him to you and told you to get rid of him. Is that correct?'

'Yes,' Patrick confirmed warily.

'How did that make you feel?'

Patrick shook his head in despair. 'Everyone keeps asking me that. I don't know. I don't remember. I'm sick of it. Of them. Of course they're mad, and I ought to deal with them, but there's never been any point. It just makes them worse.' He looked at her beseechingly: why could no one ever understand the futility of trying to change anything to do with his parents? 'How is any of this going to bring Daniel back?' he asked. 'It's not. It can't.'

'That's true,' agreed Amanda. 'But having to deal with your parents appears to make you very upset.'

'I'm used to it.' He looked stubbornly at the floor.

'Used to the fact that your parents don't care how badly they upset you?'

Patrick closed his eyes, tried to clear his head by shaking it.

'What do you do with your feelings when other people fail to care about you?' Amanda persisted.

'Nothing. Just forget about it.'

'When you left with Daniel that morning to drive to your office, what did you do with your feelings?'

'Nothing! Put everything to the back of my mind as soon as I was in the car. Forgot about it.'

'You forgot that you were distressed and angry?'

'Yes. So what?' Patrick glared at her 'What's your theory? That my repressed anger at my father made me lock my son in the car? Made me want to kill him?' His voice shook, an hysterical flush rising on his cheeks. 'That's bollocks!'

'No. Not at all. I think it was your forgotten feelings that you left in the car. Your own inner child, if you like. Not Daniel. It had nothing to do with Daniel. I think you locked the most vulnerable part of yourself up in that car, went away and forgot all about it.'

Belinda regarded Patrick strangely when he walked into the kitchen. He braced himself, not sure he could take much more in his present state of mind. He thought of descriptions in Victorian fiction of raving lunatics frothing at the mouth, and thought that very soon that would be him, then immediately berated himself. He had no right to consider himself a victim.

'Your grandmother has died,' Belinda said. 'Agnès telephoned. It was very swift, probably her heart. Agnès said you're not to worry about arrangements or anything – they'll take care of everything.'

Patrick slumped into the nearest chair. 'Poor Maman.' He disliked Belinda's scrutiny. 'Josette had little enough pity for me,' he told her. 'Frankly, it's hard to dredge up much for her right now.'

'All the same, she was a big part of your life,' observed Belinda.

He nodded. 'As a kid, sure. I'm sorry she died alone, but she chose to live that way.'

Belinda shrugged and turned back to the sink where she was peeling some potatoes. 'I begin to wonder what you'd say if I died,' she said quietly. For a moment, Patrick was unsure whether he'd actually heard her words.

'You think I have no feelings? You think I don't care?' he burst out.

'Do you?' She had turned to look at him again, observing him closely.

He jumped up and grabbed her shoulders, shaking her. 'I love you!' he shouted. 'I loved Daniel! You know that!'

'Then what were you busy thinking about all that day instead of him? What was so much more important?'

He dropped his hands helplessly.

'Not just some split second slip of attention, an accident, but hours. Hours while he – while he was all alone.'

'Do you want me to leave? I'll go. I'll go now, if that's what you want.' Part of him longed for her to condemn him, express vehemently all her anger and blame, order him to leave the house for ever. He knew the contempt she must feel and wanted to see it blazing in her face.

'Is that your answer? To duck out of it?'

He felt slightly sick with disappointment. 'What do you want me to do?'

'It's not about you! Stop making it all about you!'

Patrick was shocked. Walking home, he had mulled over all that Amanda had said. The notion that there was some part of himself that he had learnt to lock away flickered with the distant prospect of making sense, of leading perhaps to a first glimmer of understanding. But now he hung his head. Belinda had every right to condemn such self-indulgence – what could it matter whether he understood himself or not? No amount of getting in touch with his inner child was ever going to bring Daniel back to life. There was no point trying to learn anything from Amanda's psychological theories about him.

'I'm sorry if I do that,' he told her humbly. 'Really.' All he wanted in that instant was to offer whatever she needed from him. He forced himself to look steadily at her, willing himself and his feelings to disappear so that she might see how, from now on, he would live for her. She returned his gaze, but, as if searching for something in him that she failed to find, looked away at last with a despairing shake of her head. 'What?' he asked her. 'Please. Tell me.'

An image sprang into his mind of when they first met, only a few years earlier: she, a willowy figure with huge eyes and a mass of unfashionably thick and luscious hair, was seven years younger than he, but already far more sure and capable, a free spirit, full of plans, up for spon-taneous, last-minute dashes to see movies, live perform-ances, check out some new bar. Now, her eyes were too big for her face in a gaunt and unnatural way; she was too young, he thought sadly, to look like this. He reached out for her. 'Tell me,' he begged. 'Please. Let me try.'

She looked at him doubtfully, but began to speak. 'At some point,' she said, 'at some point we have to go on living. I don't know how or when, or whether I can. Whether we can do so together. But in the end we'll each have to find, or invent, some way to get past this.' Patrick started to speak, but she held up her hand. 'Maybe it's callous of me, to want that. Maybe I'm simply too shallow to die of grief. I don't care. I can't—' Patrick could see that thoughts of Daniel threatened to engulf her, but she shook her head at him to obey, and he waited for her to go on. 'I can't say goodbye to Daniel without something to cling to. Something else to live for.'

Patrick nodded, fighting back his own feelings.

'You're going to have to feel the same. To find some way, for yourself, to begin again.'

Patrick felt sick. She had asked the one thing of him that he was certain he could not do.

'What I need to know,' she continued, 'is whether we can ever dare to have another child. Even to consider it, I have to be able to trust you again. And if we don't dare,' she went on in a rush, 'if we can't, then why struggle to stay together?'

Patrick swallowed hard. 'It is a struggle, isn't it, for you to stay with me?'

Belinda nodded, sucking in her lips as she fought back tears. 'There are times I want to tear you to pieces. Just seeing you walk around the house, being alive when he isn't, when it's because of you that he isn't here, I want to rip you apart. When I feel like that, I can even believe it's a totally sane reaction.'

'It is.'

'But it's not what I want,' she cried. 'And you're the only one who can stop it. That's what you have to do. You have to stop me hating you.'

'Okay.' He put his hands on her shoulders. She wouldn't let him pull her to him, but he kept hold of her. 'Okay. I don't know how, but I'll try. I promise.'

'Good. I don't want to talk any more.' She turned back to the sink, twisting out of his grasp, but her shoulders dropped as if released of tension.

Patrick looked around the room, searching for some clue as to what to do next. His attention was caught by a cupboard door that hung too loose on its hinges and never shut properly, impeding the drawers in the fitment beside it. He knew it annoyed her, and he had been meaning to fix it for ages. Fetching his tools from the cupboard under the stairs, he set about unscrewing the hinge; the material from which the door was made had flaked away, making it impossible for a new screw to get a fixing. It was a relief to set his mind to solving a practical problem, and he spent the rest of the afternoon searching out other jobs around the house, allowing himself the delusion that, in sanding and planing, fitting and glueing, he was at least in some small way serving Belinda and easing her path.

That night, the lights were off as he slipped into bed beside her; he lay with his back to her, letting his vision adjust to the darkness. Suddenly she sat up, and he turned his head to watch as she raised her arms above her head, pulling off the cotton tee-shirt she was wearing as a nightgown. Her breasts were back-lit against the frail grey light that entered the room around the edge of the blinds. She turned to face him, and he was struck once again by how young and vulnerable she was. Belinda wriggled back down to lie beside him. 'Hold me,' she whispered.

Patrick obligingly took her in his arms, his fingertips lightly touching her naked back; he could not refuse to offer comfort, but his confused rush of sensations was paralysing. At first, to his relief, she lay still, her head tucked under his chin so that his nose was buried in her warm, scented hair. Her hand rested on his chest, her fingers gently roving across his skin. He ordered himself to relax, to doze, trying to let the undemanding physical sensations float him away from consciousness and towards sleep. But her hand strayed down his belly, and, almost with horror, he was jolted by an unbidden, deceitful jab of desire. He lay very still, forcing his breath to sound as if he were already asleep, experiencing a clear sense of salvation when she remained still, allowing his faint erection to fade. But after a little while she straightened herself alongside him, pressing her body against his. As her fingers reached lower and her stroking began to show clear intent, he shrank back, unable to prevent himself curling inwards, away from her.

'Relax. It'll be all right,' Belinda murmured into his ear, her lips touching his cheek as she raised herself to seek his mouth. He kissed her chastely, allowing her tongue to slip into his mouth as her hand softly began the attempt to tease some life into his penis. He moved her hand gently away, placing it safely around his waist, then freed his mouth from hers.

'Never mind about me,' he apologised. 'Let me concentrate on you instead.' He stroked his hand down the curve of her hip, slipping familiarly down between her thighs. She pressed against him, her lips seeking his. He kissed her back, and she moaned as he touched her, but then shifted her hand once more, hoping to find him aroused. He caught her wrist, lifting her arm up to rest upon his chest.

'No, let me,' she murmured into his ear. She pushed him back into the mattress and began to kiss his chest and stomach as she moved down the bed. In the past he would have surrendered voluptuously, weaving his fingers through her hair as she licked and sucked, awaiting the moment when she would choose to roll back, drawing him on top of her. Now the thought of such intimacy was terrible, unimaginable, so he drew her back up level with him, kissing her neck and cheeks, stroking her hair, trying to will his body to do what she wanted. After a while, as nothing happened, she straddled him, leaning down to kiss him while trying once more with her hand to arouse him.

'Please,' she said. 'I want you inside me. Just for a little while.'

'I can't. I'm sorry.'

He twisted away from her, pushing her aside, then immediately tried to atone for his ungentle reaction. 'I'm sorry, sweetheart. But it just won't happen.'

Belinda didn't move. 'At least let me hold you,' he said, attempting to pull her back into his arms. She did not entirely turn away, but drew up her knees, her arms guarding her chest. They lay like that, their bodies touching only where her head rested unnaturally on the elbow of his outstretched arm, saying nothing until both pretended to fall asleep.

Patrick's final session with Amanda was fixed for almost the precise moment when, in France, Agnès and Geoffrey were laying Josette to rest. It had been readily agreed between them all that it would be futile for Patrick to attend his grandmother's funeral. Nonetheless, he felt some regret, if merely out of a dutiful respect; all the more so when Geoffrey had rung to say that Josette had left her house and its contents to Patrick. He was perturbed by this unexpected gesture, but Geoffrey was glad to be relieved of responsibility for disposing of everything, and it appeared that Josette had discussed and agreed her decision with Agnès long before, when she had first drawn up her will. In any case, the matter would have to be considered another time: he was unable to make room right now for anything to do with Josette.

Patrick was irritated, therefore, when Amanda's first question brought his grandmother to mind. 'You told me last time that you upset people. I'd like to talk about that.'

He nodded, resigned.

'Who made you think that you upset people?' she asked.

He shrugged. 'People are better off without me.'

'Did someone use to tell you that?'

'My grandmother.'

'Grandma Hinde?'

'No. My French grandmother, Josette.'

'Is she still alive?'

'No. Though she lived to a good age.'

'Were you close?'

'I never saw much of her once I left school. Even my mother only visited once or twice a year.'

'But when you were a child?'

He nodded. 'In the holidays.'

'And she made you feel as if it was you who were to blame when people were upset?'

'Yes.'

'Can you give me an example?'

'Sometimes my mother had to go back and be with my dad, and I'd stay on with Josette. Maman hates having to say goodbye, gets distressed when people leave. Josette used to say it was my fault.'

'Your fault that your mother hated leaving?'

'My fault that she left me. That she didn't want me with her.'

'I see. What else did Josette say?'

'She'd ask what I'd done. Go on at me to own up to why they never wanted me with them. Sometimes, for fun, I'd imagine what terrible deeds I might've committed. It was almost easier to pretend they were right, like I was secretly a werewolf or a vampire or something, rather than admit that adults are all just crazy and useless.' Patrick tried to laugh, then shifted in his chair and sighed heavily. 'Even then I knew that Josette was fucked up. She'd had to be tough to survive, but she hated me. Why should she hate a defenceless kid for no reason? I must have done something.'

'Tell me how you felt about your mother leaving.'

Patrick examined his hands in his lap as he answered, 'I didn't like it.'

'Did you show that you were upset?'

'No. That would have made her worse. Made everything worse.'

'So at least, by looking after your mother, you could do some good?'

245

Patrick stared at her. 'I guess,' he said at last.

'But you never asked not to be left?'

'What good would it have done?'

When Amanda failed to ask another question, he looked up to find her observing him with a sad expression. 'I'm not going to feel sorry for myself,' he responded angrily. 'This shouldn't be about me. What about Belinda? She's the one who matters now. I want to think about her, not go on bleating away about my childhood!'

'You don't think that perhaps unravelling a few things from your childhood might ultimately help Belinda too?'

'No! Look, do I actually have to be here? Because if I have a choice, then frankly I'd rather pack it in. This just feels to me all rather like wallowing in self-indulgence.'

'The door's not locked,' said Amanda evenly. 'And you don't have to come again.' Patrick stared at her, torn. Unable to conjure up any honest justification for walking out, he stayed put. After a moment's silence, Amanda nodded, and asked, 'You feel guilty towards Belinda?'

'What the fuck do you think?' he responded belligerently, then held up his hands. 'I'm sorry, I'm sorry. But feeling guilty doesn't even begin to—' Patrick waved his arms to express the inadequacies of speech. He groaned, fighting the urge to curl into a ball and hide from the world for ever. 'I don't know what to do, how to go on,' he told Amanda. 'She wants me to, but I don't think I can. I'm totally lost. No way to go forward.'

'I suspect it would help you to be punished?'

He smiled wryly. 'Be nice to be in a prison cell!'

'What about thoughts of suicide?' she asked gently.

'Of course. All the time. But I can't, can I?' He met her steady gaze and sighed. 'But then, I think maybe it's the best thing I could do for her. I'm sure her family would agree.'

'Has she ever said so?'

'Never. The opposite.' His heart clenched and he had to look away into nothingness as the image of Belinda crying with guilt at the kitchen table washed over him. 'She blames herself for his death.'

'That must be tough.'

'She doesn't deserve this. How could I do it to her? I don't understand how she can forgive me.'

'Maybe you need to let her.'

Patrick shook his head. 'I have to find a way to make it up to her. It's all I can do now.' Sensations from the previous night flushed over him, and he tried to calm himself before going on. 'But what if I can't? However much I want to do what she wants, no matter how hard I try, I'm not sure I can.'

'What do you fear might happen if you fail?'

He stared at her, unable to find words. 'There's something bad in me,' he said at last. 'I'm no good for people.'

An hour later, on the train, a young woman caught Patrick's attention and smiled. Though he seldom responded, he was used to women putting out signals that they found him attractive. Now, however, he wondered how this girl would react if someone told her the truth about him, if she had been witness to what he had done. He shrank back into his seat, staring instead at the unfolding view through the window. It was a walk of a mile or so to Ditchling, which had no station of its own. As he neared his office, Patrick tried not to imagine how the occasional passer-by must be pretending not to notice him, then afterwards turning to stare. He kept walking, facing straight ahead.

At the entrance to the enclosed yard behind his building, he hesitated, then, his mind long made up, straightened his back and walked purposefully up the blind alley. He had never really looked at nor committed to memory this nondescript, convenient space where he had regularly parked his car. The August sun cut a diagonal line of shadow across the uneven ground. A couple of self-seeded elder saplings thrived in one corner, straw-like weeds grew out of cracks in the dry mortar of a flanking wall and bright green algae glistened below a pipe dripping from the empty flat above his office. What Patrick at first thought was litter turned out to be a rotting bunch of flowers that someone had laid on the ground. He could see a small card stapled to the cellophane wrapping, the message written in florist's biro by an immature hand, but he did not approach close enough to read the words. The air enclosed between these red-brick walls was innocent of what had happened here. Patrick remembered a teenage visit to the Coliseum in Rome when he had endeavoured to extract from the stones some tangible trace of all the years of fear and savagery they had witnessed. But they were just stones: any awareness of what had taken place was in his own head.

He went back down the alley and turned out onto the narrow pavement. He stopped at his office doorway beside the brass plate. He had his key ready in his pocket, but it was a few moments before he could will his arm to move. He had to push the door open against a small mound of mail collected on the mat. His half-drunk mug of tea was on the desk where he had abandoned it. Thick mould covered the surface of the once milky liquid. The message light on the phone flashed. When he touched the keyboard, the computer screen sprang to life, the cursor blinking at the end of the sentence where he had left off writing up his notes on a new patient. He could still remember his thoughts about her. For a second it seemed as if time had stood still, and his heart gave a wrenching leap – It was not true! It had not happened! – before jolting him back into reality. He bent to pick up the post. Among the bills were quite a few handwritten letters that he assumed would be abusive.

Sitting down at his desk, he decided to deal with those first. The majority turned out to be letters of condolence. He read each one quickly before dropping them all into the waste bin. Some of the phone messages, too, expressed sympathy and regret, though most were about appoint-ments that he had failed to cancel. To begin with the tone was of annoyance, replaced by shock and embarrassment as the news spread, and finally by self-interest as concern for their own migraine or sciatica closed over the unnatural chasm of his personal tragedy. 'Please let me know when you're coming back,' requested one voice with faint apology. 'I'd much rather keep coming to you, Mr Hinde, but I do need more pills.'

Patrick found himself amused: for once, his patients' self-involvement was refreshing. Here at least he could be of use, could carry on with some aspect of his life that was not about him. He had not fully appreciated until now how vital a refuge his work provided nor how deeply he would have mourned its loss. If his patients were to go on entrusting him with their intimate troubles, then here was some vindication of his continued existence. For time was his real enemy now, his task to find some way to get through each of the thousands of days that lay ahead; without work, he wondered how on earth he would fill the void.

He felt the impact of the past thunder through him, all the weight of distant unresolved traumas, of other unforgiven deeds and insufficient atonements. Recognising in himself the destructive symptoms of inherited predispositions, he realised he must fight against becoming an outcast, a leper. Though he knew he lacked the objectivity to prescribe for himself, he could safely assume which miasmatic remedy a colleague would suggest, and went to fetch it for himself.

Swallowing the pills gave him enough courage to deal with the list of his patients' queries and complaints, and gradually he found an easeful distraction in the practical concentration on other people's problems. Although not yet ready to speak to any of his patients on the phone, he wrote the necessary messages in emails or on cards. Offering new appointments – though God knew whether they would be taken up – constructed a framework around which he could foresee himself building a future; which, he reminded himself, was what Belinda wanted. An hour later he found himself sticking stamps onto envelopes in a luxurious interval during which his mind had not once been snagged by pain. He silently blessed each and every patient for the gift they had unwittingly bestowed.

A short account of the inquest appeared in the local Brighton paper. It reported how the coroner had delivered a narrative verdict, finding no evidence of gross negligence or reckless disregard, and also confirmed that no criminal charges were to be brought. The following day, Belinda told Patrick, the parents of one of her music pupils withdrew their daughter from her private lessons and harangued the principal to dismiss her from the school. Although the principal refused, she felt she should not keep Belinda in ignorance of how the couple had vented their belief that Patrick was guilty of child abuse and that Belinda, in not divorcing him, must be complicit.

Despite the coroner's sympathetic handling of the

process, the inquest had left Patrick feeling wretched. Belinda had wanted her sister there, and by the end of the proceedings Patrick half-agreed with Grace's poorly concealed belief that Belinda needed to be protected from him. It had been hard enough giving his own evidence, trying to weave a meaningful account of his actions that day, but even worse to witness the strain on the faces of the young police officers, and even of the experienced paramedics, as they recorded, with valiant attempts at objectivity, their horror at discovering Daniel's body.

He had stared at the floor, burning with shame as each of these well-meaning and diligent people attempted to account for his crime of forgetfulness – a crime he remained unable to explain. When one of them happened to catch his eye, Patrick wondered how the man could so successfully hide the disdain he must surely feel. Listening to the pathologist recount the details of the post-mortem, with Belinda sitting rigidly beside him, Patrick had thought his heart would burst as she endured the list of atrocities inflicted on her child.

After the coroner's verdict, he and Belinda had emerged from the court into the oblivious September sunshine, standing like lost children, unable to comprehend the bizarre nature of their freedom.

Grace had shepherded Belinda across the road to a coffee shop, making it plain that Patrick might follow or not as he pleased. Belinda had sat staring into her mug, shut off from her surroundings, while Grace fussed over her, helping her off with her jacket, offering to fetch more milk, urging her to drink before the coffee went cold. Grace had ignored Patrick until Belinda got up to go to the loo. Then she had immediately leant in towards him. 'Why are you here?' she had hissed at him. 'If you loved her at all, you'd clear off.'

Patrick had been taken aback. 'Is that what she wants?'

'Can't you see how much she must hate you?'

He had swallowed hard and nodded. 'If it's really what she wants, then of course I'll go.'

'None of us can understand why you're still here. How can you face her? How can you face any of us?'

'Has she told you she wants me to go?'

Patrick had watched the struggle in Grace to be fair. 'No,' she had conceded.

'I can only do what she wants.'

'No! You have to decide what's best for her! Give her some peace. Leave her free to rebuild her life. If you had any true feeling, you'd know what was right!'

Seeing Belinda making her way back to the table, Grace had retreated. Belinda had glanced curiously at the two of them, but when Grace made an effort to smile and appear relaxed, had let it go.

For the rest of that week Belinda was withdrawn, clearly undergoing some tense inner struggle of judgement and conscience. Patrick watched her closely, turning over Grace's furious admonition and wondering despondently what to do. Towards the end of an unhappy weekend, Belinda came out to him in the garden where he was trimming the hedge. While she waited for him to switch off the whirring blades, he was certain that this would be his dismissal.

'I want to apologise,' she said.

'What?'

'I couldn't be sure, couldn't make up my mind to be sure, that I believed you. I had to doubt you, for Daniel's sake, do you understand?'

'Of course. Sweetheart, you don't have to do this.'

'I do. I want to say I'm sorry for the terrible thoughts I've had. And that they're over now.' She stroked his cheek. If he had not been holding the hedge trimmer with its dangerous teeth, he would have struck her hand away.

'Don't!' he implored her. 'Please. You've nothing to be sorry for.'

'I still love you,' she told him. 'But there is one thing you have to do for me.'

'Anything. Whatever it is, I'll understand. And I'll do it. No matter what. Don't be afraid to say it.'

'I want you to forgive yourself.'

Patrick never imagined the effect that words alone could have upon the body: he was so overwhelmed that for an instant he believed Belinda's words must send him mad. When the red mist cleared, he found himself standing in the garden, the electric tool in his hand, and Belinda retreating into the house. A little later, she called him indoors for supper, and he made himself obey her summons.

V

It was not long after dawn when Belinda and Patrick made their way up the steep footpath to the place on the Downs where they had picnicked less than three months earlier. As the slope evened out, they stopped to get back their breath, turning to look at the view. Though the early morning mist obscured the horizon, they could see how the landscape was bleached and yellowing, already autumnal.

It would be a long time before either of them could bear to bring to mind any detail of Daniel's cremation the previous afternoon. Overnight, they had placed his ashes in his room which, except for Belinda cleaning and tidying it as she would have done were it still occupied, had been left unchanged. Both of them liked to sit alone there occasionally, finding comfort in the touch of the bright cotton duvet cover or soft toy animals, and the sight of his plastic play figures, folded clothes and cast-off shoes. Belinda had wished to carry the metal canister, and she hugged it to her now. They had easily agreed that this was where they wanted him to be – up high near the sky, blown by the wind across the grassy masses of the chalk downs. This was where they would be able to come and find him, part of nature, not under some memorial stone in a municipal cemetery. But now that the time had come, its inconceivable finality gripped them both. They sat on the grass, not touching but not apart, and stared out at the rising mist, trying not to shiver in the damp early morning chill. Belinda's fingers were white where she gripped the canister.

'I don't think I can do it,' she said, handing it across to him.

Patrick accepted it from her. 'Now? Are you ready?'

Belinda nodded. He pulled off the close-fitting lid. The contents made him feel faint and distant from himself. He sat still, fearing collapse if he attempted to stand.

'Do you remember how he rolled that day?' he asked.

'Yes. He loved it.'

'If we think of him tumbling down, like he did that day, do you think we can do it?'

'Yes. Go on. Please.'

Patrick rose and took a step or two down the slope. Belinda came to stand behind him, her hand resting lightly on the small of his back. He bent forward and gingerly shook some of the pale ashes from the container. There was very little wind, and only the finer dust was picked up and carried further off. Belinda reached out and took her turn and together they emptied all that remained of their child's once small and vivid presence across a short stretch of cropped grass. They went back a little way up the slope and sat down. Patrick grasped Belinda's hand, the clutch of each other's fingers communicating their struggle to subdue an animal howl of repudiation. They remained there, watching each tiny gust of wind until at last the breeze had left nothing that would be remarked on by any walker straying from the main pathways.

Neither of them spoke for the rest of the day, but that night they slept in one another's arms.

For Belinda's twenty-ninth birthday a week or two later Patrick bought tickets to hear a soloist she admired at the Royal Festival Hall. It was his only gift – the kind of presents he might usually have chosen for her seemed trite and pointless – and he hoped it would re-ignite her enthusiasm for teaching now that the school term was underway. They sat together on the train to London, watching as fields and woods gave way to Thirties ribbon developments and then to yards full of used car tyres and white vans.

They arrived into Waterloo as the first rush-hour crowds were beginning to fight their way across the concourse, and Patrick put his arm around Belinda's shoulders to guide her through the onslaught of elbows, laptop cases and backpacks heading ruthlessly for the platforms or Tube entrance. He liked having something real to protect her from, while simultaneously feeling guilty that it was he who had brought her here. This was how he often felt these days. When he had presented her with the concert tickets, she had been pleased – she wanted them to 'get back to normal' – but he was aware that the prospect of a pleasure jaunt to London was daunting, and that she had not suggested setting off any earlier in the day so that they might go shopping beforehand or meet up with one of her family for lunch. Escaping the commuters at last as they emerged from the underpass to the South Bank, she already looked anxious and exhausted.

They had a drink in the bar overlooking the river, though neither could bring themselves to suggest or want champagne to toast her birthday. It was a pretty view, the twinkling décor accentuating the lights of the city that were already beginning to be reflected in the choppy water, and the place was animated and noisy. In the past, their shared silence as they took in their novel surroundings would have been understood and enjoyed, but now it was brittle and unhappy. They did not belong here. But this, they had promised each other, was what they must force themselves to do – to join in where they no longer belonged.

Belinda had returned to work and Patrick, to his grateful surprise, had patients to see, but with the resumption of their regular activities it had begun to sink in at last that their pain was no aberration; that it was not going to come to a convenient end, and that it wasn't possible to experience grief once and for all and be done with it. This is what their lives now had to encompass, and always would.

During the recital, Patrick found himself unaffected by the sweeping romanticism of the music, and was unable to detect whether Belinda was similarly unmoved. He took her hand and continued to hold it until the time came to applaud. During the interval they mingled with the rest of the audience. When Belinda commented appreciatively on the pianist's technique, admiring his interpretation of one of her own favourite pieces, Patrick began to hope that maybe he had not after all made a mistake in bringing her here. On the hour's train journey home, she rested with her head on his shoulder while he stared at their flattened reflections in the darkened glass, trying to penetrate the blackness beyond.

In bed later that night, Patrick submitted to the ordeal of Belinda trying to make love to him, and had again to endure his own chronic failure to respond to his beautiful young wife. Eventually she turned away and wept into her pillow, refusing all his frail offers of comfort. He lay awake long into the night, wondering if the Judas goat were similarly impotent.

Two removal men in liver-coloured uniforms beckoned to the driver of the Swiss pantechnicon to back it up into the narrow driveway of Agnès and Geoffrey's new home in Esher. Standing by their front door, caged canaries at their feet, and intent on the encroaching vehicle, neither of them noticed Patrick's approach on foot from the distant station. He had stopped to buy flowers, and carried an insulated picnic bag full of home-made soups and vegetable stews that Belinda had prepared.

Geoffrey shook Patrick's hand. 'Hello, there,' he said, looking up at the pale sky. 'At least we've got a clear day for it.'

With a pang, Patrick realised that his father was glad to see him. He presented his flowers and kissed Agnès, who looked distractedly over his shoulder at the men opening the van's vast rear doors. As a boy, Patrick had seldom been permitted to take part in the family's transcontinental moves, but he had seen enough to know that, legitimately occupied with checking and re-checking, Agnès was in her element.

Sure enough, once the open doors had been secured, the foreman handed Agnès a clipboard, and, laughing and joking, followed her into the house carrying the cardboard box nearest to hand: it was clearly labelled, in French and in his mother's rounded letters, 'Kettle, mugs, tea, coffee and biscuits'. Patrick smiled at his father and stood back to take a proper look at the house. Although he suspected that his parents' bland Euro-furniture would sit oddly against the Edwardian flourishes of this compact red-brick cottage, he could imagine them settling here.

'What do you think?' asked Geoffrey. Amazed, Patrick wondered if retirement had dismantled his father's supportive hierarchies to such an extent that he was now prepared to tolerate his son's opinions, and hoped that the loss of an executive infrastructure was not about to catapult Geoffrey into helpless old age. He kept at bay the knowledge that it was more likely his own culpability that had dealt the blow.

'You'd better give me the tour,' Patrick responded cheerfully. 'Stay out of the way until Maman's made the tea.'

The neatly proportioned rooms would need little in the way of refurbishment, and the small gardens, both pretty and relatively private, were manageable, which, Patrick guessed, was what had appealed to his father about the property. 'I hope you'll be happy here, Dad,' he said, daring to place a hand on his shoulder.

Geoffrey nodded. Though he crimped his lips, he did not shrug off the physical contact. 'I'm worried about your mother,' he said abruptly.

'Why, what's up?' When Geoffrey did not immediately reply, Patrick went on. 'I haven't spoken to you properly since Josette's funeral. How did it go?'

'Fine, fine. I mean, she was upset, naturally, but it all went off okay. No, you'll see. Once the boxes are unloaded. The men do all the packing, but she likes to label them herself.'

'I don't understand.'

Geoffrey led the way from the garden in through the open French windows to where the uniformed men were already efficiently stacking up cardboard boxes. 'See?' he asked, showing Patrick where, on at least three of them, Agnès had written simply *ces choses* – those things.

Patrick stared at the words, but the meaning Geoffrey intended him to take from them eluded him.

'You know how organised she is,' Geoffrey said, an almost badgering tone creeping into his voice. 'She has it down to a fine art. Won't let me interfere. It was the foreman who pointed it out. When I ask, she insists she knows exactly what's in each box.'

'Maybe she does,' said Patrick, realising as he spoke how ludicrous a wish that was, given how many identical boxes there were. 'It's just stress,' he corrected himself. 'She's had a lot to deal with. She must be worn out.' He half-expected his father to round on him, accuse him of causing his mother's latest aberration.

'You don't think I ought to take her to a doctor?' It dawned on Patrick that Geoffrey's hectoring was an appeal, that what his father wanted from him was reassurance, command, to be relieved of responsibility.

'Sure, why not, once you're settled?'

His father nodded, uncertain.

'I had some tests recently,' Patrick hazarded, not wanting to detonate the tripwire of Daniel's death. 'Amazing what these scans and things can show.'

Geoffrey sighed heavily, shaking his head. 'If only you'd stuck with medicine. Such a waste.'

Patrick almost laughed. The familiarity of blame was a relief, and evidence that his father was recovering his poise. 'But why not wait a week or so?' he suggested, making sure he sounded bright and optimistic. 'She may be fine once everything's sorted. After all, she's been pretty positive about the move, hasn't she?'

'Yes. Yes, maybe you're right,' said Geoffrey dismissively, ready now to turn his back on the inconclusively labelled boxes.

Patrick took his cue. 'I really wouldn't worry about it, Dad.' He watched in regretful amusement as, lacking the mechanism to show gratitude, Geoffrey expressed his renewed confidence by going out to the driveway to instruct the men that the dining table should be taken into the dining room. Feeling in his pocket for the remedies he had remembered to bring for his mother, Patrick wished it were possible to offer his father some kind of help.

An hour or so later Patrick went to assist Agnès in making up their bed. All the boxes stacked against the wall correctly declared their contents: duvet, pillows, sheets and towels. But when, delving into an opened box, he asked her which pillowcases she wanted, she looked at him wide-eyed.

He held up two cotton cases. 'Do you want these plain ones on first, or just the ones that match the duvet cover?'

She looked from one piece of fabric to the other, then at him. 'What are they?' she asked. 'What are they for?'

His heart sank. 'It's a covering for the pillow you're holding, Maman.'

'Of course!' She laughed, and held out her hand, but then watched as, deliberately instructive, Patrick picked up a pillow from the bed and began slowly to encase it. Seeing her concentrate on following his example, he wondered how many hundreds of times she had put on and taken off pillowcases in her life. Yet an uninformed observer would have to conclude that she had never done this before. Usually, if somehow made to feel lacking or out of her depth, she would become agitated and apologetic, but Patrick realised that she was too engrossed, too intrigued by the novelty of her actions, to be anxious. In a way, perhaps it was a blessing.

The bed made, Agnès sat down while Patrick flattened and folded some of the unpacked boxes to get them out of the way and make more space in the room.

'I hope you'll be happy here, Maman,' he said.

'I think so.' She smoothed the surface of the duvet beside her. 'And you, Patrice? Can you manage to be happy again one day, do you think?'

'I'm trying. For Belinda.'

'Now you can sell Josette's house and not worry about money. Spend some of it on yourselves. Go on a nice holiday.'

'Maybe,' he agreed diffidently. When Josette's lawyer had first written to enquire about Patrick's plans for the property, a decision did not seem urgent, so he had put off replying. As a second letter and then a third followed and went unanswered, he had begun to admit to himself the possibility of keeping the place. He had no idea why – it was impractical, and he certainly had no sentimental attachment to it – but he found increasingly that he liked the notion of possessing it.

'I'm sorry I wasn't with you at the funeral,' he told his mother.

Agnès nodded. 'Josette should have married again. She was wrong to shut herself off from life the way she did.'

'Did you ask her to leave the house to me?' he asked, still struggling to believe that his grandmother's bequest had been meant as a genuine gesture of affection.

'No. It was her decision. She only consulted me so I should not feel passed over.'

'I never thought she cared for me.'

'She loved you. She just didn't know how to show her feelings.' Agnès twisted round to look across to the other side of the bed. 'Pass me my—' She waved her hand impatiently.

Patrick looked where his mother indicated. 'Your handbag?' he queried.

She nodded. 'That's it. Thank you, *mon chéri*.'

He fetched it from the bedside table, and she searched in its depths, drew out a manila envelope, then patted the bed for Patrick to sit beside her. She drew from the envelope several small, creased black and white photographs, the edges of the stiff paper crinkle-cut in the fashion of the 1940s. She handed the first one to him.

'Your grandfather, Patrice Broyard.'

He looked at the image of a reasonably handsome man in his late twenties, wearing wide flannel trousers and an open-necked white shirt with rolled-up sleeves, smiling politely at the camera. Patrick took the second photograph, and smiled. 'This is the one I used to have. Remember how I used to love old-fashioned adventure stories? Biggles and

265

Sherlock Holmes and Rider Haggard? To me, the heroes always looked like this. I used to badger Josette to tell me more about him, but it just made her cross.'

'I found these in a drawer of her desk. She never really liked me looking at them,' explained Agnès. 'You must sell the house now she's gone.'

'Do you miss her, Maman?'

Agnès looked up and out of the window for a moment at the new and disorienting view. 'I wish I'd had more people in my life,' she answered, studying the drifting clouds. 'A bigger family when I was growing up. Maybe, if I'd been less alone, I'd have been stronger. A better mother.'

'Hush, Maman. Don't talk like that. It's bad luck to be sad in a new house!'

'But it's true.' She looked at him as if surprised that he should discourage her thoughts. 'I should never have left you so often with Josette. She was too harsh.'

Patrick was surprised: Agnès had never spoken of her mother so plainly before. 'I always felt I disappointed her,' he started cautiously. 'To begin with, when you left and I'd cry – like any child would,' he added hastily, 'she'd tell me I was a coward.'

'She had no way of tolerating weakness. She'd shake me when I was little, tell me never to be afraid of anything.' Agnès smiled in self-derision. 'But I grew up afraid of everything.'

Patrick looked down at the photographs in his hand. 'I tried so hard to be brave, like him. But I never matched up, wasn't ever good enough.' He touched his mother's arm. 'I wish I'd known you were grieving for the baby you lost. Maybe, instead of thinking it was my fault you were sad, I could've helped you.'

Agnès laughed sadly. 'I was too afraid of upsetting you. Josette said I mustn't let you see my grief.'

She shuffled through the remaining photographs, passing them to him one by one. They were all of Patrice Broyard, either alone or with Josette, a young couple standing awkwardly in their best clothes. The last one, the largest, had been taken on their wedding day, and showed Josette glowing with optimism and pride.

'Such a shame,' observed Patrick, handing them back. 'You could've done with a dad.' Instantly, he was pierced by his own failure as a father.

Agnès seemed to sense his shame. 'I'm glad I can be near you now. Be of help at last. Not that I'm much use at anything.' Her right hand fluttered to her earrings then down to her shirt buttons.

'Of course you are!' he told her brightly, trying to keep on breathing. 'Let's go back down. I'll get the TV and stuff wired up for you.'

'I shouldn't have been so afraid to have another child,' she went on, ignoring his move towards the door. 'You and Belinda, you mustn't be afraid.'

He gripped the door handle behind him.

'You mustn't shut yourself off from life like Josette,' she said with sudden, wild determination. 'Like I did.'

'Of course I won't.'

'Promise me, Patrice?'

'I promise,' he answered automatically. He glanced at his watch. 'Come on. I bet Dad's ready for a drink.'

After the empty pantechnicon had lumbered away, they ate Belinda's soup leaning against the kitchen counters. Rinsing out his mug at the sink, Patrick announced that he must be heading home.

'I'll give you a lift,' offered Geoffrey.

'No, you're tired. You've done enough today.'

'Order a cab, then. I'm sure we can find a number.'

'Honestly, Dad, I'm fine, thanks.'

'It'll be dark any moment.'

'I'd like to stretch my legs. Really.' Meeting his gaze, Patrick wondered if his father was being deliberately obtuse.

'Do what the hell you like,' declared Geoffrey.

'Anything you want me to do before I go? Shall I help you lock up first?' Patrick said, following the direction of Geoffrey's anxious glance.

'Thanks,' Geoffrey accepted curtly.

They went around the house together, Patrick reassuring his father that all the doors and windows were secure. Reaching to rattle the arm of a window catch, Geoffrey spoke without looking round. 'It's not exactly where we thought we'd end up, but it'll do.' He cleared his throat; his hand shook slightly and he withdrew it into a trouser pocket. 'I always tried my best, you know,' he told his reflection in the pane of glass before him.

'I know, Dad,' Patrick acknowledged quietly. He wanted to say more, to thank him perhaps, or tell him everything would be okay, but felt too depleted to come out with something he didn't believe.

Patrick welcomed the lengthy walk back to the station. As the evening darkened and the autumnal dampness chilled his face, he lengthened his stride, releasing the tension between his shoulder blades. He emerged wearily from the cumbersome train journey back to Brighton into heavy rain blowing in off the sea, and prayed that Belinda would no longer be awake by the time he reached home.

In the morning when Patrick came into the kitchen Belinda gleamed up at him with what he quickly saw was a precipitous excitement. She reminded him of how Daniel used to be when he was over-tired.

'I've had an idea!'

'Oh?' he said moving past her in search of coffee.

'Let's be like your parents. I thought of it yesterday, while you were over there.'

What?'

'We can move house. Make a fresh start.'

Patrick reached for the loaf and cut slices of bread with extra care to give himself time to respond. 'Do you think it would make such a difference?' he asked. 'Would a new house really change very much for us?'

'We can use the money from your grandmother's house.'

'I'm not sure how easily it'll sell,' he prevaricated. 'We'd have to wait and see what we get for it.'

'We can always rent first. Better anyway to be cash buyers.'

'You've got it all worked out!'

'Yes! I've been talking to Grace about it. She thinks it would be good. Said I should go see an estate agent right away. At least find out what this place is worth.'

'Okay.' Patrick slowly unscrewed the lid of the marmalade jar. An insanely simple solution had taken sudden root in his mind. Recognising its treacherous perfection, he just as quickly suppressed it, clinging instead to the vague notion that selling a house was a long-drawn-out process that could be halted at any stage. Leave well alone, he instructed himself. Don't open the door to crazy ideas. Feeling as if he were moving through a thick fog, he reached for the half-full cafetière. 'More coffee?' he offered. 'I can make fresh.'

'No, thanks,' she answered impatiently. 'Well, what do you think?'

He poured a cup for himself and sat down, unable now to avoid her scrutiny. 'I don't know,' he said. 'It's all a bit unexpected. Let me get used to the idea.'

He made himself smile. A fresh start promised only failure. Better not to puncture Belinda's euphoria today; better to let her carry on and maybe realise for herself further down the line that they were fine as they were, just about managing to cling on to what they had. But a second look at her face confirmed his first impression that her excitement was febrile and short-lived, that it hid some more strident despair. 'Has something happened?' he asked.

She hung her head, pushing a crumb around her plate with one finger. 'One of the kids at school yesterday had a birthday. Brought me a slice of cake.'

He knew immediately what she had been thinking. Daniel's birthday was not until the beginning of February, but this was the house to which they had brought him after his birth, in which they had celebrated his first birthday, first words, first steps. Belinda was right: she could not wait here for constant reminders of loss. Of what he, Patrick, had taken from her. He acknowledged that, in her own way, Belinda wanted to escape as much as he did. Knew deep down that Grace was right: Belinda would be better off without him.

'I'll do whatever you want,' he said.

'No.' She looked at him straight, as if she had anticipated this answer. 'You have to want it, too. It's not just for me. You can't live through me.'

Patrick began to walk further and further. Whatever the weather, it was the only way he knew not to succumb to the panic that robbed him of breath and filled his head with both dread and liberation. He still took the remedies he had prepared for himself when he first went back to his office, even though they did not help. He knew that his failure to look clearly into himself was to blame for the lack of a beneficial response, and that he ought to consult a colleague, but now that his sessions with Amanda Skipton were concluded he was unable to face speaking to anyone else.

In his worst moments, on days when he knew that Belinda pictured him busy at work, he strode along the South Downs Way trying to walk away from himself. He sought to conjure up an image of himself that he could like, to recover some instant in time when he could regard himself as innocent, as possessing some modicum of goodness, but none came. Instead, the alluring idea sang to him over and over again, a siren call that filled his real self, his better self, with guilt and self-loathing. He sensed a monstrous *Doppelgänger* in pursuit at his heels, whispering that he deserved to suffer, deserved to be alone. Its eyes bore the same triumphant expression as Josette's when she had watched him stand, numb with homesickness, as his mother's taxi drove away; the same hatred as Grace, hissing at him across the coffee mugs. As he walked, trying to outpace the demon, he was lured by the temptation to let it catch him up, and to surrender to it.

Once the For Sale sign had gone up outside the house, and buyers began to come and look around, Patrick used their invasion as a further excuse to walk. Mostly he intended merely to go as far as the seafront and back, but once in a while he found himself going in the opposite direction, on the outskirts of the town, heading along public footpaths towards the Devil's Dyke. When the real-isation of where he was broke through his body's narcotic rhythm, it was an effort to stop and, with a yearning look at the path ahead, turn for home.

There he did his best to shelter Belinda's brittle enthu-siasm for a move. Half an hour of looking over her shoulder while she displayed for him computer images of houses for sale, of places where they might live, was enough to leave him stupefied from the effort of appearing to show an optimistic interest. He apologised that the French lawyer was being so slow to process the paperwork necessary to sell Josette's house, and pointed out the advantages of renting somewhere for six months so they could take their time finding what would suit them best. With cash in the bank, he urged her, they would be in a good position as buyers, and renting would give them the opportunity to see whether they liked living in the area she favoured. Belinda conceded, yet, when they received a good offer on their house, she hesitated, suddenly afraid of her own desire for change. With a show of cheerful resolve, he persuaded her to accept the offer, assuring her that he would take care of everything.

Belinda was grateful to leave all the necessary legalities to him, and his vigour in dealing with the banks, lawyers, utility companies and all the rest seemed to persuade her that he was re-discovering some confidence in life itself. Seeing how this pleased her, he reacted positively when she suggested they invite one or two friends for supper, readily agreed when she asked him to accompany her to a party for her elder sister in London, and willingly talked about where they might go on holiday in the spring. In bed one night after they had been out to the cinema together, she began to kiss and stroke him seductively. It had been some time since she had attempted love-making, and he had been thankful that, after repeated annulments, she seemed to have grown tolerant of his evasive tenderness. But now, unable to respond as she wished, he lifted her hand away, kissed her wrist and murmured, 'Once we've left here, I promise, it'll all be different.'

They agreed to rent a small flat in Hove for six months. They would be cramped for space, but it had a hypnotic view of the sea and, they decided, they might as well enjoy on a temporary basis something they could not afford as a permanent home; as it was, Patrick explained, the lease had to be in Belinda's sole name because he could not demonstrate sufficient self-employed income for the current year. He told her not to worry; as soon as they had completed on the sale of their house, there would be plenty of capital in the bank to tide them over potential difficulties.

One task remained about which they did not speak: dismantling Daniel's room and packing up his things before the move. When almost everything else had been done, and they were boxing up the contents of the airing cupboard on the landing, they found themselves standing together in the open doorway to his bedroom.

'Shall we leave it 'til the very last?' suggested Belinda. 'I don't want to see it empty and bare any longer than I have to.'

Patrick nodded, and closed the door.

By tacit agreement, after a half-eaten lunch the day before the move, they made their way unwillingly upstairs. Patrick started with the newer toys and unread books, talismans that possessed the least connection with Daniel, while Belinda opened a drawer and began to take out his clothes, their smallness already alien and incomprehensible. Folding a favourite pair of pyjama leggings, the baggy cotton still holding the ghostly imprint of his knees, she started to cry. Patrick crawled across the space between them and took her in his arms. Holding tight to one another, they wept, barricading themselves inside a shelter of whatever items they could drag near to them.

After it was done, and the sealed boxes marked with Daniel's name, they drank wine, exhausted, in the glare of a bare bulb, the kitchen light shade already packed away. Though neither spoke, they shared the bond of having accomplished their task. Patrick was impatient now for the morning. Belinda's instinct to give up the house had been right, and he couldn't wait for these final hours to pass. They switched off the lights and went up to bed. Their room, emptied of half its contents, was echoey and strange, already half-belonging to other people. Belinda lay on her side facing the window. Tucking himself around her from behind, Patrick lay watching for the last time the watermarks on the blind illuminated by the street lamps outside. He felt the full impact of their immediate predicament – rootless, exiled, adrift – and experienced a sense of respite, a prospect of safety. Belinda's body lay heavy and still against him, and he felt the twitch of an erection against her warm skin. 'You do know I love you?' he murmured into her shoulder. 'No matter what?' She stirred slightly in response, and he kissed her shoulder. He began to stroke her arm and then caressed her breasts, but she failed to reach for him in return, nor did she twist around to face him.

In the middle of the following morning, Belinda called the removal men into the kitchen for mugs of tea. Patrick dodged past them in the hallway and went outside, his feet crunching on the gravel. Rain drizzled in a fine mist, muting the usual background sounds of traffic and calling seagulls. He glanced into the van where their furniture and other belongings, draped in grey felt blankets, were securely piled in unlikely juxtapositions. Their solicitor had already called to confirm that the buyers' funds had been received and forwarded to their joint bank account. Everything was in order. He went back into the hall and stood listening for a moment to the men's banter in the kitchen, before picking up the rucksack into which he had placed various documents and other chosen items for safe-keeping. Plucking his waterproof jacket from its hook, he went out the door and walked away.

PART FOUR

London 2011

I

'You'll never guess who I ran into today,' said Leonie, as she placed two glasses of wine on the table and sat down beside Stella. They were in the paved garden of a pleasant pub around the corner from Stella's north London flat, where Leonie had also been living for the past few months.

'Who?' Stella asked. 'Cheers.'

Out of ancient habit, Leonie clinked her glass against Stella's. 'Greg.'

'Gosh, I haven't thought about him in a long while! How is he?'

'Rather spruce. Lost a bit of weight. Looked well.'

Stella gave a teasing look. 'And?'

'And he was holding hands with a sweet-looking woman wearing an engagement ring.'

'How did that feel?'

'Fine, actually. I'm glad for him. And it helps in a way, seeing him back to his old self, the Greg I once cared about.'

'No regrets?'

'No. Pang of envy, maybe, that he's found someone, but no regrets. We weren't right for each other.'

Stella raised her eyebrows but, when Leonie failed to notice, apprehensively watched her stare into her wine. 'How would you feel if you bumped into Patrice like that?' she asked carefully.

Leonie's surprise was not at hearing Patrice's name, but that her friend had so accurately read her mind. She laughed a little shakily. 'Okay, I hope.'

'Really?'

'I think so.' She glanced sideways at Stella. 'Why?'

Stella gave in reluctantly to Leonie's shrewd look. 'I suspect he may be in London.'

Leonie flushed, and then went icy cold.

Stella leant over and rubbed her arm. 'I'm sorry, Lennie. I couldn't decide whether to tell you or not.'

'You've seen him?' Leonie could already sense the monsters mustering around her head, forcing her to inhale the stale air whipped up by the beat of their nasty little wings, driving out all the sweet, sensible progress she had made these past months.

'No,' said Stella. 'It was someone at work. Courtney. She goes to some holistic spa in Islington, for Reiki or Shiatsu or whatever, and was praising the homeopath there.'

'Doesn't sound like the kind of place Patrice would work,' said Leonie breathlessly.

'Calls himself Patrick now. Patrick Hinde. Courtney said he was tall, good-looking. Can only be him, don't you think?'

Leonie nodded, misery fighting excitement as her heart juddered sickeningly against her ribcage.

'I wouldn't have said anything, except that Islington's so close. What if you did literally run into him?'

'Oh, God, why can't it all just go away!'

'I'll drink to that. Here, knock it back.' Stella pushed Leonie's wine glass closer, raising her own: 'Here's to kind, honest men.'

Leonie drank obediently, gazing distractedly around the cluster of tables as if some unexpected miracle might burst forth from among the early-evening drinkers to clear the static in her head.

'What else did Courtney say?'

'Nothing. Only how helpful he was. But then she's always raving about some new therapist she's discovered.'

'What's the place called?'

'Don't know – and I'm not going to ask.' Stella spoke sternly, though she regarded her friend with concern. 'Please tell me you won't go tracking him down?'

Leonie forced a smile and shook her head.

'You've been so much better lately,' Stella went on. 'It won't do you any good to see him again.'

'No. But somehow I imagined he'd be lost somewhere in France. I never pictured him here in London. Not for a moment. And now it's so strange, knowing he's a mile or so down the road.'

'Don't, Lennie. Let it go.'

'I will. Promise. I need time to get used to the idea, that's all. Another drink?'

'Good idea. My turn.'

While Stella went inside to the bar, Leonie tried to shake off the dread that gripped her. Her worst fear, until she had read the brief report of the inquest into Daniel Hinde's death, had always been that she had driven Patrice away. But the discovery of his tragic secret had enabled her to convince herself that he had fled not from her but from his own demons, allowed her to believe that she had not been entirely deceived in his integrity. Leaving no clue as to his whereabouts, he had gradually almost ceased to be real flesh and blood.

But, from now on, every time she went through a shop doorway, he might have slipped by and out of sight only a second before. In a darkened cinema, he might be seated two rows behind. Every street corner she turned, every Tube or bus she travelled on, she could be breathing his air, and he hers, without ever being aware. But there also lurked a more intolerable notion: what if he had seen her, and chose to let her walk on by with no greeting?

Stella came back with replenished glasses. 'Okay?' she asked, studying Leonie's expression.

'Fine.' Leonie smiled confidently, while her heart sank at the utter certainty of how incapable she was of out-pacing this unbearable jangling alertness to his proximity. Whether he ever thought of her or not, she was his captive.

*

It took Leonie only three calls to discover at which holistic centre in Islington Patrick Hinde was the resident homeopath. Accepting there was no other escape from Stella's information, she asked the receptionist for the times of his last appointments, and was also told which evenings the Angel Sanctuary stayed open late.

A few days later, having calculated when he was likely to leave at the end of the day, she hovered on the pavement opposite. It was almost midsummer and the streets were busy with people making the most of the light evenings. Exactly as she had planned, she watched him come out, an achingly recognisable figure in his usual black jeans and jacket. He appeared unchanged, seemed relaxed and at ease, and she drank in his familiar stride as he loped off towards Highbury. Had she expected him to appear harried, guilt snapping at his heels? She couldn't work out what she felt, what she ought to feel. Anger, desire, fury, hatred and pity were all mixed up in the tightness in her chest. What she wanted was for him to turn instinctively, notice her, then cross the road to where she was waiting, eager to say the welcoming words that would make her whole again. She stood immobile, unable to gather her wits enough to negotiate the traffic and catch up with him. He walked on, and was lost to sight behind a wall of buses and cars.

On Friday evening, two days later, she watched again for him to appear; it was fear of her own obsession, of turning into a stalker, that propelled her swiftly across the road the instant she spotted him. She hurried up behind him.

'Patrice.'

He turned, ready with a pleasant, meaningless expression; clearly he had not recognised her voice, and, to her distress, it took him a moment or so to place her.

'Leonie!' He looked beyond her, over her shoulder, up and down the street, as if she might not have come alone. 'What are you doing here?'

Afraid of being tongue-tied, she had rehearsed precisely what to say, deciding after much reflection that she could not bear the dishonesty of pretending to him that the encounter was accidental.

'I'm a Londoner, remember! And I heard this was where you were working now.'

'What a coincidence. Are you over on holiday?' he asked with devastating politeness.

'I left France. For the time being, anyway.' She lifted her chin. 'And you?'

He flushed, his lips drew tight and he stared down at the pavement.

'How about a drink?' It was a suggestion she had also carefully prepared. 'There's a bar up the road.'

For an awful moment she feared he was going to refuse, but, flicking his gaze up and down the street once more, he agreed. 'I'd prefer a coffee, though, if you don't mind?'

'Of course not. Whatever.'

In miserable silence Leonie walked beside him a hundred yards or so along to an Italian café, where they sat inside at a small table beside the window. A girl sallied out from behind the counter to take their order. Leonie took the opportunity to glance covertly at Patrice – Patrick, she corrected herself. This was her first chance to observe him since learning what had happened to his son, and it was as though the face she had loved and memorised so minutely was now overlaid by the shadow of his dreadful past. Her anger melted into compassion. Yet she also realised how the shadow had always been there – in the guardedness, the hesitation, the soreness she'd glimpsed in the set of his features – but he had always directed her away from any intimation that might have deciphered it, sent her off chasing after imaginary hares instead. Had that misdirection been instinctive, she wondered? Or calculating.

As soon as the waitress was busy with the espresso machine behind the counter, Patrick took a deep breath. 'I expect you're here to ask why I haven't been in touch.' He regarded her warily.

'I thought you might want to know how I am.' Involuntarily, Leonie glanced down at her flat stomach. When she looked back at him, he seemed confused. 'I'm no longer pregnant,' she said. 'That's what I came to tell you.'

Patrick exhaled. 'But you were?' he blurted out.

'Yes.' Her guts churned: had he imagined her a liar?

'I thought maybe you'd had it already.'

'I lost it. Otherwise I'd have been as big as a house by now. But I didn't want you thinking you were about to be a father when that's no longer going to happen.'

'You decided not to go ahead?' he asked with a mixture of concern and suspicion.

'No. I had a miscarriage.' Saying the word still made her want to cry. 'Back in January. Early miscarriages are quite common, apparently.'

He nodded, staring inward as if untying some internal knot. 'I'm glad you didn't end it,' he said. Leonie couldn't tell whether his relief was for her or himself.

She regarded him as steadily as she could manage. 'I really wanted this baby. Losing it was horrible. It hurt. And I was on my own.'

Patrick kept nodding until reprieved by the waitress bringing their coffees. 'I'm sorry,' he said, once she had gone. 'But you're all right now?'

'Yes, I suppose so. Gaby's been wonderful. And Stella.'

'Good. I'm glad. You've a lot of strength. I always admired you for that.'

Leonie was stung by how easily he dismissed her empty sadness, how readily he imagined that she lacked the imagination to suffer. He must have seen her feelings in her expression, for he reached out to take her hand where it rested on the table beside her foaming cappuccino.

'I never lied,' he said. 'You must believe that.'

'But you stayed silent,' she answered. 'About a lot of things.'

'You must think very little of me,' he responded, stroking her fingers with his thumb. And I don't expect you to forgive me. But I never lied to you.' His skin was warm and dry. 'I do care about you, you know.'

Confused and smarting from disappointment, Leonie withdrew her hand.

'I had to go when I did,' he went on insistently. 'You were better off without me. I never meant to hurt you, I just collapsed. I don't know why.'

'I do,' she said softly, but he appeared not to hear, not to conceive of a world where his secret might be known.

'And see,' he went on, 'here you are, safe and sound!' Leonie wondered whether his expression was an appeal for rescue. 'You are fine now, aren't you?' He reached for her hand again, and she let him take it.

'I guess so, more or less – but I wasn't.' She raised her chin again defiantly, determined not to be his fool. 'That's why I left France. Stella took me in. I've had one or two small commissions from translation agencies, but finding a proper job has been really hard.' She could see he wasn't listening, but she wanted him to fully appreciate her predicament. 'To pay the rent, I work part-time for a posh estate agency that needs my language skills.'

'Good. I mean it's good you've found something.' He let go of her hand to glance at his watch. 'Look, I'm sorry, but I have to be somewhere. Give me your number, and we'll meet up properly. Go out somewhere and have some fun.'

He smiled at her kindly. When she did not respond, he seemed to scan her face as if searching for resolution; or maybe, she thought with a certain bitterness, for permission to disappear and leave all this behind. 'I appreciate your coming to find me,' he said. 'I'm glad you told me what happened, and I'm so sorry you've had a hard time.

It's good that you're okay.' He pushed his chair back and stood up.

Prepared to be stubborn, she remained seated.

'I turned out not to be who you thought I was. I wouldn't blame you for hating me, but I swear I never lied to you,' Patrick repeated, and Leonie wondered whether this frail self-defence were all that truly mattered to him, whether he cared for her at all. 'Do you need anything?' he asked suddenly, sitting down again. 'Money, or something? I'll help in any way I can, if that's what it is.'

But for the transparency of his desire to make practical amends, she would have been insulted. 'No,' she said, getting to her feet in turn. 'I'm fine.'

'Look, I really do have to go. It's a charity thing I'm involved in. But give me your number, and I'll call.' He took a pen and notebook from his jacket pocket. 'Then we can talk properly.'

Leonie obediently dictated her number, then lingered beside him at the counter as he paid for their coffees. She had a sudden longing to lean in against his shoulder, for everything to be simple.

Out on the pavement, the sky had turned a dark, rich blue, and the crowded street sparkled with lights from passing cars and buses and from the local shops and restaurants. As Patrick bent to kiss her, she offered her cheek, but instead he touched his lips to hers. 'Bye for now,' he said. She was still his captive.

*

Patrick had walked half-way home to Stoke Newington before his head cleared enough for him to consider Leonie's unheralded appearance. He realised with some surprise that he had barely entertained a single thought of her during the past months. He was embarrassed that she had tracked him down to the Angel Sanctuary. His role there was belittling, and he disliked being identified with such a frivolous place, but with very few contacts in London he had needed the work and a colleague had tipped him off about it. He intended to use it to build up a clientèle before opening a practice of his own again.

He recognised how shallow it was to be vain about his professional image, but sometimes his work seemed like the only honourable achievement in his life; he needed it in order to look himself squarely in the eye, and often worried what would happen to him if, as he increasingly feared, his daily interactions with patients were to become sterile and meaningless.

He didn't want Leonie to think of him like that, or to imagine that their time together had been inconsequential. Last year in France he had savoured the image of himself reflected in her eyes; it had given him an essential shot of courage, something he'd desperately needed to dare to live again.

Too late to cut through the park, he skirted its perimeter, reflecting on the muddle in which he had left Riberac. He knew he was solely to blame. He should have handled things differently. But he couldn't have stayed to watch Leonie's pregnancy progress without telling her about Daniel, and it had been impossible to reveal the truth. So he had taken the only route left open to him. Several times, he had begun a second letter to her, but had always given up, never sure what to say. It had been a shock to discover her waiting for him tonight, but he realised he was glad to have been found. While he had expected a blaze of recrimination right there in the street, it was clear she had recovered from the shameful way in which he had fled. It was a relief to see that she had been so resilient, that he had evidently caused no lasting harm.

He was late, and Rob was waiting outside his flat, lounging against the gatepost in the soft dusk light, intent on the music on his iPod. His precious bike was chained up nearby. The boy – Rob was twenty, but Patrick couldn't help thinking of him as a boy – removed the earpiece when finally he noticed Patrick, raised a languid hand in greeting, and followed him obligingly indoors.

'Sorry to keep you waiting,' said Patrick, turning on the lights.

'No problem. I was late anyway.' Rob smiled his winning smile, making Patrick laugh.

'That's all right then.'

'Mum says hi.'

Patrick nodded.

'Did you check out those steel frames?'

'Yes. Impressive, but I'm not spending that much on a bike.'

Rob grinned. 'You'll come round to it.' He opened the fridge in the room that served Patrick as both kitchen and living room and surveyed the contents.

'Hungry?' asked Patrick, not minding the way the boy assumed he could make himself at home. 'There's some soup I made yesterday.'

'Great, thanks. If you're sure you've got enough.'

As Patrick removed the pan from the fridge and set it to heat up on the stove, Rob went unthinkingly to the cutlery drawer and laid the table. Patrick reflected again on how well Vicki had brought up her son; despite his ragged art-student clothes and pierced eyebrow, she had taught him wonderfully old-fashioned good manners. When the soup was hot, Patrick poured it into two bowls and put them on the table along with bread and cheese. Saying 'Cheers', Rob pulled closer the morning's discarded newspaper, picked up his spoon and started to devour the food while simultaneously flicking through the pages. As Patrick ate his own meal, enjoying the easy silence, he observed the boy's appetite, the unself-conscious way he laughed or frowned to himself at items in the paper.

Rob's vitality led Patrick's thoughts back to Leonie. When they first met she, too, had this same engaging robustness; she had breathed new life into him after those terrible years of stagnation. He had tried to resist her, battling his sense of unworthiness, his fear of self-exposure, but the moment he had sensed her desire for him, he was overcome. He had trusted her, and his lonely body had chosen life. He looked back on his first years in France with real dread, amazed that he had ever survived such isolation, and certain he never could again.

He admitted to himself that he was still dangerously attracted to Leonie, perhaps even more so now that her youthful glow had been tempered by an appealing air of fragility. While it eased things to see her so well, it was completely out of the question to allow himself to become involved with her again, though eventually he probably ought to give her a call. She might well choose to tell him to get lost, but he owed her at least the opportunity to talk things over further, if she so wished.

Rob folded the newspaper and laid down his spoon. 'So are you really going to ride fifty-four miles on that old bone-shaker?'

Patrick was amused. 'I've managed okay in the past.'

'But if you got a steel frame, it'd be worth getting better gears. The technology's beautiful. You'd love it!'

'Thanks, but it's not a race. I just have to cover the miles. How's your recruitment coming along?'

'Lots of people at uni have signed up to ride, but it's no good if they don't get enough sponsors. How are you doing?'

'Only one or two, so far, I'm afraid. I'm not gregarious enough. But one client is down for fifty pence per mile.'

'Not bad. Most of mine are, like, five pence.' Rob got to his feet. 'Give me your application form, then, and I'll add it to the bunch.'

'Thanks.'

While Patrick searched out the form, Rob cleared the table, stacking the dishes by the sink. 'Want me to wash up before I go?'

'No, leave it. It's fine.'

Rob hesitated, as if unwilling to forgo the ritual. 'Well, thanks for feeding me. See ya.' The boy let himself out. He was like a cat, Patrick decided – amused – as the front door banged shut behind him; a creature that reserved the right to be nurtured whenever and by whomever took his fancy. Such compartmentalised promiscuity seemed to Patrick to contain a restful quality which he coveted for himself.

Leonie crept into the flat like a thief. She was not ready to confess to Stella how she had bearded Patrick, yet felt bad about her clear intention to lie. She was no good at deception and was sure to be caught out. She hugged to herself the bigger secret of his kiss. She had worked hard, with Stella's help, to put behind her all those sleepless nights during which she had flayed herself for being blind, clumsy, stupid, unlovable, when she yearned for confirmation that he had loved her. The touch of his lips tonight had transformed the past, assuaging all the horrible stored pain and filling her with elation that she had not been to blame for her abandonment. She was sure Stella would understand how wonderful it felt to be released from months of self-hatred but, for now, she was desperate to guard the sensation, to keep it private and pristine.

'You seem different,' observed Stella when Leonie appeared for breakfast the next morning. Stella, in her dressing grown, was reading the Saturday papers, which an admiring downstairs neighbour insisted on delivering.

Leonie had showered and thrown on sweatpants and an old tee-shirt. She placed her mobile on the counter as discreetly as possible, before opening the fridge. 'I'll go out for more milk later,' she offered. But Stella had clocked both the phone and Leonie's self-conscious manner. With a slight raise of an eyebrow, she returned to the article she was reading. Leonie, contrarily, was disappointed not to be pursued for information. As she rinsed out the teapot and waited for the kettle to boil, she tried phrasing a confession, but each attempt confirmed that Stella could only condemn her action. Of course seeing Patrick again had been a huge mistake, but it had been inconceivable not to.

She made toast then sat down with her mug of tea. Stella appeared to be reading, but there was something ominous in the hunch of her shoulders.

'Do you think,' Leonie began in a deliberately vague tone, 'that if people around Patrick had known about what happened to his son, he would have behaved differently?'

Stella's head jerked up. 'He's not Patrice any more, then?'

'You said he was Patrick now,' stumbled Leonie.

'You've seen him, haven't you?'

'I wanted to tell him I'm not having his child,' she defended herself. 'It seemed only fair.'

'Fair?' Stella made a huge effort. 'Okay, so how did he react?'

'He was relieved I was okay.' Leonie told herself it was mere pride that made her withhold the full story of how lightly he had dismissed her ordeal, but she didn't dare meet Stella's eye.

'And that's it? You won't see him again?'

'I doubt it.'

'I won't have him here. I'm not going to watch it happen all over again.'

'It won't.'

Stella's chair shrieked against the tiled floor as she stood up. 'Then why are you waiting for him to ring?' She seized Leonie's phone from the counter and slapped it down in front of her. 'Why even consider seeing him a second time?'

'It's not that easy.'

'Jesus, Lennie, you were suicidal after you lost the baby. And even before that, at Christmas, too, when he'd buggered off. Face facts! This is the man who walked out on you without a word, who stuck his baby in a car and left him to die.'

'Not deliberately!'

'Oh no? How can you possibly be sure?'

'Because I know him!'

'Oh, for God's sake!'

Leonie clenched the hot mug between her hands, refusing to raise her head. Stella stood her ground, frowning down at her. 'I'm sorry, Lennie,' she said at last, a little more calmly. 'But I can't go through it all again. I realise it's not about me, shouldn't be about me, but the fact is that I sacrificed all this year's holiday time because that selfish shit wasn't there for you. You're truly welcome to all I've got to give, you know that, but I don't want Patrice, or Patrick, or whatever he calls himself, back in my life. He's bad news and always will be.'

'I'm sorry. I'm so sorry. I do appreciate how much you've done for me.' Leonie made mewling sounds in an effort not to cry.

Stella took pity, and pulled up a chair beside her, rubbing her shoulder. 'It's okay. Really. I shouldn't have spoken like that. I'm just so angry at him.'

Leonie nodded miserably. Stella fetched some kitchen roll for her to blow her nose. 'We've been over this a million times. You have to have the courage to face up to the fact that you made a mistake with Patrice,' said Stella. 'It doesn't matter, we all do it. But he's never going to be the man you hoped he was. You have to move on. Change. Don't get hooked back in, or you won't survive.'

Leonie nodded again, trying to breathe normally. 'Do you seriously believe he was to blame for his son's death?'

'What did he say?'

Leonie busied herself with the kitchen roll.

'You didn't ask him about it?' Stella was incredulous.

Leonie defended herself. 'We were in a small café. It was hardly the right time or place.'

Stella sat back, exasperated. 'Answer me this: if you'd been told before you met him what he did to his son, would you ever have dreamt of getting involved with him?'

Leonie shrugged. 'I'd've felt sorry for him.'

'Honestly?'

'It was an accident.'

'An accident happens in a split second. He left that poor kid for hours. The whole day, Lennie. How does any sane, normal parent forget his child for an entire *day*? What kind of forgetting is that?'

'If it was deliberate neglect, he'd have gone to prison.'

'How do you know he didn't?'

'The inquest report in the paper said it was a tragic accident.'

'It's still macabre. There has to be more to it,' insisted Stella.

'Like what?'

'I don't know. Resentment. Some passive-aggressive controlling thing against his wife. Catastrophic thinking. Like those fathers who kill the whole family rather than lose custody.'

'Patrice isn't like that.'

'No? How can you be sure? I'd like to hear his wife's side of it!'

Leonie had no response.

'Look what he did to you! His disappearing act was pretty passive-aggressive. Certainly wasn't normal.'

'But it did make sense once I found out what had happened, how he'd feel about being a father again. Imagine what it must have been like for him, when I told him I was pregnant!'

297

'Frankly I was rather too busy witnessing what the consequences were for you! And asking myself, if he hadn't upset
you so much, whether maybe you wouldn't have lost the
baby. I'm sorry, Lennie, but his selfishness runs pretty damn
deep.' Stella rose to her feet and began shakily clearing
the table. She dumped the plates and mugs in the sink
and rested her hands on its rim, bowing her head. 'Why
defend him?'

'Because I have some sympathy with what it's like to
lose a child,' said Leonie quietly. 'So I do see why he couldn't
bear to stay, couldn't face having another child.'

Stella turned back to her, clear-eyed. 'Fine,' she said. 'If
that was the reason he left, then face up to telling you
the truth. Don't just vanish.'

Certain that Stella had only her best interests at heart,
Leonie tried to account to herself for why she defended
Patrick. She had sensed from the very beginning how
wounded he was, how his reactions were those of someone
badly damaged, but she hadn't cared. Had that been stupid?
Or was that what love was about? She needed to know,
once they had spoken and the tragedy of his son's death
no longer lay between them, whether their connection
was as strong as she hoped. She still believed in him, in
his essential goodness and desire to heal. After his kiss,
she would be mad to walk away before she was sure of
what she was discarding. She recalled how well and happy
Greg had looked beside the woman he was about to marry,

how altered from the pasty, resentful man she had left. It *was* possible to be transformed, and much as she loved and trusted Stella she owed herself a chance at that kind of love.

She concealed her silent mobile in loose pockets where she could feel it vibrate. Patrick had not offered her his number, nor mentioned where he lived, but she could always find him again at the Angel Sanctuary. Pushing away the silly fear that he would flee from her a second time, she allowed herself to rehearse the conversation they would have about his son, to anticipate his relief at no longer having to live alone with such guilt and grief. Stella was right: however carelessly she had sprung on him the news of her pregnancy, he should have told her the truth. Or, after his first panic, at least come looking for her again to make sure she was all right.

And yet, while Leonie could hardly blame Stella for condemning him, she was not wholly convinced it *was* cowardly to seek to avoid contaminating others with the unthinkable manner of his son's death. Why should he have burdened her with such knowledge? Yet, equally, why should his need to protect himself from exposure bar him from closeness and intimacy? Would Stella honestly wish to shun him, deny that he deserved a second chance, and expect him to lock himself away from all human contact?

These were questions Leonie had asked herself many times. She possessed remarkably few concrete facts about his former life, and nothing beyond the barest circumstances of his son's death, but, now that she knew the worst and could release him from the past, he would be free to tell her everything.

Her mobile rang the following week while she was showing a wealthy couple from Mauritius around a flat in St John's Wood. She took the phone from her bag. Not recognising the number, her heart leapt at the thought that it might be Patrick. She excused herself and went swiftly out to the hallway to take the call in private, leaving the clients to discuss the size of the bedrooms.

'Hello?'

'Hello, it's me, Patrick. Patrick Hinde.'

Leonie felt a rush of sweetness at his notion that she wouldn't have recognised his name or voice. 'Hello!'

'How are you?'

She laughed. 'I'm fine. How are you?'

'I thought we could meet for a drink. If you'd like to.'

'I think I would, yes.'

'There's a pub on the corner of Primrose Hill, The Queens. See you there tomorrow? At seven?'

'Okay.'

Patrick said goodbye and rang off. Leonie felt the past months recede like a wave from the shore, dragging away with it all the gritty, sore detritus. She returned to her clients, smiling confidently.

The following evening Leonie's mobile rang again while she was getting ready to go out. Debating whether to wear her new summer slippers decorated with silver sequins took her back to how Patrick had had to push her on his bike after she'd decided to wear unsuitably high-heeled sandals. She instantly recognised the voice.

'Hello, sweetie. It's ages since we spoke. How are you?'

'Gaby! I'm very well. And you? And Thierry?'

'Well, not so great. That's why I'm calling. Thierry had some tests, and the doctors think he may need a heart by-pass.'

'Oh no!'

'There's no immediate danger, but that's the way it is.'

'I'm sorry, Gaby. You must be worried.'

'We've been doing a bit of re-assessing our lives,' she admitted. 'Thierry thinks he may retire.'

'That wouldn't be so bad, would it?' asked Leonie. She remembered Thierry's many interests – local history, wine, the peach and apricot trees espaliered against the high stone wall in their garden, over which he fussed about winter frosts and pollination and marauding insects.

'I suppose not. Everyone thinks they're immortal, that's all.'

'Are you okay, Gaby?'

'Fabienne, the girl I took on when you left. She's hope-less.' Gaby paused. Sensing what might be coming, Leonie hesitated to fill the silence. 'I may semi-retire, too,' Gaby went on. 'So Thierry and I are free to go off and do things together. Sweetie, none of my kids are interested in the business, so I'd like to make you a partner. They're all happy with my decision. What do you say?'

Hearing the pleasure Gaby took in making her offer, Leonie swallowed hard. 'Thank you, Gaby. So much. I'm very touched. And I really admire how hard you've worked to build up the agency.'

'So you'll come back?'

'I don't know.' She registered Gaby's involuntary little gasp and winced guiltily. 'Gaby, I'm honoured. It's a wonderful offer, but please may I think about it?'

'Are you still working part-time for that estate agent?' Never one for flannel, Gaby had cut straight to the bone.

Leonie felt terrible. Gaby had been unbelievably kind and generous and understanding: she owed her a proper explanation. 'The truth is, I've just seen Patrice Hinde again.'

'No! Oh, sweetie, no, you mustn't.'

'I know, I know. But I have to—' Leonie sought the right words. 'I have to finish it. So I can pack it away.'

'Stay away from him, Leonie. I beg you. Think of what you told me about his son!'

'I know you're protecting me, Gaby, and I'm terribly grateful.' Leonie struggled with conflicting impulses. 'Give me a day or two, and you'll have your answer.'

There was a long silence before Gaby spoke again. 'Something else you should know about him. Something I learnt a little while ago. I wasn't going to rake things up again, but—'

Leonie could just imagine Gaby pursing her lips with a shake of the head.

'It's about his grandfather,' Gaby went on. 'Madame Broyard's husband.'

'Yes?'

'He had nothing whatsoever to do with the Resistance. He shot himself.'

'Suicide?' Leonie was astonished.

'Yes. When his poor wife was eight months pregnant. Even worse than what his charming grandson did to you.'

'My God!'

'Whether or not you come back to Riberac, you should stay away from that man.'

'But he had no idea about his grandfather! And it was hardly anything to do with him!'

'Bad blood, all the same.'

'Please, Gaby, let me have a few days. I just want to clear stuff up first.'

'Think things over very carefully, sweetie. It's a good business. A good life here. Thierry joins me in sending big *bisous à toi*. We'd all love to have you back.'

'I'll call soon, I promise. And thank you. For everything.'

Gaby rang off. Leonie dropped the phone on the bed and put her hands to her face. It was all too much. And now she was running late and Patrice – Patrick, she corrected herself again – would be waiting.

As she sat on the bus towards Camden, from where she intended to walk along the canal, Leonie attempted to examine the tumult that besieged her feelings. She hated being so ungrateful to Gaby; and she had lied to Stella about what she was doing tonight. And what was she supposed to do with this latest revelation about his grandfather? A suicide more than sixty years ago, how could it possibly affect her? Yet she was certain it did. There had been too many long dark nights when her sanity had rested on the attempt to understand how anyone could be capable of such indifference, how Patrick could have been able to abandon her so completely, yet still persuade himself that he had acted for the best. She was sure the reasons lay in his damaged childhood, and that this suicide, kept secret, was yet another of the toxic adult emotions that had swirled and curdled above his head when he had been a homesick, lonely little boy.

And there still remained Patrick's own secret to take into account: his son's death, and the way in which he had left his marriage and, according to him, walked to Riberac; his horrific nightmares; his refusal to travel in a car; his reaction to Gaby's grandson clinging onto him that night at dinner; his panic at the prospect of fathering a second child. All things he must still assume she could not possibly link together. She hoped he would trust her to understand.

The bus reached its stop and Leonie pushed her way off. She went down the steps to the tow-path, awakening to the fact that it was a beautiful June evening and the canal side was thronged with kids out to enjoy themselves.

Threading her way between the various tribes sprawled out along the path, she felt charged with special power and energy. This grappling with damage and memory, with secrets and despair, was all about what makes people who they are. It was a privilege to see beyond the veil of everyday superficiality and be vouchsafed a glimpse of the real stuff of life. She was determined to respond with every scrap of courage and wisdom she possessed.

Patrick was waiting for her on the wide pavement outside the pub at Primrose Hill, his stance rigid with self-consciousness. Leonie was immediately taken back to how he had leapt up from the churchyard bench the evening of their first date. If only she had known and understood then what she did now, had herself possessed more self-confidence. He gripped her arm and kissed her cheek, and she noticed a rucksack in his other hand. He threw a glance of distaste towards the bellowing drinkers occupying the pub and displayed the rucksack. 'We don't have to stay here,' he said. 'I brought a picnic. And a bottle of wine.'

The flimsy barricades she imagined she had constructed so carefully around her heart melted, and she walked in happiness beside him up the grassy slope of Primrose Hill, letting him choose a spot beside some scrubby thorn trees where they sat down, the panoramic view of London spread out below them. She stretched out her legs, wriggling her toes so she could admire her glittery new slippers. She caught him looking at them askance and curled her feet away out of his line of sight.

'They're a bit silly,' she apologised. 'An impulse buy.' But instantly she admonished herself: there was no point being here if she let herself feel inauthentic because of what he might like or dislike.

'Impractical, but very stylish,' he teased. 'They suit you. Though I hope it wasn't a trek for you to get here,' he went on. 'Where do you live?'

'Caledonian Road,' she told him. 'Up near Holloway. So not too bad. Anyway, it's worth it. This is lovely, isn't it?'

'Yes.'

She noticed that he didn't offer in turn to inform her where he lived. All too aware that at some point she would be answerable to both Stella and Gaby, she vowed to keep her wits about her.

Patrick busied himself opening and pouring the white wine. 'You're not hungry yet, are you?' he asked. 'Though I brought some olives.' He removed the lid from the delicatessen's little plastic tub and nestled it into the dry grass between them. 'Help yourself.'

'Thanks.' Her impulse was to fill the silence, but she made herself wait for him to speak first.

'I don't suppose you can ever really forgive me,' he said abruptly. 'You must be very upset with me.'

'I had a very bad time. I was hurt and frightened. I didn't understand why you'd gone. Had no idea even where you were. But your silence was the hardest thing. It felt like a punishment, like I'd done something wrong, something unforgivable.'

'No! It wasn't you. It was all me.'

'Did you mean me to feel like that? Is that why you kept silent?'

'No!'

'I wondered if that's how you must've felt, when you were left, as a child? And maybe other times?' She glanced at his face, but his expression gave nothing away.

'I'm sorry for what I did to you,' he said, sounding genuine and sincere. 'But there were reasons. I couldn't help it.'

Leonie waited, but he sipped his wine, drawing her attention to the antics of a dog chasing a stick nearby.

'I spoke to Gaby this evening,' she told him. 'Gaby Duval?'

'Oh, yes.'

'She told me something.'

Patrick licked his lips and nodded cagily, his eyes darting over her shoulder. 'Really?'

'About Josette, about your grandfather.'

'Ah.'

'Remember, you wondered if there was some secret about his death? That maybe he'd been a collaborator, and not a hero at all?'

'Yes.'

'Well, apparently, it was neither. He killed himself.'

Patrick gave a short laugh. 'Of course! I should've worked that out for myself. It makes sense of all kinds of things.'

'Must've been awful for your grandmother.'

'Yes. No wonder she closed up so tight.'

'How much easier her life would have been if the secret hadn't been kept.'

He nodded. 'Amazing how everything just falls into place once you know the truth.'

'Your life, too,' she prompted.

'I suppose things become unsayable.'

'Surely nothing is truly unsayable?' Leonie held her breath. 'Not in the end?'

'Josette never trusted anyone enough to tell them the truth.' Patrick caught her look, and seemed to Leonie almost to perceive that it held some intent.

'I can see now why she always insisted it was selfish to feel sorry for oneself. How my being homesick and miserable must have goaded her! That time I drove her too far and she snapped, said I was evil, like him. And my poor Maman! No wonder she was so anxious. I used to believe it was me, that I'd failed her. But she never stood a chance, born right into the middle of that inferno.'

'Just weeks after he shot himself,' agreed Leonie, swallowing her disappointment at Patrick's deflection. 'What incredible selfishness, to do that to his unborn child, never mind leaving Josette to cope on her own.'

'Or despair. The impossibility of a future.'

'Perhaps. But still . . . '

'It's extraordinary really that it could remain hidden for so long,' Patrick went on, deflecting again from his more painful truth.

'You don't think your mother knew, or ever suspected?'

'No.' Patrick shook his head, pondering. 'No. I'm pretty sure she would have told me. By the time she was old enough to understand, it had probably been swept right under the carpet, and the longer a secret is kept, the harder it becomes to speak about.'

'Keeping secrets takes up a lot of energy,' said Leonie. 'I can't even begin to imagine the effort it must have taken for Josette to hide it from your mother. *And* to pretend that your grandfather had been a hero.' She observed his face intently. 'Never to drop her guard, never to slip up.'

'Blocked energy,' agreed Patrick. 'It's what I see in my patients all the time.'

'If only that energy had been free to flow into other aspects of your grandmother's life,' said Leonie. 'How much happier you all could have been.'

Patrick nodded, but failed to see the true bearing of her words. Instead, he sighed. 'I went to see Maman the other week. She recognises who I am, but that's about it. Her memory's gone. Fragmented like a computer disk.' He stared out at the soft evening sky for a moment. 'Dad never visits her.'

'Do you see him?'

'Not really. Speak on the phone. He's not interested.'

'Did he ever come to see you in Riberac?'

'No. Are you hungry? Shall we eat?'

He rooted in the rucksack, bringing out bread, tomatoes, mozzarella and a tiny bottle of olive oil. Instead of being enchanted by his consideration, by the picnic and its magical setting – lights glimmered in the city below, while above them, on the hill's summit, a party of students had lit a ribbon of candles, all in glass jars to protect against the breeze – Leonie noted how fluently he managed to distract the conversation from dangerous topics. It was as though she had been taken to some spellbinding theatrical performance, and all she could concentrate on was the flare of the footlights and the creaking of the scenery. And yet somehow, sensing the strength of Patrick's desire for this all to be real, remembering how hard he had always worked to win her favour and applause, to distract her attention from the flimsy backdrops of his life, her heart went out to him all the more. His evasions were not fraudulent, their aim not to deceive her but, by beguiling her, to deceive himself. This performance gave him something, too. It had become, by degrees, by force of repetition, fundamental to who he was. Maybe, the idea struck her, it had become all he was.

Patrick tore the bread, moistened it with a few drops of olive oil and, explaining that he'd only brought one knife, layered on slices of tomato and cheese. Watching, she longed to reach out and touch his wrist or the warm skin at the nape of his neck. The memory of his body against hers was intensely present, reminding her of their undeniable physical connection, a connection in which she had to believe he had been truly himself. Taking the food from him, Leonie would not contemplate that he could have forgotten how his hands still held the memory of her flesh, just as hers did of his. She knew now that Patrick was not the shy wild creature she had imagined in Riberac; his real self was far more deeply buried than she had ever thought, and the love that would heal such wounds might not be easy. For it to be possible at all, much more than patience would be required. But he had chosen to be here with her, to share this moment. In return, she must keep an open heart.

'Gaby wants me to go back to France,' she told him. 'She's offered me a partnership in the business ready for when she retires.' She was gratified by the way his eyes widened in surprise, but, just as he opened his mouth to respond, his mobile rang. Distracted, he pulled it out of his pocket, checked the screen, then switched it off.

'Sorry,' he said.

'Take it,' she said. 'I don't mind.'

'No, no, it can wait. It's not urgent.' He put the phone back in his pocket and shot her a quick, searching look. She smiled back reassuringly. He took her hand. 'Are you going to go?'

Leonie squeezed his hand. 'I haven't decided.'

'You're leaving already!' He laughed and lifted her hand to his lips, kissing it. 'Just when you found me again!'

Leonie studied his face. His expression was as fond and sincere as she could wish, yet she could not dispel the sense that this gallantry was an act put on to convince himself of his authenticity. 'I haven't decided yet whether or not to accept,' she repeated.

'Then you should go. Don't listen to me.'

'We could stay in touch. Work things out,' she offered, trying to formulate a way to ask him now about his son's death.

'No. You deserve someone much more reliable,' he joked anxiously, letting go of her hand to reach for bread and oil. 'I'm starving!' he said. 'Dig in!' The mood shifted and the moment was lost again.

They ate, then sat watching the stars emerge from the night sky, hearing the murmur of other voices in the darkness around them. They finished the wine, and Patrick packed away the remains of the picnic. He took her arm for the walk to Camden Town Tube and sat holding her hand in the carriage until King's Cross, where she changed lines. He made no suggestion that she stay with him and it was impossible to invite him to Stella's, so they parted on the train.

Leonie got off at the next stop and, as she stood in the lift ascending from the platform, the couple standing in front of her were kissing; she could see, from the way their bodies swayed into one another, their confidence that, after a few streets' walk, they would be in bed making love. Though she had steeled herself all evening to remain watchful, to guard against being swept away, when she observed the anonymous lovers exit the station and walk off together, she indulged in memories of herself with Patrice. Walking the short distance to Stella's flat and spying into some of the lighted windows of the residential streets where other people had lovers, spouses, families, she couldn't help feeling that her wishful imaginings were just a mirage.

II

Rob let Patrick in. 'Hiya. Mum's in the kitchen.' He disappeared back into the sitting room, returning, Patrick assumed, to his computer. Patrick went through to the large, uncluttered kitchen where he found Vicki putting a supermarket concoction into the microwave. She smiled and waited for him to kiss her.

'I brought you some herbs.' He showed her the tray of pots balanced on one arm.

'Thank you!' She touched the leaves caressingly and made space for the tray on the counter beside an ordered pile of files which Patrick knew concerned her role in planning an annual conference for her professional association. He was well aware how much time and energy she channelled into such voluntary commitments, needing a variety of outlets, he suspected, for her cool-headed intelligence.

'You'll have to remind me what each one is for,' she said, lightly rubbing some of the leaves to release their scent. 'It's so long since I did any proper cooking.'

'Sure. I'll plant them out later for you, by the back door, then it's easy to grab what you need.'

'Would you?' Vicki seemed to take such delight in his offer that he almost turned away. And yet he seldom found her expectations burdensome, as Leonie's had sometimes been. Vicki's demands were pliable, short-term, realistic: meeting them gave him pleasure, made him feel that, with her, he could be his best self.

'Be nice to dig out some of my old recipe books,' she said. 'Don't know why I ever let myself get out of the habit.'

'Always too much else to do first,' observed Patrick. She smiled at his teasing rebuke as he put an arm around her shoulder and nuzzled her neck.

Rob slouched in as the microwave beeped. 'You're not cooking tonight?' he asked Patrick, disappointed.

'You could always learn,' Vicki said to him.

'Sure. Patrick can teach me.' The boy was matter-of-fact, his back already turned as he fetched cutlery from the drawer.

'Ready for tomorrow?' Patrick asked him.

'Yes. You? We'll set off from here, right?'

'No. My bike's at my place. I'll go home tonight.' Patrick glanced at Vicki, but she continued to reach smoothly for drinking glasses. 'Have to see you at the start point.'

'Text me when you arrive. There'll be nearly two hundred of us.'

Patrick was impressed. 'Not bad for a local cause.'

Vicki ruffled Rob's hair with one hand as she placed a jug

of water on the table. Though Rob bent his head away, Patrick noted how easily he accepted his mother's proud affection. He could imagine how her own self-contained reticence must win the confidence of the self-conscious children with whom, in her day-job, she worked as a speech therapist.

'Should be a blast,' Rob told them, surveying the table setting, making sure he'd missed nothing. 'And the fore-cast says there'll be a bit of cloud cover, which is good.'

'You still have to wear sunscreen.'

'Yes, Mum.'

Patrick gave him a wink and turned to Vicki. 'I'll watch out for him.'

'You won't be able to keep up,' riposted Rob. 'Not on your rusty old wheels!'

Vicki added bagged salad to the servings of ready-made fish pie and handed them their plates. 'I called you after work last night, in case you had wanted to bring all your gear over here,' she said to Patrick as she sat down.

'Yes, sorry, I meant to call you back.' He indicated his plate. 'Thanks for this.'

'Oh, it doesn't matter,' she said mildly. 'It was only to save you to-ing and fro-ing. It might've been easier for you, that's all.'

'Someone from France turned up unexpectedly. Someone who used to send me patients. We met up for a drink.'

'I would have been at yoga anyway, even if you had called back. There's a new teacher there. I'm not so sure I like her approach. Maybe I'll change to a different class.'

'It would be nice if we both had Friday evenings free.' Patrick touched her hand.

'Really?' Vicki sounded pleased. 'Okay then, I'll definitely try out a different class.'

Patrick caught Rob's glance of surprise. Though Vicki gave no sign, Patrick was sure she, too, had registered her son's reaction. Rob's attention returned to his food, but, in the softening of his expression, Patrick could unmistakably detect a measure of gratification and even relief. It had never been discussed, but Patrick had gathered from the uncomplicated way in which Rob's father was never mentioned that he had probably never been on the scene. Patrick was pretty certain that Vicki had not been married and, apart from a series of occasional lodgers, of which he had been the most recent, had never lived with anyone. Like him, she seldom referred to the past.

When he had first arrived from France just after Christmas, a silent, wraith-like figure, Vicki, with her busy life, had remained a largely invisible presence, and it was Rob who had gradually enticed him out of his top-floor room. He had stayed barely a couple of months before renting his own place nearby, but Rob found a series of reasons to stay in touch.

Later, when the boy had wandered into his mother's room one Sunday morning a couple of months ago and discovered Patrick drinking tea in bed beside her, he had merely smiled his secret smile and asked Vicki what had happened to the favourite jeans he'd put in the washing basket. Since then, Patrick could not help but be aware of Rob's tacit encouragement. In many different, subtle ways, the boy made it clear that he was happy for Patrick to usurp his role as the man of the house.

To his surprise, Patrick had found that he enjoyed living in London. He had never done so before and he relished – at least until Leonie had turned up outside his work-place – the heady sense of anonymity that its endless variety produced, finding it restful to pass unnoticed among people ruthlessly intent on their own desires. Since he landed up here, he had begun to sleep more soundly, to find a clearer energy inside himself. It seemed incredible that six long years had passed since Daniel's death. The very fact that he had succeeded in emptying those two words of nearly all significance and could now reference the event calmly as 'Daniel's death' without experiencing the old crucifying implosion, showed the distance he had travelled.

His exile in Riberac had been his penance, his prison sentence. In Josette's house he had known what it was to be unforgiven. But the isolation had been too much, and he had stood on the brink of being lost to himself when Leonie had reprieved and revived him.

It was a strange coincidence that she should show up right at this moment with a solution to the riddle of Josette's carefully tended anger and contempt. It had never occurred to him that his grandfather's death might have been suicide. Who could explain why he would put a bullet

317

in his own head? Some ancient miasm at work. All the same, the information enabled Patrick to look back with some compassion not only at his grandmother, but even at himself as the child who had taken on himself all the blame for her coldness. Leonie's re-appearance with this revelation from the distant past seemed like another signal of redemption.

In spite of his foreboding about seeing her again, it had been bewitching to sit beside her on the grass the previous evening, watching the stars brighten against the glow of London. Leonie attracted him still, but she also challenged him, invaded him, wanting something that he simply did not have to give. Vicki, who was five years older than he, was less demonstrative sexually and easily satisfied, but she also left him unencumbered, making room for him to grow into his new urban self.

After they had stacked the dishwasher after supper, Vicki stood leaning against the kitchen door in the evening shadows, watching as Patrick planted out thyme, sage, rosemary and mint in the patch he had cleared the previous weekend. When he straightened up, he caught her observing him, but her expression, though soft, was completely neutral. Finding her unreadability liberating, he wished that he could, after all, spend the night with her.

About two hundred cyclists were already gathered on Clapham Common next morning when Patrick located Rob among them. All had found sponsors for a bike ride in aid of a children's performance project in Hackney that was under threat from council funding cuts; Rob and several of his friends who volunteered there and were determined not to see it close had, through various digital networks, recruited impressive support for their cause. Patrick had agreed to take part when Rob asked him to several weeks ago, and only afterwards had learnt from Rob's email, luckily when he was alone in his flat the next day, that their destination would be Brighton. He had felt a nauseous urge to hit the delete key and obliterate the message, deny that he had seen it, avoid seeing Rob and his mother ever again.

He had left his flat and taken a long walk around the park, during which he managed to push the bulging pain of memory to the back of his mind and barricade some inner door against it. But so completely did he manage to forget that proscribed mental compartment that, when Rob had called a couple of days later, he had answered his call without hesitation. Not remembering to have an excuse ready when Rob mentioned the charity ride again, Patrick had surprised himself by his decision to let events take their course.

One foot on the ground, Patrick rested on his saddle in the shade of a chestnut tree. His hands shook as he pulled the yellow safety tabard over his head. He took a deep, unsteady breath, blowing out through his mouth, hoping his stress levels would drop once he got underway. Normally he loved walking, running, cycling – forms of exercise that allowed his consciousness to fall away – but today he feared

319

that the sight of familiar Sussex landmarks would overwhelm him. He was not sure what he would do were he
to be engulfed by the memories of his previous life.

'Come on,' said Rob beside him. 'We're off!'

The unwieldy crowd of cyclists took some time to thread
its way out into the Sunday traffic. Heading south and
concentrating solely on keeping the right distance behind
Rob, who pedalled smoothly ahead of him, Patrick was
relieved to drop into a regular, solid rhythm. Although the
weather was cloudy, the summer morning was already
warm, and soon he was able to focus on the physical sensations of his muscles and lungs. Despite his anxiety about
seeing Brighton again, he realised also that he felt oddly
optimistic. Cycling a long distance was different from
walking. When, before, he had taken to the road and walked
for days, the impact of each step upon the ground had
reverberated organically, closing him off cell by cell from
the lives – with Belinda, with Leonie – from which he fled.

But now the road speeding beneath his front wheel
seemed paradoxically to offer the possibility of a return.
He could not undo the past, but perhaps the time had
come to lay it aside and accept that he had been scourged.
As the grey tarmac unfurled before him all he had to do
was scan the uneven surface a few feet in front of him; if
he raised his head he could make out Rob's lithe, yellow-
helmeted figure amongst the group of riders ahead. In a
moment of revelation, Patrick saw that he could have, if
not regeneration, then at least a life of sorts. With each

push on the pedals, he lectured himself that he must cauterise any remnants of memory that threatened the present. It might leave him impaired, less than whole, but it might be enough to stay where he was.

The miles passed in a satisfying haze. Even when the evocative slope of Ditchling Beacon came into sight away to the east, Patrick was able to subdue his incipient panic by concentrating on the pulsing, rhythmic movements of his aching legs. They were on a minor road, not far now from traversing the main south coast arterial route, and the jumble of cyclists had thinned out into small bunches of riders separated by increasing gaps.

Rob was still ahead of him, speeding along with four or five others. An overtaking car caused one rider to veer closer to the others. Patrick didn't see precisely how it happened, but suddenly Rob went skidding diagonally towards the scruffy grass verge where his front wheel caught and jammed between the tines of a storm drain, upending his machine and sending him diving head first to the ground. Patrick braked hard and came to a stop. Rob lay ominously still. Patrick dismounted, threw his bike down on its side on the verge and ran to kneel beside the boy, who lay with his head tucked at an unnatural angle into one shoulder, the helmet pushed forward and blood seeping from behind his ear and down across his cheekbone. Other riders were already there, shouting at each other not to touch him, not to move him in case of spinal injuries, to call an ambulance. The younger men seemed

321

capable and in command, so Patrick stood aside. When he looked up he was confronted by the looming, accusatory mass of Ditchling Beacon.

Sitting beside Rob at the hospital in Brighton, Patrick could scarcely believe that he had climbed blindly into the ambulance, pushed there by Rob's friends, and squeezed himself in next to the still unconscious boy, who lay strapped into a collar on a spinal board, his face smudged with blood. Throughout the journey Patrick had been in shock, unable to speak a word to the paramedics.

In A&E, after Rob had been whisked away, he had waited to be told the worst. Some time later, a nurse came out to explain that Rob had woken up and, apart from a fractured ankle and some stitches to his scalp, his X-rays were clear and he had escaped more serious injury. Patrick had stared at her, unable to process what she was saying. Now Rob was propped up on a hospital trolley, picking listlessly at the cotton blanket as he waited to be taken across to the orthopaedic wing for surgery to pin his broken ankle.

'Mum's going to go berserk,' he warned. 'She hates any kind of fuss.'

At the reminder of Vicki, Patrick stood up abruptly. 'Back in a minute,' he said, and made for the double doors that led out of the department, out of the hospital, away from Brighton. The reminder that he had broken yet another woman's trust, had allowed a second mother to see her child come to harm through association with him, was intolerable. He felt possessed by that hideous but invisible self that polluted his every attempt to be good. He could not face Vicki, could not face seeing all his repeated failures and treacheries reflected in her eyes. But as he strode towards the exit, he saw her enter the building through the doors at the far end of the corridor. He looked about him wildly, but it was impossible to avoid her. Her face was white, but she seemed calm. She spotted him, and Patrick waited for the expected change in her expression as she held him to account. But her face softened. Trapped by her mistaken kindness, Patrick began to weep.

'What's the matter?' she demanded in terror. 'They said he was okay. Has something happened? Tell me.'

'No, nothing,' he gulped back the sobs, trying to catch his breath. 'He's fine. He's through there. Waiting for you. I'm just so sorry.'

At that, she laughed, and put her arms around him. She let him cling to her for several moments as he heaved with sobs, then pulled away to fish a tissue out of her bag. 'Here,' she said matter-of-factly. 'Blow your nose. I want to see Rob.'

Patrick wiped his face and followed her sheepishly back through the doors. Still somehow awaiting their contempt, he stood at a distance watching as Vicki bent to kiss Rob on the cheek, shaking her head at him in mock reprimand. 'I might've guessed you'd take a tumble.' She turned to Patrick, smiling: 'It's all right now. There's nothing more to worry about.' She patted Rob's arm. 'See what you've done?' she scolded softly. 'Given Patrick a horrible fright.'

Seeing Patrick's distress, Rob added his consolation. 'Wasn't your fault, mate. You were nowhere near. Wasn't anyone's fault.'

Patrick managed to nod but, seeing from their shining faces how they fondly imagined that he cried for them, cried not from guilt but from relief, he began to weep afresh.

Later, in the bedroom of the local B&B that Vicki, with her usual quiet efficiency, had found for them, they stood by the window, taking in the paltry view. 'Thank you for everything you did for Rob today. It was sweet of you to be so concerned.' She laid a hand tentatively on his arm. 'When I got your call, well, it's the call every parent dreads, isn't it?'

Patrick nodded. The sincerity of her gratitude was more than he could bear. He felt himself floating, and shut his eyes against the lure of escape.

'That glimpse of a future you can't begin to imagine,' she went on.

'Don't think about it,' he said, pulling her round to him and folding her in his arms. 'It didn't happen.'

'I'm so glad you're here,' she said, hugging him in return. 'If I'd been on my own, even though I've seen for myself that he's going to be all right – oh, you have no idea how good it is not to be alone! I've never had that before.'

He kissed her hair, stroking her spine. 'Hold as tight as you want.'

'Really?' She spoke into his shoulder, hiding her face, and he sensed that his concern mattered to her in some fundamental way that he did not possess the means to comprehend. He took her chin and turned her face up to him. The gleaming hope in her eyes was intoxicating.

'I'm not about to run out on you,' he said. 'Rob's got his operation tomorrow. You don't have to do this alone. I'll stay until you know everything's over and he's all right.'

'I've always managed fine, fending for myself. But I have to admit how nice it is to have a knight in shining armour for once!' She laughed a little shakily, regarding him with such beseeching faith that he yearned to be everything she wanted.

'Then you should get used to it,' he said. 'I promise I won't leave you. Not for as long as you want me around.'

'Do you really mean that?'

Patrick hesitated, feeling a prickle of retrenchment run across his scalp, then found himself laughing. 'Yes!' he cried. 'Yes, let's be a family! You, me and Rob. Why not?'

She also laughed, clearly taken aback by his impulsive words. She pushed her fingers up into his hair and pressed her breasts against him. 'That sounds wonderful!' she said. 'We'd love to have you around!' She kissed him, sealing the promise.

Patrick's sigh of self-retreat, water withdrawing from a hated shore, became a deep, searching kiss. He felt as if a

fortified door had locked tight behind him with a whisper
of escaping air: he prayed that, in the act of shutting himself
in, he had also closed out his demons. He pulled her to
him, desperate to lose himself completely inside her.

The next morning, walking together back to the hospital
to see Rob, Patrick took out his mobile. 'I must ask them
to cancel my patients.' He dialled the number for the Angel
Sanctuary, and spoke to the receptionist. 'I'm sorry, but I
have to be in Brighton today.' He paused to flourish a
glance at Vicki. 'With my family.' He grinned in satisfaction as Vicki's lips melted open at the word *family*. 'My
partner's son is in hospital here, after an accident . . . a
broken ankle . . . I should be back the day after tomorrow.
If not, I'll call you again.' He ended the call and hooked
her arm into his, replenished by her smile.

A seagull's cry reminded him of the proximity of the
sea. He could hardly believe that he was walking here in
Brighton, unscathed. He felt as if, over the past twenty-
four hours, he had been through a baptism of fire, emptied
out and re-filled, made anew. It seemed impossible that
he had survived the trauma of a second ambulance journey,
another wait in A&E, and yet, miraculously, all had turned
out well. For the first time he wondered if perhaps he had
been wrong all these years to regard himself as a leper, an
outcast. Maybe that was what Belinda had wished him to
understand in her insistence that he had to want a life for
himself. He rolled the words around his mouth: 'My family.'

'My partner's son.' Here were roles others wanted him to play. Worthy roles in which he could be of use, could *serve*, maybe even win some small measure of redemption.

They found Rob groggy after the anaesthetic, and stood hand in hand beside his bed. Rob glanced at his mother, apparently reading in her face a confidence that pleased him. He held out his hand formally to Patrick.

'Just wanted to say thanks, mate.'

Touched by the gallant gesture, Patrick shook the proffered hand. An image of how Daniel might have turned out at this age streaked across his mind, but he let it go, made no attempt to seize it, smiled steadily through the pain.

'I called in at a chemist and bought you a couple of remedies,' he told Rob, placing the tiny bottles on the bedside locker. 'They won't interfere with whatever medication you've been given, but they'll stimulate your body's healing responses and help your bones mend more rapidly.'

'My own personal physician!'

Patrick smiled. 'And why not?'

Vicki grinned. 'I think we're in good hands now.' She turned to Rob. 'Is there anything else you want? There's a shop downstairs.'

'Wouldn't mind some chocolate. And something to read.'

Vicki patted his arm. 'Back in a minute.'

Patrick pulled up a chair and sat down, unsure what to talk about. Rob was frowning, biting his lip, and Patrick wondered what he was psyching himself up to say. 'What's happened to my bike?' he asked finally. 'Did anyone say?'

Patrick laughed. 'No. I had to abandon mine, too. I was hoping one of your mates would've dealt with them.'

Rob frowned again, unsure.

'If not, then I'll buy you a new one!'

'Watch it! You have no idea what mine cost,' Rob warned. 'Not with all the modifications I made.'

'Just don't worry about it, okay?'

'How come? You an international jewel thief or something?'

Patrick grinned, but spoke solemnly. 'No. I sold a house in France recently, that's all. An inheritance. The money should come through soon.'

Rob shrugged, scrutinising Patrick's face. 'Sounds like you're planning to stick around?'

'Yes. I am. I'd like to take care of you and your mum, if that's okay?'

Rob relaxed back against his hospital pillows. 'Sure. Fine by me.'

Later that afternoon, as Vicki sat playing whist and rummy to pass the time with Rob, Patrick took a bus to one of the bigger villages north of Brighton. There he asked directions in a local newsagent before walking a few streets to a wide horseshoe of small detached houses, settled enough in their landscape to look no longer new. Diagonally across from them was an open area of grass with some swings, a rubbish bin, and a bench on which he went to sit. From this vantage, he could see driveways, garages and curtained front windows. Belinda had written to him when she remarried, a brief and considerate note explaining that she thought he ought to know, and wanted him to hear it from her. He had been gladdened by her news, hoping it meant she had recovered from the worst of her grief, that he had been right to go and leave her free. Since then he had heard no more from her, but, knowing her married name, it hadn't been difficult to find her address.

He sat in the July sunshine, his gaze resting comfortably on the place where Belinda dwelt, the unremarkable house onto which he projected his wishes for her peaceful and contented life. It was a quiet Monday lunchtime, and few people came or went, only a postman intent on finishing his round and a few passing cars. He had no real idea quite why he wanted to be here. There was nothing he needed to say to Belinda and he didn't expect, or even especially want, to catch a glimpse of her. It didn't occur to him that she might notice or recognise him. He felt like a ghost, invisible, unconnected. His mind registered the fact that a half-drawn blind at an upstairs window was printed with the kind of cheerful, primary-coloured design that usually signified a nursery, but he chose not to speculate further. After nearly an hour, he got up and strolled back into the centre of the village. As he stood waiting for the three o'clock bus, he watched several mothers pushing small children in buggies, and hoped that Belinda now took her place amongst them.

Riding back into Brighton, looking out at the streets and houses and thinking of all the lives led in them, Patrick allowed himself the indulgence of imagining for himself what he so sincerely wanted for Belinda – a safe haven, an absence of grief and alarm. Yet he also recognised the old thoughts and feelings churned up by such wishes: the terror that it was dangerous even to entertain such a vision, that to do so invited catastrophe and punishment, and that catastrophe and punishment were all he deserved.

He cast his mind forward to Vicki playing cards with Rob and waiting for him to return, and instructed himself that accidents could and did happen without fatal consequences. The bus lumbered past endless terraced streets: how many of these houses had seen tragedy? Not every one, surely? There must be some houses in which life passed uneventfully and in relative security, where people did not live constantly on the edge of panic.

Patrick acknowledged how impossible it had been after Daniel's death to let go of the terror that had possessed him, body and soul, and to believe in a future where the worst might not happen. He thought of Josette, eight months pregnant in 1944 when her husband shot himself; of Agnès born into a time of acute anxiety, anger and guilt. But, recalling with sharp regret his own inability to accept Belinda's generous compassion, he could summon no admiration for Josette's iron resolve. He saw clearly now how his grandmother's rigid self-control, her lack of forgiveness, disguised a cowardice for which others had paid the price.

He no longer blamed himself for his refusal to allow Belinda's forgiveness in those first few months after Daniel's death. He had been deranged by shock – as no doubt Josette had been by her husband's suicide. But afterwards? Then he had unwittingly copied the example she had set and been as culpable as she in clinging to a secret that barricaded out anyone who offered comfort. Images of Leonie came to mind, of how successfully she had broken through his isolation; and with them a painful flash of recognition that he had failed her more severely than he cared to acknowledge.

The bus drew up outside the station where its route ended, and, relieved, he got to his feet. As he stepped down, he knew that this was his last chance, that if he did not make good his promises to Vicki and her son he would be lost.

III

The evening was sweltering, and Leonie was with Stella heading for an after-work swim in the Ladies' Pond on Hampstead Heath when Gaby called again. Stella listened with a deepening frown to Leonie's awkward side of the conversation and, when she ended the call, stood on the path staring at her oddly. 'You never told me Gaby wants you to go back.'

Leonie swallowed guiltily. 'It's more than that,' she confessed. 'She's offered me a partnership. Take over when she retires.'

Stella was too generous not to dismiss her own hurt feelings. 'But that's wonderful, Lennie! Amazing! Congratulations!'

'Thanks.' Leonie returned Stella's embrace with an uneasy conscience.

'So what are your plans? Will you have to buy her out, or what? You'll be set up for life!'

'Yes, I guess so.'

'Then what's the matter? The agency's on a pretty solid

footing, isn't it? And you loved living there, wanted to stay.'

'I am very tempted, but . . . ' Leonie sighed and looked down at her feet – red toe-nails and flip-flops.

Stella coloured. 'Jesus! It's him, isn't it? You've seen him again.' She walked away, hugging her bag of swimming gear tightly against her chest.

'Stella, wait!' Leonie caught her arm, but she refused to stop. 'Listen. I knew you'd be angry. That's why I didn't tell you.'

'You bet I'm angry. You lied to me!'

'I didn't lie. I just didn't tell you.'

'What's the difference? Don't split hairs with me!'

'Okay, I didn't tell you the truth. I'm sorry. Please, Stella, don't make me choose. You're my best friend. No one could ask for better. But . . . I'm not sure yet whether I might still be in love with him.'

'How can you be?'

'I can't help how I feel.'

'After what he's done? That's pathetic.'

'No, it's not!' Leonie almost had to run to keep up with Stella. 'That's what love is. You can't help it. You have to go with it.'

'No, you don't. That's fantasy.'

'It's what life's about, isn't it?'

'No, it's like women who stick with some bloke who beats the shit out of them, just because he says he's sorry afterwards!'

'What if he can change?'

'So let him change. Then see what *you* want.'

'You're jealous!'

'Oh, please!'

'You are! Because you're too scared to try again, to risk getting hurt! Afraid of love!'

Stella rounded furiously on Leonie. 'Look, when I was a kid I dreamt of being a prima ballerina, but I'm not whining that my whole life's been wasted because I'm too tall to dance at Covent Garden. Sorry, but this is just so much romantic crap!' Clearly making a huge effort to curb her tongue, Stella appealed less harshly to Leonie. 'Jesus, listen to us.'

Leonie took a deep breath and, in turn, spoke as reasonably as she could. 'It's not crap to want to see him again. To give it a chance. Make sure I'm not throwing away something precious.'

'And then what?' demanded Stella.

'I honestly haven't decided.' She hung her head again. 'What if he wants me to stay?' When Stella did not reply, Leonie looked up apprehensively, expecting contempt, but this time saw perplexity and concern.

Stella waited until two other women approaching along the path and watching them with open curiosity had gone by. 'Has he said plainly that he wants you to stay?' she asked.

'Not quite.'

'Not quite?'

'He doesn't want to influence my decision.'

'This man who's failed ever to tell you the truth about himself, who killed his son and abandoned you when you were pregnant?'

'But what if he loves me?'

Stella regarded her incredulously. 'So what if he does? You might as well believe in fairies at the bottom of the garden.' Then her voice softened. 'Lennie, how much of this is about losing the baby?' she asked in a gentler tone. 'About wanting another child?'

'Maybe.'

'So what *did* he tell you about his son's death?' Stella waited in vain for an answer, then, perceiving the truth, shook her head. 'You still haven't asked him,' she stated flatly.

'Not yet.'

'Why not? Don't want to upset him, I suppose,' she observed sarcastically. 'Too afraid he'll do another runner? How can you bear it that he never tells you the truth?'

'How do you start to tell a thing like that?'

'How do you live with yourself if you don't?'

'Can't we go and swim?' pleaded Leonie miserably. 'Talk about this later?'

'If you like.' Stella shook her head in frustration, but they set off again along the path. 'Though listen, Lennie. You still have stuff in storage in Riberac to sort out, right?'

'Yes.'

'So why not go do that?' she urged. 'Stay and help Gaby

for a few weeks. Talk through her offer properly. Get some perspective. Hardly like you're giving up much here work-wise.'

'Maybe.' Leonie had to admit to herself how unbearable it would be to turn down Gaby's offer.

'If Patrick's feelings *are* real, then he'll still be here, won't he?'

Leonie nodded, glancing sideways at her friend. 'But Stella, don't you want to fall in love again?' she asked, desperate to understand. 'Long to really feel? To *live*?'

Stella shot her a resentful look, but then evidently thought better. She sighed and shook her head. 'Doesn't seem worth it to me,' was all she said.

The following evening Stella returned home looking shame-faced and agitated. Her hand shook as she poured herself a slug of wine from a bottle left unfinished the previous night. Leonie was slicing vegetables, and Stella nervously eyed the large kitchen knife in her hand.

'Lennie, I have something to tell you.'

Leonie put down the knife. 'Go on.'

Stella knocked back a mouthful of wine. 'I went to see Patrick today.' She held up a hand to forestall Leonie's protest. 'I realise it's none of my business. I'm not sure what on earth I supposed I was doing, but I felt I had to do *something*. See for myself just what he's playing at this time.'

'To warn him off!' said Leonie furiously.

'Kind of. But he wasn't there.' Stella took a deep breath. 'Oh God, this is awful. I don't want to tell you, but the receptionist said—' Stella took another deep breath, then went on, articulating very precisely, 'The receptionist said he wasn't in today because he was down in Brighton with his family.'

'His *family?*'

'Lennie, I'm so sorry.'

'But it'll be some mistake. She must've got him muddled up with someone else.'

'No. We had quite a chat. When she saw how surprised I was, she said she had no idea either that Patrick was with anyone. Explained that his partner's son was in hospital there with a broken ankle.'

'I don't understand. How old is this son?'

'No idea.'

'Did you tell her about me?'

'Of course not.'

'You should've done!'

'Well, she made a note of my name. Said she'd tell him I'd been in, so maybe he'll work it out for himself. I'm so sorry, Lennie.'

Leonie's mind was already racing ahead, trying to keep up with the rapidly changing geography of her emotional world. 'In Brighton, you say?'

'That's where he lived before, isn't it?' Stella echoed her thoughts. 'Where his son died?'

'The bastard.' Leonie collapsed into a chair, beginning

to tremble uncontrollably. 'I can't believe it. Why couldn't he just tell me the truth?'

'I've been dreading having to upset you all over again.'

'You did warn me! And I knew. Deep down, I knew none of it was real. How could I be so stupid?'

Stella leant across to squeeze her arm. 'I'm sorry.' She got up and poured a second glass of wine. 'Here.'

'He chose to see me again. Took me for a picnic on Primrose Hill. Held my hand. I believed he was being so kind because he loved me. He knew that's what I felt, and did nothing to stop me.'

'It's cruel.'

'Someone phoned him when we were together. It was probably her!'

'I wish I could help.'

'You tried your best, and you were absolutely right.'

'Doesn't give me much comfort now.'

'We sat there for hours. He talked and laughed and we star-gazed. And all the time none of it was true. None of it. Why? Why do that?'

'Did you sleep with him again?' asked Stella cautiously.

'No. But I would have. Jesus, it makes me feel sick.'

'A lucky escape.'

'Thank God I hadn't said no to Gaby.'

'Absolutely!'

Leonie shook her head in disbelief, absently sipping her wine. 'I can't imagine how he does it,' she said at last. 'Was he actually congratulating himself on how clever he was being, spinning his lies and making such a fool out of me? Of her, too, if that was her on the phone. Is that really who he is?'

'Some people keep separate compartments,' offered Stella. 'If he doesn't want to think about something, he just doesn't. Like he didn't think about his son that day.'

Leonie stared at her, dumbfounded. 'But what does he get out of it?' she asked herself. 'That's what I can't figure out.'

'Nor me.'

'Though I suppose I did know it was some kind of act,' Leonie admitted. 'It was just as much me convincing myself that night, wanting to believe in my fantasy of happy-ever-after.'

'That doesn't excuse him,' observed Stella. 'He doesn't care about anyone but himself.'

'Maybe he can't.'

'Such a shit. He's never going to change.'

'Nor me, pinning all my foolish hopes on love.'

'Well, it's not stupid to act in good faith,' declared Stella. 'And that's all you've ever done.'

Leonie shrugged, feeling suddenly and intensely bereft.

'His loss, not yours,' Stella insisted.

Leonie smiled at her in gratitude, and wistfully agreed.

Three weeks later, Leonie waited again outside the Angel Sanctuary. At first, she had intended never to see Patrick again. Nor had he called her, though whether from further cowardice or some tardy sense of honour, she had been unable to decide. But even Stella agreed that she deserved 'closure'.

To begin with, Leonie had been aware of a huge emptiness within her, a blank space around her heart which until recently had been filled with yearning and conjecture. Though the lack of activity now felt odd, it had taken surprisingly little time to colonise the space with new plans and ideas. As a future partner in Gaby's business she would be able to afford to rent, or eventually buy, somewhere much nicer to live than her old cramped apartment. Audra could help her buy interesting pieces to furnish a new home. She could have a garden. Martine had mentioned that her brother, who had recently re-located from Paris, was eager to be re-introduced.

She was forced to realise how much of her energy had been swallowed up by the black hole of trying to second-guess a deeply hidden man who covered his tracks to an impenetrable degree. Nevertheless, she retained a nagging curiosity about how Patrick would react to his secrets being uncovered, and, as Stella pointed out, why should she, out of consideration for his feelings, relinquish a final chance to put her own emotional affairs in order? And so she waited here, ready to ambush him, before her flight to Bergerac the next day.

Patrick came out more or less when Leonie expected and headed up towards Highbury. She crossed the road and fell into step beside him. 'Patrick?'

He swivelled, eyes wide with alarm.

'I came to say goodbye. I'm going back to France tomorrow. I've accepted Gaby's offer.'

His alarm subsided but he glanced at her doubtfully. 'I'm sure that's a good decision,' he said carefully.

'Yes, I'm certain it is,' she said with emphasis. 'Do you have time for a drink?'

He checked his watch, then forced a smile. 'Of course. Come with me.' He turned and led the way determinedly back in the opposite direction, turning into a side street where a small pub sported several picnic tables on the wide pavement outside. 'Why don't you grab a seat and I'll get you a drink. White wine?'

'Thanks.'

He disappeared inside, and she pictured him breathing a sigh of relief at the moment's temporary respite, imagined him trying to work out what she might want from him. She wondered if he had any suspicion how much she knew, whether the receptionist at the Angel Sanctuary had said anything to him about the conversation with Stella.

To Leonie's surprise, her own hands trembled and she felt dry-mouthed with tension. Why had she always been so porous to his emotions, so compliant when he wished to avoid topics or situations? She had wondered recently if it were to do with her parents' divorce, her desire to please her largely absent father, her sense of abandonment at her mother's decision to emigrate. If so, then Patrick had picked her because he had recognised an innate ability to tolerate and excuse his whims in a way in which a Stella or a Gaby would never do. She looked down at her sequinned slippers, which she had worn deliberately as a small act of defiance, curious to see how their conversation would go once he saw that she was no longer prepared to play along.

Patrick returned with two glasses of wine, and climbed onto the bench seat across from her. He raised his glass: 'To Riberac. And your return.'

'Thanks. There's something I wanted to talk to you about before I go.'

'That sounds serious!' He tried to make a joke of it, but there was already a wariness in his expression.

She spoke softly. 'I know more about you than you probably think I do.' She saw a glint of repudiation in his eyes, even the hint of a snarl in his hunted smile. 'You've let me believe things that aren't true,' she told him.

'I never made any promises to you.'

'No, but you let me think you had no children.'

'I don't.'

'That you never had a child.'

He gazed at her, blinking rapidly. She could almost see his mind working, turning over phrases that he could use, desperate for some form of words that would fend off the truth, keep her close, but not be a lie.

'Patrick, I know what happened.'

He looked down, his head jerking slightly. It struck Leonie that, in the same way that her map of the world had altered irrevocably when she discovered his betrayals, maybe what she was witnessing now was him being wrenched into having to reconfigure his world in the light of her knowledge of his past. She watched, almost too fascinated to be angry, waiting for him to find words. Finally he looked up, and she could not help being moved by the sadness in his expression.

'I should have told you,' he said. 'But I couldn't. It was impossible, even when I wanted to. And I did want to. I never set out to mislead you.'

'And now?'

'It's in the past. I can never atone. Though I can go on.' He paused, regarding her intently. 'I have you to thank for that,' he went on. 'Seriously, it was you who brought me back to life. Showed me how to go forwards again.' He leant across and took her hand. 'I'll be for ever grateful.'

Leonie beat down the bitter memory of his abandonment, the hurt and loss and disappointment of her miscarriage, and forced some composure into her manner. 'Will you tell me now what happened to your son?'

Patrick withdrew his hand, retreating inside himself for a long while. 'I'm not sure I can add to what I assume you've already been told,' he said formally. 'I can't explain my actions. I forgot that Daniel was in the car, and as a result, he died.'

'What did make you remember he was there?'

He licked his lips. 'I didn't. Not until they tried to rescue him. Not even then. I never realised he was there. Didn't

understand what they were doing. And then it was too late.'
He paused. 'I loved him very much. He was a perfect, adorable
little boy.' He crossed his arms, closing his eyes for a few
seconds. 'I'll never forget the feel of him.'

Leonie waited, rocking the wine in her glass, putting
no pressure on him, but he said no more.

'Is that how you could leave Riberac the way you did?'
she asked finally. 'No warning, no explanation, just two
lines in a letter? Did you manage to forget about me, too?'
Leonie watched as Patrick pensively rubbed at the dry wood
of the picnic table with his fingertips.

'I failed you,' he said at last. 'I was wrong. But I was
afraid something terrible would happen if I stayed; that
I'd be punished again.'

'But was it the same? Forgetting I was pregnant by you?
The same as forgetting about your son?'

'Possibly,' he admitted, shamefaced.

'And your wife,' Leonie went on. 'You told me you walked,
when you left England. Walked to France.'

'I didn't want to do any more harm.'

'Did she know you were leaving?'

'She knew I'd inherited Josette's house. Eventually she
got in touch with me there.'

Leonie heard the familiar evasion slide underneath his
words, and was overwhelmed by a rush of both pity and
distaste. 'And what happened to her?'

'I was no good to her. To anyone. Her sister said so, told
me to go. I make people unhappy. And I was only capable

of putting one foot in front of the other, my belongings reduced to what I could carry on my back. That's all I was, for a long time. That and, in time, my work, my patients.' Patrick gave a twisted smile and reached across the table again to touch her arm. 'I warned you I wasn't reliable. Not a good bet.'

His touch depleted her and she moved her arm. He didn't seem to notice. 'I know I hurt you, and I'm sorry,' he said, circling the surface of the wood once more with his finger. 'You do believe that?'

She nodded. And it was true: she did not doubt his sincerity. But it felt woefully inadequate, and she had nothing to say in response.

'I'm glad you're going back to France,' he went on. 'You were happy there. It suited you. And Gaby and her husband seem like good people.'

'What about you?'

Leonie's heart beat against her ribs with the urgent wish that he tell her everything, tell her the truth – that he was already with another woman, a *family*. If he could only do that, want her to share in his life, trust her even to be glad for him, then she felt as if some old and malign enchantment would be broken and she could depart in peace, could feel that he had proved himself worthy of how desperately she had loved him.

'Oh,' he said. 'Don't worry about me. I'll get along.'

'Will you be happy here in London?' she persisted, striving to keep the quaver of disappointment out of her voice.

'Yes,' he smiled. 'Thanks to you.' He raised his glass to hers, his gaze seeking reassurance.

Leonie held tightly to her glass, feeling the lethal chill of contempt. She knew this was the best she could expect, that Patrick's habits of guardedness and misdirection were too ingrained, but she suddenly felt she owed it to herself to rebel, to rip to shreds his carefully constructed web of untruthful silences. 'Only me?' she demanded scornfully. 'No one else?'

Patrick, surprised, shook his head, as if trying to shake some tinnitus irritation from his ears. 'It was you who saved me,' he answered, giving her a wounded look. 'No one else.'

'You're such a liar!' Leonie pushed her wine glass away, swung her feet around, free of the narrow seat of the picnic bench, and, relieved now that she was unlikely ever to see him again, walked away.

IV

Rob reclined on the settee, looking out of place against the boldly patterned cushions. His plastered leg was stretched out ahead of him and he tucked enthusiastically into Patrick's vegetable lasagne. Patrick watched, amused: enforced inactivity made the boy restless but had done nothing to diminish his appetite.

'So when are you planning to move back in?' Rob asked between mouthfuls.

Vicki, sitting with Patrick at the table, glanced across at him. Caught up in Rob's surgery, and the logistics of bringing him home from Brighton, neither of them had yet re-visited Patrick's promise of commitment. Struck by the poignancy of Vicki's expression, Patrick grinned at them both.

'Still sure you want me?' he asked.

Vicki looked to her son, who waved his fork in the air. 'Your call, Mum. Nothing to do with me!'

'What about your flat?' she appealed to Patrick.

'The lease still has a few more months to run, but I don't suppose that matters.' Patrick reached for her hand. 'Whenever suits you.'

'If you wait till I'm out of plaster, then I can give you a hand with your stuff,' offered Rob.

'Great.'

Patrick was rewarded with a smile from Rob that lightened some of the flatness he'd felt since his leave-taking drink with Leonie. Her final anger had been well deserved, but what lingered in his mind was speaking about Daniel. Apart from his parents and a couple of work colleagues, it had been years since he had even been in the company of anyone who knew what had happened. Although a part of him felt absolved by her knowledge, for a day or so it had made his present life seem unreal, made the guy-ropes that attached him to it feel dangerously frail. Rob's easy hold on life renewed his confidence.

'We could throw a party,' suggested Rob. 'A kind of house-warming.'

Vicki looked to see Patrick's reaction. 'Easy, tiger!' she rebuked her son. 'One thing at a time.'

'No, why not?' asked Patrick. 'Be good to meet your friends.'

'I'd like you to meet my brother,' said Vicki shyly. 'He lives in Northumberland, but he's all the family there is left now.'

'And I'll take you to visit my mother, if you like,' offered Patrick. 'Not sure I can face socialising with my dad and his lady friend. We haven't seen eye to eye for a long time.'

'That's a shame,' Vicki observed. 'But you must do exactly as you please.'

Patrick felt comfortably encircled by her determination to make everything easy for him. While it made defection impossible, it also relieved him of responsibility. 'Let's have a party! Invite as many people as you want,' he promised her gaily. 'I want you to be happy.'

Hearing the slightly too-high note in his voice, Patrick realised he was attempting to skirt his sense that his gesture that evening in the guesthouse now seemed to him faintly ridiculous. He wasn't sure what he wanted – wasn't even sure whether it mattered what he wanted. His mind flashed back to his younger self, moving in with Belinda, going along quite naturally with plans to get married once she became pregnant. He remembered how, waking up and finding her beside him, he had felt for the first time in his life as if he had not a care in the world. Perhaps that's how he would feel again if he allowed himself once more to go with the flow of other people's wishes.

'Is there anyone you want to invite over from France?' asked Vicki, her mild tone nonetheless betraying a twinge of anxiety.

As Patrick hesitated, Rob blithely interrupted. 'I'll have some more, if there is any.' He held out his empty plate. 'And don't forget Elizabeth,' he reminded his mother before turning to Patrick. 'She's my godmother. Lives in Ipswich. You'll like her.'

Vicki jumped up to take Rob's plate, laughing at him. 'You just want as many people around as possible to wait on you hand and foot!'

'Sounds good to me.' Rob lay back, smiling at them like a well-fed cat.

The following week, as Patrick left the Angel Sanctuary at lunchtime, intending to grab something to eat between patients, he remembered to stop and tell the receptionist to block out his appointments for the dates when he and Vicki had booked a week's holiday together.

'Oh, lovely!' exclaimed the girl when she heard the reason, then drew a sharp breath. 'By the way, did that woman ever get hold of you?' She flicked back through the large appointments diary. 'Stella Deacon. She came in asking for you. Sorry, I completely forgot. It was while you were down in Brighton.'

'Stella Deacon?' It took Patrick a few moments to place her as Leonie's friend, whom he had met in Riberac. His spine tensed.

'I told her we weren't sure when you'd be back,' the receptionist continued. 'She wouldn't say what she wanted, but she seemed rather agitated.'

He became aware that the young woman's radar for gossip was on high alert. 'Oh, yes. She did find me, thanks.'

Patrick went out, pausing on the pavement as the

lunchtime crowds surged impatiently around him. His appetite forgotten, he made for Islington Green where he managed to find space on a bench. He sat down, thinking hard. He had seen Leonie after his return from Brighton. Was this why she'd called him a liar? It hurt him that Leonie might feel betrayed. By denying her such a mundane, simple truth – that he was seeing someone – he had repaid her generosity with a meanness of spirit that she would rightly despise. At least she was now back in France, safely away from him. He wondered how long his inability to speak would go on inflicting damage on others?

A new thought stabbed him: did Vicki know about Leonie? Might Stella, or Leonie, have felt it her duty to track Vicki down and warn her? He could not bear that Vicki and Rob might also be hurt by his dereliction. Josette's voice echoed in his ears, and he felt pursued again by the monstrous *Doppelgänger* that was his worst self. Vicki had shown little curiosity about his marriage or past relationships. It was one aspect of what he found so restful about her. So why had he not simply been open with her about his past, about Daniel, about seeing Leonie again? He had wanted to live with Vicki because of the self he saw reflected in her eyes. A self he wanted to be. He didn't want that reflection to be spoiled. He was tired of being this monster who upset everyone, who left his own son to die in a hot car.

Patrick slowly became aware that people around him were scrunching up their sandwich bags and heading back to their jobs. He had a patient due at two o'clock, but he sat on, exhausted. A filthy pigeon with a dismembered claw pecked about the ground beside an over-flowing rubbish bin. He could not bear it if his life were to be reduced again to the simple act of heaving himself to his feet and putting one foot in front of another. Where would he go this time? Josette's house was sold. If he were in Brighton he might consider walking into the sea.

The thought of his two o'clock appointment tugged at him. He struggled to focus his attention, to remember who he was due to see. Yes, Rebecca, a 'yummy mummy' with two small children, a borderline anorexic who ricocheted from one type of therapy to another. But he had seen her twice and believed his remedies had already made a difference. He might help her yet. He should go. It was all he could do. It was unfair to keep her waiting.

That evening, although due to see Vicki, he called to say that he wasn't doing very well, that maybe he was going down with something. He went back to his own flat where he occupied himself catching up with domestic chores.

The following day he called her as he left work, said he was going to get an early night, then, instead of taking his usual route home, he crossed the road and made his way down to the canal, heading east. On this high summer evening there was an attractive desolation about the unfolding vista of crumbling Victorian brick, ramshackle industrial units and cheap-jack new-build flats. Every so often a cyclist coming up behind him would ring their bell, which, even in his distraught mood, Patrick couldn't help experiencing as a particularly merry sound. For the canal was not a lonely place: he passed moorhens, ducks, runners, young office workers in business suits carrying backpacks, lovers, gossiping friends. He slowed his own pace, determined to fight the compulsion to enter the trance-like state that his walking so often induced. Something in him recognised that if he disappeared from himself, this time there would be no return.

He forced himself to leave the tow-path at the next set of steps, and found himself on a busy main road. The noisy traffic confused him and for a moment he felt helpless and overcome. But he no longer wanted to feel like this, and it was his determination not to yield to the siren voices that whispered to him to surrender that propelled him to a bus stop and onto a crowded bus that took him close to Vicki's house.

She had returned to him the key he'd had previously as her lodger, yet he rang the bell before letting himself in. Rob craned forwards to look into the hallway from his position on the settee.

'Oh, hi,' he greeted him. 'Feeling better?'

'Yes. Thanks.'

'Mum's upstairs.' Rob returned his attention to the laptop balanced on his thighs.

Patrick climbed the stairs and found Vicki in her bedroom listening to the radio whilst ironing. He went straight to her and, but for the hot iron, would have taken her in his arms.

'There you are!' She kissed him, laughing as she suspended the iron awkwardly in the air away from them.

'Wanted a bit of time to myself, that's all,' explained Patrick.

Vicki busied herself with unplugging the iron. 'Of course.'

'I was upset over some news about an old friend.' He steeled himself. 'Someone who was close to me in France.'

'But it's all right now?' Vicki's glance seemed to contain a warning not to trespass across some invisible boundary.

'Yes.'

'Good. Can you help me fold these duvet covers?'

Patrick took two corners of the fabric in his hands and, as he helped shake it flat, said into the billowing cotton, 'We never seem to speak about the past.'

Vicki took his corners from him and folded the cover neatly. 'Well, there's no rush, is there?' She patted it smooth and turned to scoop a second one from the pile of laundry.

'There are things about me I want you to know,' he implored her, desperate now to tell her about Daniel.

Her concentration was absorbed in untangling the fabric, and she held out the corners to him again with a smile. 'When the time is right.'

Patrick experienced a sudden rush of rage, not against Vicki but against a world that had conspired to shut him up and suffocate his need to speak, to be heard. He wanted to smash up every object in the room. Instead, he handed back the cover and turned to the window, hoping somehow to discharge the sour metallic taste of his fury. As he did so, he caught sight of his reflection in the mirror on Vicki's dressing table and glimpsed in his own face his father's thin mouth and high cheekbones, his father's aggrieved sideways glance. Patrick's sense of being thwarted became vicious and dangerous, threatened to overwhelm him. He turned back to Vicki.

'We won't have secrets from one another, will we?' he pleaded. 'We must be able to speak to one another.'

She paled slightly, but nodded seriously. 'I promise. You can tell me anything you like.' Before he could say more, she came to him, lying her hands lightly against his chest. 'All in good time.' She touched her lips to his, then turned to pick up a pile of folded linen from the bed. 'Here,' she said, thrusting it at him. 'These go in the airing cupboard.'

As Patrick put away the clean sheets his anger ebbed as swiftly as it had risen. Although forced to acknowledge that once he would have welcomed Vicki's reticence and found it endearing, now he felt utterly dejected by it.

Rob looked up as Patrick came back into the kitchen. 'You making supper, then?' he asked.

'Sure.' Patrick opened the fridge to see what was there. Little on the shelves appealed, and he shut it again, sighing, then saw Rob regarding him candidly.

'Mum clams up when she's upset,' Rob informed him. 'You'll get used to it.'

'I've been fairly guilty of that myself,' Patrick admitted.

'Can I ask you something?' asked Rob.

Surprised by the boy's serious expression, Patrick sat down at the table, facing him. 'Of course.'

'I never paid much attention to what Mum got up to when I was growing up,' Rob began. 'She told me who my dad was, no big deal, and then, like you do as a kid, I assumed it never bothered her to be on her own because she had me.' He stared down at his hands. 'She's stopped doing yoga on Friday night, right?'

Patrick was taken aback by this non-sequitur. 'Right. She didn't like the teacher.'

'She's *always* done some kind of regular class on a Friday. Always. Guess why.'

Patrick shook his head, mystified where this was leading.

'Because her married lover was never going to see her over a weekend. The tosser!' added the boy. 'Eight years he told her he was going to leave his wife and kids. And she believed him. Until he dumped her.'

'When was that?'

'I was about fifteen. She got ill. Lost weight, cried all the time. I was terrified she had cancer and was going to die, so she told me. It's the only time she's ever talked about it.'

Patrick nodded. 'Did you meet the guy?'

'I'm not sure. Once, I think. But—' Rob sighed. 'I love Mum,' he said, 'but it can be pretty heavy, being all she's got.'

'I know exactly what that's like,' said Patrick, grimacing.

Silence fell between them. Patrick looked at Rob, seeing the vulnerable teenager visible beneath the surface of the young man he was becoming.

Patrick took a deep breath. 'I had a son.'

Rob looked at him with mild curiosity. 'Really? So where's he now? With his mum?'

'He died. When he was eighteen months old. An accident for which I was responsible.'

'Wow. Sorry. That must've been tough.'

'Yes. It was.'

Patrick glanced at Rob and saw only sympathy in his eyes. There seemed to be no reason to say more, not at this moment, but he felt lighter than he had in years.

'So what was it you wanted to ask me?'

Rob bit at his lower lip before replying. 'D'you reckon Mum settled for second-best with that tosser because of me? To have more time for me? So I wouldn't have to deal with a string of boyfriends?'

Patrick looked into his earnest face. He thought of a childhood spent negotiating silence, living someone else's lie. 'No,' he told him decisively. 'If she was that broken up about the affair ending, then I reckon she was with him because she really wanted to be. She maybe just thought you were too young to understand.'

Rob nodded, his whole body appearing to relax.

'Do I let on you've told me?' asked Patrick. 'Or is it a secret?'

'Nah!' Rob shook his head. 'Mum'll kill me, but I don't care. I mean, what's the big deal?'

Patrick laughed with relief. 'Ridiculous how easy it is to believe that the world will end, just by saying something.'

When Vicki came downstairs five minutes later she found them arguing amicably over the best way to chop an onion. They turned to her, their easy grins automatically including her in their intimacy. She peered over their shoulders at the ingredients for a pasta sauce laid out on the chopping board, then slipped out of the back door, returning a moment later with sprigs of rosemary and thyme. She stripped the leaves from the soft stalks ready to add to the pan, but was prevented by Patrick covering her hand with his.

'Wait,' he counselled her. 'All in good time.'

'Okay.' She smiled and kissed him lightly. 'Smells delicious.'

In October, Leonie came to London to spend a long weekend with Stella. On the Saturday, as planned, they drove to Brighton for a day out. They found a space in an underground car park and walked down to the promenade. Stella insisted on buying them ices from a van, a chocolate Flake stuck into each sculpted wave of sugary cream, and they leant against the railings, looking across at the pier. The clear autumn weather had brought others like them to stroll on the beach, and there was a pleasant sense of companionship about the scene.

'No regrets?' asked Stella.

'About going back to France? None at all.'

'And the rest?'

'No. I decided just to remember the good times, forget the bad stuff. A selective memory has its benefits.'

'You're more forgiving than I am.'

'I forgave myself. That's what matters.'

'Sure.'

'Couldn't have done it without you.' Leonie put her arm through Stella's and hugged her closer.

'If only goodness really were a match for damage. If we could just kiss it all better,' Stella observed.

'You'd be out of a job.'

Stella laughed. 'True. You certainly tried, anyway. Gave it your best shot.'

'I did, didn't I?'

'No shame in that.'

'No.' Smiling, Leonie looked out to sea where the sun made the waves sparkle above the cold depths.

ACKNOWLEDGEMENTS

This book owes much to Elizabeth Buchan for her encouragement, generosity and all-round wonderfulness. For their time, insight and expertise, I also wish to thank Claire Baker, Tina Burchill, Lisa Cohen, N.J. Cooper, Dr Peter Dean, Alan Dunnett, Maggie Hilton, Bernard Lever, Jackie Malton, Sarah Medford, Angela Neustatter, Laline Paull and Caroline Willbourne; and, not least, my editor Jane Wood and agent Sheila Crowley.